The Soldier's Refuge

SABRINA YORK

D0971028

HARLEQUIN

SPECIAL
EDITION

If you purchased this book without a cover you should be aware
that this book is stolen property. It was reported as "unsold and
destroyed" to the publisher, and neither the author nor the
publisher has received any payment for this "stripped book."

HARLEQUIN®
SPECIAL
EDITION™

Recycling programs
for this product may
not exist in your area.

ISBN-13: 978-1-335-72470-0

The Soldier's Refuge

Copyright © 2023 by Sabrina York

All rights reserved. No part of this book may be used or reproduced in
any manner whatsoever without written permission except in the case of
brief quotations embodied in critical articles and reviews.

This is a work of fiction. Names, characters, places and incidents
are either the product of the author's imagination or are used fictitiously.
Any resemblance to actual persons, living or dead, businesses,
companies, events or locales is entirely coincidental.

For questions and comments about the quality of this book,
please contact us at CustomerService@Harlequin.com.

Harlequin Enterprises ULC
22 Adelaide St. West, 41st Floor
Toronto, Ontario M5H 4E3, Canada
www.Harlequin.com

Printed in U.S.A.

Sabrina York is the *New York Times* and *USA TODAY* bestselling author of hot, humorous romance. She loves to explore contemporary, historical and paranormal genres, and her books range from sweet and sexy to scorching romance. Her awards include the 2018 HOLT Medallion and the National Excellence in Romantic Fiction Award, and she was also a 2017 RITA® Award nominee for Historical Romance. She lives in the Pacific Northwest with her husband of thirty-plus years and a very drooly Rottweiler.

Visit her website at sabrinayork.com to check out her books, excerpts and contests.

Books by Sabrina York

Harlequin Special Edition

The Tuttle Sisters of Coho Cove

The Soldier's Refuge

The Stirling Ranch

Accidental Homecoming
Recipe for a Homecoming
The Marine's Reluctant Return

Visit the Author Profile page
at Harlequin.com for more titles.

Chapter One

Natalie Tuttle pulled to the side of the road at the crest of the hill and stared down at the quaint little town of Coho Cove, tucked neatly into a curve of the Washington coast just north of the Columbia River. After seven years, here she was, looking down the barrel of a long-avoided homecoming to a town she'd never liked.

Surely, the churning in her gut wasn't trepidation...

It must be hunger.

Yeah. Hunger.

When had she last stopped to eat on the twenty-plus-hour drive from Los Angeles? Somewhere in Oregon, if fast food counted. Not that she'd been in such an all-fired hurry to get home, but Celeste's tone, when she'd shared the news of Momma's stroke, had been worrisome. When Dad had died, and their brother Nate,

Celeste had been the only one who hadn't lost it. That telling quaver in her voice was probably why Nat had plowed through the drive with hardly a potty stop.

And now she was here.

Yay.

Only a medium-sized part of her wanted to turn around and flee.

From up here, it looked like an ideal place to live—a charming, slightly rustic seaside town with the picturesque pier and marina, and the southern curve of the bay where the old mill once stood. It was especially pretty, bathed as it was in the orange and pinks and purples of the setting sun. But looks could be deceiving.

Her jaw tightened as old feelings arose and compressed in her chest; memories swelled in her mind.

No.

She pushed that detritus away. Natalie wasn't that girl anymore. She'd left this town in her dust the day after graduation and never returned. She'd remade her life, her self-image, her *everything* once more. As a military kid, the instinct was second nature and Nat had become exceedingly good at it.

She liked who she was now—established, successful, sure of herself. Totally independent of anyone else. She didn't want to go back to feeling like a misfit. She would not become the butt of their jokes again just because she was different.

With any luck, she could remember that.

Fortunately, this was only a quick visit to see Momma—who'd had a stroke just as their decades-long housekeeper broke a hip tripping over one of her

Chihuahuas—and to give her sisters a hand with care-giving for a bit. It was wrong to leave everything on their shoulders, even if being here—without grinding her teeth to the nubs—was going to be a challenge. It was only right that she pitched in for a week or so to help Amy and Celeste—mostly Celeste—negotiate this life change.

It was good timing, too. The TV show she worked for as an art director was on hiatus. Normally, she'd have gone on a long European jaunt and visited a thousand museums, or met her family members somewhere fun when the show was on hiatus. Instead, this.

Ah, well. There was no putting off to tomorrow that which you dreaded doing today. She glanced over her shoulder to make sure Pepe was still asleep in his car-rier in the back seat, then pulled back onto the road and started down the hill into town—with a stop at her favorite burger joint on her mind. As anxious as she was to get eyes on Momma, it wouldn't be fair to show up this late in the evening and expect Celeste to make her dinner.

If she had missed anything in this town—other than her family—it was a Sparky's burger. She'd had *dreams* about Sparky's burgers and woken up salivating. Besides, after that drive, Nat fancied more than a quick PB and J to restore her soul.

She was practically drooling as she neared the 1950s throwback malt shop on Main Street, so it was particu-larly annoying to realize it wasn't there anymore. Oh, the building was still there. But instead of Sparky's, the neon sign read Bootleggers: Craft Beer for the Rebel in

You. A sign on the door indicated they did, indeed, sell food, but since Natalie had always hated the smell of beer, she decided to drive a block to the east in hopes that Smokey's, the local barbecue joint, was still there—and thank God, it was.

It made sense to get her barbecue to go—the Smokey's dining room was notoriously...sticky—so she made her way up the rain-spattered, slick steps, pulled open the creaky door and sauntered up to the counter to order. Her eyes widened in surprise as she recognized the man in the Smokey's Keep it Blazin' apron. It took a second to find his name in her mental file cabinet, but when their eyes locked, it came to her.

"You're Baxter Vance." She didn't mean to say it. It just came out.

He nodded but his eyes were blank. "Have we met?"

"Yeah. We went to high school together." *You used to call me Butterball. With the emphasis on butt.*

"Really?" He shot her a grin. Gosh, he looked like such a nice guy. Too bad she remembered what he really was. "What's your name?"

"Natalie Tuttle."

His eyes went big, really big, and he gaped at her. His shock was hardly insulting at all. "Nuh-uh."

"'Fraid so."

"Wow," he said. And then, "Wow."

"Yeah. It's been a while." Seven years, to be exact. Time enough to replace every cell in her body—she'd read on the internet.

"Wow." He nodded. Come to think of it, he had always been something of a one-word wonder.

"I'm back for a visit," she said, even though it was none of his butterball business. Momma had ingrained etiquette into her offspring's souls from birth, with chants of *Mabel, Mabel if you're able, keep your elbows off the table*, exhortations to wear white gloves on Easter Sunday, and other nonsense. Dad had been an army officer, and everyone knew that an officer's kid served as a reflection of his effectiveness as a leader. How things *looked* in their household had always been paramount. Certainly, more important than how they actually were. This deeply rooted ethos usually served Nat well, but since she was polite by default, it sometimes irritated her. Like now.

"Wow. Well, you really look…great." His eyes flicked over her in a way she really didn't like, especially because it was him.

"Thanks." She sucked in a deep breath to indicate a change of topic and said, "Okay. So, I'd like a half rack of the Smokey Pigs, with coleslaw and a couple of those cornbread muffins."

"Sure," he said, for some reason still agog. And, "Wow."

"And I'd like that to go," she added as he continued to gawk. Honestly, she wasn't *that* different. Was she? She'd matured a little, slimmed down a little…gotten a stylish haircut, contacts. But basically, beneath all that, she was the same nerdy girl she'd always been. Wasn't she?

"Oh, yeah. Sure. Sure."

She leaned in and gave him a wicked smile. "And I'm really hungry, so if you could hop to it, that'd be great."

She never would have said something that snarky—bordering on rude—if she hadn't been nearly cross-eyed with fatigue. And, dare she mention, starving. Still, politeness reasserted itself. "Sorry. Kind of in a rush. The family is expecting me."

"Sure. Sure." He took her payment and went to work on her order. At least he didn't make those little piggy noises he used to make whenever he saw her in the high school cafeteria with actual food on her tray. If he had, in her current mood, she'd probably have clocked him. She was no longer a shrinking violet. She was no longer an easy mark for bullies.

She sat down at a sticky table and scrolled through her phone as she waited for her order—not because she had any urgent texts to read, but because if she looked busy, he probably wouldn't try to talk to her. She needed some time to process this surreal moment.

Because this was *Baxter Vance*, one of the reasons she never wanted to come back this town. Somehow, he wasn't quite as, well, *tall* as she remembered. And nowhere near as impressive.

He'd been the leader of the pack back then. The instigator of all her misery. Mr. Most Likely to Succeed, Prom King, THE stud on campus…and now, he lived in the same small town and worked at the rib place where the uniform was, apparently, a filthy apron.

Facing him hadn't been as hard as she'd expected. Maybe she could do this homecoming thing without too much angst. Maybe?

But then, Baxter Vance wasn't the one she'd dreaded meeting most. Not by a long shot. Lola Cheswick and

Sherill Scanlon leaped to mind. And, of course, Jaxon Stringfellow. He, however, didn't have to leap to mind because he was always there for some bizarre reason, burrowing in her memories, popping up at the most inopportune times.

Heat scorched her cheeks at just the thought of him. Her whole body went hot and cold, as it always did when thoughts of Jax danced through her mind.

Quit it, she told herself. Don't forget what he did to you.

He still lived here. She knew it. Her friend Sheida had mentioned in passing that her brother had returned to town after a stint in the army. Amy had mentioned him as well, with fondness in her tone.

How flipping awkward would it be to see him again? Talk to him? With actual words? It was probably going to happen, sooner than later, so she might as well prepare. She could probably say something blasé like, *"Oh, hey, Jax. Nice to see you again."* Or, *"Remember that time you kissed me on a bet? Oh, yeah. That was hysterical."*

But it hadn't been hysterical, had it? Not to her.

She should have known better. The captain of the football team kissed cheerleaders like Sherill, not the chubby, awkward "newcomer" who never quite found her place or her*self* in this alien universe filled with people who'd all grown up together.

Nope. Guys like that didn't kiss girls like the girl she'd been. Not on purpose anyway. Not unless he did it on a bet. Which was, clearly, hilarious. But only to him and his crowd.

For Natalie, the utter chagrin had been just one more reason to get the hell out of Dodge the second she could. And for seven years, it had served as a reason to not return.

Not because some snotty football players had laughed at her. She couldn't have cared less what *they* thought. It was Jax's part in the debacle that had crushed her. For some reason, she'd thought better of him. She'd thought their friendship, at least, had been a real thing.

But like most men, he'd let her down.

Whatever. Ancient history. Suck it up, Buttercup. Move on.

If she did see him again, maybe she should just pretend not to remember him? Maybe that would be best.

When Baxter brought over her order, he hovered while she collected her things, as though he wanted to talk to her. Pity she was too tired and hungry to linger. Even if she hadn't been, lingering with him did not appeal. It never would. Nat grabbed the brown paper sack, already spotted with grease stains, tossed a too-cheery "Thanks" over her shoulder and pushed through the door.

She should not have been in such a hurry to escape a conversation with her painful past. She should have remembered how slick the steps had been when she'd come into the joint. But she was and she didn't, and as a result, she slipped on the middle tread; her foot—and her food—went flying, and she landed on her butt, hard, in the mud at the bottom of the stairs.

The impact made her head spin for a second. The pain made her woozy. That was probably why it took her a minute to realize that the man standing in front of her holding out his hand to help her up, with a look of concern on his—gorgeous—face was not an angel as she might originally have assumed.

He was, in fact, Jaxon Stringfellow himself.

And damn it all anyway. He was even hotter than she remembered.

It was an instinctive reaction, Jax supposed—when one saw a woman fall down three stairs and land that hard—to reach out a hand to help her up. He did so without thinking. But then, their gazes met and locked, and a thunderbolt hit him. Hit him so hard that he was incapable of saying anything other than a purely instinctive "Are you all right?"

Natalie Tuttle. Her name rang in his head like a bell. She'd finally come home.

He'd known she was coming, so he wasn't sure why he was surprised, or stunned, or whatever the hell this gut-wrenching emotion was.

She'd changed, he had the presence of mind to notice. She'd grown up. Gone from cute to drop-dead gorgeous. She'd lost the straight-across bangs that had always clashed with her glasses and added a diamond nose ring, declaring the rebel she'd always been, albeit secretly. Her hair was slickly styled, sadly missing the careless ponytail and random nibbled pencil behind one ear—sometimes both—and she'd become, well, svelte. He wasn't sure he liked that part, or the fact that she'd become someone he nearly didn't recognize.

But those eyes didn't change.

Maybe they were the source of his discombobulation.
They cut right through him. They always had.

He saw the exact second she recognized him. The
muscles around her mouth tightened. Her cheek bunched.
She swallowed.

Oh, and she totally avoided his hand as she helped
herself up—thank you very much. Then she nodded
primly, collected her bag of food and made her way to
her car. In a hurry.

He could hardly blame her. He'd been a jerk back
then. A stupid kid. And obviously, she remembered.

His buddies had egged him into kissing her—dared
him, really—there behind the bleachers in the gymnasium. And he'd done it. Partly because they encouraged it, and partly because he'd wanted to kiss her.
There'd always been a connection between them. He
could not deny his attraction to her—at least to himself.
But he'd never acted on it because, well, he hadn't had
the strength to stand up to his friends and step outside
of expectations.

After having been an outsider his whole life himself, he was suddenly, now, one of the cool kids, and
she hadn't fit the narrative.

But he'd wanted to kiss her, and so he had. And it
had been, well, wonderful.

Until—a second after his lips left hers—his friends
had surrounded them, howling like hyenas…at her.
Laughing at *her*.

She'd stepped back, away from him as she'd realized
that she was the butt of a stupid joke…again. And he

had been the agent of her humiliation. He hadn't meant it to be that way, but intention changed nothing.

The memory of that moment—her wounded expression—was burned onto his brain. The regret, the embarrassment of his rotten behavior had haunted him for years. He'd wanted, needed to apologize to her, to explain, but had never had a chance. She'd left home for LA right after graduation, and she'd never come back. Not once in seven years.

But now she was here. Now he had the opportunity to clear his conscience, make things right with her—if he could. If she'd even listen to him, which was a big if.

His heart leaped as she paused by her car, blew out a breath and headed back to him. Well, stormed back to him. He sucked in a breath, steeled his spine. This wouldn't be easy, but then, when were apologies ever easy? She paused beside him, but before he could open his mouth, or form the words he'd been practicing forever, before he could say anything, she bent down, picked up her keys, which had fallen in the mud and, without even a nod this time, turned around and walked away from him again.

Damn.

Damn, damn, damn.

Natalie Tuttle had finally come home.

He had no idea why that thought scared him to death.

Or he did.

Hard to tell which was worse.

His boots were heavy as he headed into Smokey's to pick up his order—Amy and the boys were waiting for supper and he was already late—but his mood was heavier. Nat's reappearance had kicked up old feelings about her and insecurities about himself—things he'd rather ignore.

But he couldn't.

Baxter's reaction to his entrance to the restaurant didn't help. His eyes went wide and his jaw dropped. "Jax?" He slapped his forehead. "Man, this is a weird day."

Jax held back a sigh. He wasn't in the mood to deal with Baxter's melodrama. Especially not while he was still reeling from his encounter outside with Natalie, and that upheaval of old guilt. Aside from that, he hadn't slept well the night before—the nightmares again—and he was just plain tired. "Hey, Baxter. Just here for Amy's pick up," he said, hoping that would be enough to move things along. He should have known better.

"You'll never guess who just left." Baxter leaned forward, his expression alight. The dude had always loved gossip, so it was hardly a surprise. It was almost a shame to burst his balloon.

Jax did anyway. "Natalie Tuttle?" And, when Baxter beetled his brows, "I saw her in the parking lot."

"Doesn't she look hot?" Baxter shook his head. "Who'da thunk it? Natalie Tuttle. Wasn't she was the dorky nerd you kissed on Senior Skip Day?"

He knew damn well it was, so Jax didn't reply.

"How bizarre that you *both* show up on the same day."

Was it? Was it really? "I live just down the road, Baxter," Jax felt compelled to remind him. Sure, when he'd returned home from Afghanistan, totally wrecked emotionally and spiritually, he'd shut himself in. To heal, he'd told himself. He'd deliberately avoided other people as much as he could, focusing on his work. Oh, he let in some folks, like his best friend Ben and his sister Sheida and Pops. And Amy and the boys, of course. They'd been central to his healing, those boys. Other than those exceptions, he'd made it a point to avoid people.

But things were starting to change now. He was making a deliberate effort to get out into the world more. Forcing himself to open up, at least a little. Baby steps, right? Hence, his very simple offer to run to Smokey's to grab dinner for Amy. The last thing he'd expected was an emotional ambush in the form of Natalie Tuttle…

"Dude." Baxter, who seemed to have no inclination to get Amy's order, leaned on the counter and blew out a chuckle. "I haven't seen you in forever. No one has. You're like that rich guy who holed up in his mansion and let his fingernails grow super long." And yeah, he even glanced at Jax's fingernails. "Was it really that bad over there?"

Yeah. Yeah, it had been bad. But Jax and Baxter weren't friends anymore. At least not close enough for Jax to share the dark details of his trauma. Or the lingering PTSD and night terrors. In his estimation, no one needed to know about the things he'd seen. And, frankly, it was no one else's business how he was coping. Maybe his demeanor got thought Baxter's thick head, because he sobered.

"Well, it's good to see you," he said as he reached for the bags that had been sitting under the heat lamp throughout the conversation. He handed them over. Finally. But he wasn't finished. "It's just bizarre that you both came in *tonight*, you know?"

Jax nodded as he gathered the food. Yeah. It was bizarre. If he hadn't been running late he would have missed her. He wasn't sure if that would be better or worse.

He'd known Nat was coming back to town. Amy had mentioned it. He just hadn't been prepared for a face-to-face with her. Not at all. But, as awkward as it had been, that altercation in the parking lot, he couldn't deny that somewhere, deep in his soul, a sliver of excitement lurked.

Because Natalie Tuttle had finally come home.

Natalie had no idea how she arrived at Momma's house. The shock of seeing Jax again had taken over her brain for the entire drive, and habit had just taken her through the streets until she pulled up to her old home. But here she was. In the driveway. Sitting in the dark in her car. Thinking about him.

He didn't deserve her attention, but that didn't seem to matter to her poor pathetic heart, which insisted on this obsession. She'd thought about that day, about him, about what he'd done, a thousand times, and her adult brain could process it for what it had been. A stupid joke for stupid boys to cackle over. They'd all probably forgotten about it long ago. Jax had probably forgotten about it.

It was pretty clear Jax had forgotten about *her*, too, given the fact that he hadn't said a word to her, other than "Are you all right?"

Are you all right?

No, dammit. *You made me cry. You wounded me to the core. You warped my self-image and all my relationships with men since.*

That was a heavy load to dump on an eighteen-year-old boy. She knew it. Heck, she'd done some pretty foolish things at eighteen. She also knew that, now, she was the only one carrying the load. No one else even cared—about ancient shenanigans or her resultant pain.

Wouldn't it be wonderful to just let it go? To be free of those bad feelings? She was a grown woman now. She'd had a boyfriend. Had had several since that debacle with Jax.

She should be able to move on. She'd tried. It hadn't worked. But then, letting go would have been a lot easier if she hadn't been half in love with him.

Half in love? Could she not even be honest with herself? She'd been totally, completely, head over heels in love with him.

And he'd kissed her on a bet.

It could be amusing. It should be. But some tiny part of her reptilian brain clung to it. Damn it all any—

She jumped as someone knocked on her window, and then gusted a laugh as she saw her sister Celeste press her nose against the glass like a puppy. "Are you coming in?" Celeste said in a playful plea.

"Of course. Yes."

Celeste opened the door and, as Nat stepped out, pulled her into a hug. Oh, it was warm and long and lovely. Celeste had a way of sowing calm to all around her and Natalie reveled in it. "It's so awesome to see you again," she chirped in her chirpy voice. "Thank you for coming. Momma's so excited. We all are. The boys especially. Oh. Can I help you?" she asked as Nat reached back into the car to grab her dinner.

"Could you take this?" she handed over the Smokey's.

Celeste took a deep whiff and moaned.

"And I'll get Pepe."

Her sister's brow rumpled. "Who?"

Nat opened the back door of her sedan, pulled out the cat carrier and lifted it aloft. "Pepe, meet Celeste."

"OMG. He's so cute," she said, though not much of Pepe's adorable black-and-white face was visible through the peepholes. Celeste reached for the carrier.

Nat caught her hand. "Oh no. Don't get too close. He bites."

Her sister lurched back. "Why do you have a cat that bites?"

"He doesn't always bite. Only when he's in the carrier."

"Hmm." Celeste's smile was infectious. She shifted the ribs under her arm and led the way into the house after Nat locked the car. "Momma hates cats," she said apropos of nothing, and Nat grinned.

"Does she?" They both knew damn well. Other than Mr. Bunnynose, who had not lasted long, they'd never had any pets. "I couldn't leave him alone in LA." Not knowing how long she'd be staying.

"In that spacious one-bedroom mansion you own?" Celeste's brow wrinkled. "And what do you do with—what's his name again?"

"Pepe. As in Le Pew?" Because he was black with

a white stripe. And she'd always had a fondness for French skunks.

"Ah! And what do you do with Pepe when you travel?" One of the reasons Natalie had never come home was that her work often required her to travel—most of the shows she worked on were filmed on location, usually a sound stage, far from LA.

Or, at least, that was the excuse she used for the last seven years. Sometimes it was true.

"My neighbor keeps him. He has two cats as well."

Celeste waggled her brows as she opened the door. "Tell me about this neighbor. Is he cute?"

"Super cute."

"And…"

"And he's married."

"Rats."

"To Steve."

She deflated. "Of course."

As they engaged in this nonsensical prattle, Nat took in the living room of her mother's house. The first thing that hit her was the smell. Momma's house had a certain odor. The scent of familiarity, perhaps. It smelled like…home.

Nothing had changed. At all. The Hummels still marched across the mantel, interspersed with family photos. Even the chimneysweep was there, his little ladder glued on—a trifle askew—marking the time Natalie had broken it while dance-dusting.

Momma always said, "You don't need to dance when you dust," but Natalie did. Otherwise, dusting was just work.

Grandma's Clovelly plates—etched with quaint scenes from her hometown in England—rested on a shelf above the arch into the dining room. Grandma met Grandpa during WWII and they'd lived in this house until the day they died. Most of the tchotchkes sprinkled about had been theirs, which was probably why Momma couldn't bear to let them go.

Natalie had hated dusting them all, but now they were a warm reminder of two people she'd loved very much.

"Well?"

She glanced at Celeste, who was staring at her. "It's the same," she said.

"Your room is the same, too. Don't be embarrassed by all the posters."

"Oh, Lord." There had been no teen idols for her. Her posters had all been of the nerd variety. Such as the one with two crows, titled "Attempted Murder." She'd always been a dork. Still was. But now she was a dork with glee. And she got paid for it.

"Where's Momma?" she asked as she set everything down.

Celeste sighed. "In her room. She was tired so she went to bed, but she made me promise to wake her when you got here." And then, when Natalie headed for the stairs, Celeste caught her arm and tugged her to toward the back of the house instead. "She's in the guest room. Since she needs a walker, it's…easier for her to stay on the ground floor. Come on."

She needed a walker? Natalie swallowed heavily as they made their way down the hall. Even though Celeste had tried to prepare her, she knew that it would be difficult to process all the changes the stroke had wrought. Momma had always been a strong, independent woman. And, indeed, just the sight of the walker, with its tennis ball feet, parked at the end of the bed in the shadowed room was a gut punch.

"Momma?" Celeste said softly. "Nat's here."

"Natalie?" Momma's voice was a little slurred and her face was slack. As she struggled to sit up, her left arm hung slackly.

Nat, biting back her shock, sat next to her on the bed and took her mother's hand. "Hey, Momma. I'm home," she said softly.

"Natty," Momma said on a sigh. "It's so good to see you. How was your drive?"

"Long," she said on a laugh. "How are you doing?"

Momma blew out a rude noise and gestured to her body.

"Better every day," Celeste said in a chirp that might have been a little forced. "We were able to get her to the hospital right away. That's important with a stroke you know, because they can mitigate the damage with intervention and treatment, if you're quick."

Momma barked a laugh. "I didn't want to go," she said. "Celeste insisted."

Nat nodded. "It's nice having a nurse in the family. I'm so glad Celeste realized what was happening."

Momma nodded, but said, "I hate hospitals." And then she yawned.

"You're tired," Nat said. "I should let you rest. Unless you're hungry? I brought Smokey's…"

"Yum," Celeste said encouragingly, but Momma made a face.

"You go. Eat. We'll talk more tomorrow." She practically pushed Natalie away.

"Are you sure?"

In response, Momma snuggled deeper into her pillows. "I'll see you tomorrow." But then, as Nat stood and headed for the door she called out, "Oh, Natty?"

"Yes, Momma?"

"I'm glad you're home."

It was heartwarming and sweet and a wonderful thing to hear, and it nearly brought a tear to Nat's eye. "I'm glad too, Momma."

"Come on. Sit down. Eat." Celeste pulled out a chair at the old dining table.

"Will you eat with me?" Nat offered.

Celeste glanced at the grease spots on the brown paper bag and licked her lips. "I couldn't."

"I got a whole rack…"

For some reason, Celeste set her hand on her tummy. "Oh, I really shouldn't…"

But in the end, she did. She got a plate for Natalie and one for herself too, poured two glasses of red wine—after a short discussion about which vintage best accompanied Smokey's barbecue sauce—and went at those ribs like a velociraptor coming off a vegan diet.

When there was nothing left but a boneyard and a couple corn muffin crumbs, Nat brought in her bag and Pepe's food and litter box, but though she was dead tired, she couldn't go to bed. She'd always loved chatting with Celeste and face-to-face was so much better than phone calls or Zooms; it had been the better part of a year since she and Celeste had been together.

While she loved all her siblings, growing up Nat had always been closest with Nate and Celeste; she and Amy had always seemed to rub each other the wrong way. The worst of it had been the horrible fight they'd had right before Natalie left.

It was better, now that they were adults, especially since the boys had come along, but even then, conversations with Amy could be a minefield. Natalie tried to stay in the safe zones which resulted in somewhat superficial interactions.

With Celeste, on the other hand, she could talk about almost anything, so this evening was a treat.

Nat let Pepe out of his cage so he could avail himself of the litter box and explore, then refilled their glasses.

"I gotta say," Celeste said, rolling her wine between her palms. "You look really great."

Nat lifted her glass. "Thanks."

"What's so different?"

"The nose ring?" Nat said with a grin.

"Ahh. It might be that." Celeste attempted a smile. "I'm surprised Mom didn't mention that."

Nat nearly laughed out loud, because in the past, Momma had made quite clear how she felt about loose girls with piercings. She'd always been prim and proper, the perfect military wife. Everything in their lives had been precise and SOP—standard operating procedure, in military speak. Dinner at six—right after Dad came home. Lights out at eight. When they were little, the four of them had worn matching outfits, and there were many "casual" photos of them lined up by height. Something as radical as pierced ears had been taboo. She grinned at her older sister. "I'm a grown-up now. I make my own decisions."

"Well, I'm glad you decided to finally come home."

Nat made a face. For her this was a tender point. "I've come home lots," she reminded her sister. "We did Raging Waters for John J's birthday last summer. Remember? And that family trip up to Victoria on the Clipper two years ago? That weekend in Friday Harbor for whale watching? I always come home when I can—"

"I meant here. Coho Cove. Home."

Nat took a breath. "This town isn't home. Not for me. It never was." It was the end of the world. It was the place where you moved after your father died and the perfect, magical life you knew dissipated into the wind.

It hadn't helped that, shortly after they'd settled in Coho Cove, her twin brother, her partner in crime, Nate, had died from a totally unexpected case of anaphylactic shock. Nat had been left to navigate this unfamiliar landscape, and high school, without him. Just another empty space in in her heart. Another reason why it was too painful to be here. Nate's death had hit everyone hard, especially following so closely after their father's passing, but Nat had never really recovered.

Celeste noted the downturn of her mood and frowned. "I really have missed you."

"I've missed you, too."

"It's only the four of us now. We've got to stick together."

Well, hell. What could she say to that? She couldn't think of anything, so she said nothing.

But Celeste wasn't done making her point. She took another sip of wine, then blurted, "You could have come home, you know. At least for Christmas."

Nat stood up and wandered to the fireplace. Her gaze landed on the family picture they'd taken while skiing in the Alps. Dad had been alive then. Nate, too. She stopped herself from tracing her brother's face with her finger, but just barely. "My job is demanding," she said, and not for the first, or the tenth, time.

Celeste wasn't placated. "You always make us come to you."

Natalie forced an evil grin. "But I have Disneyland."

Celeste narrowed her eyes. "Fine. Okay. I did love Disneyland. And the boys—" She trailed off because they both knew what their sister's boys had thought of Southern California's collection of theme parks. They'd hit every one. Multiple. Times.

"Even Momma had fun in Disneyland." Was it wrong to remind Celeste of that? Even if it was to gloss over that niggling shred of guilt about not coming home for so long. But honestly. No one in her family understood how miserable she'd been in this little town. When they'd moved here after their father had died—massive heart attack while they'd been stationed in Stuttgart—everyone else had simply slid in, found their place, as though they belonged—even Nate. And no one in her family had had a clue why Natalie been so miserable here, because it had been far too painful to explain.

Simply put, her world had shrunk. One day, she'd

been living in Germany, taking weekend jaunts to Paris or Munich and the next, she lived in a Podunk mill town—that wasn't even a mill town anymore. Regardless, she'd known, immediately, instinctively, that she didn't fit in here.

Even if she had been able to put words to her discomfort, her family, undoubtedly, would have pooh-poohed her reason—they'd always pooh-poohed her reasons. She was Natalie, after all. Dad's little drama queen, the family goofball.

So, she'd lived here, in this tiny little universe, surrounded by people who didn't understand her.

There had been one bright light, though, in those early days.

Back then, before he joined the football team, Jax had been an outsider, just like her. He'd been the person who had come up to her empty table at lunchtime on her second day in Coho High, and asked to join her. They hadn't talked much, other than to discuss what was in their lunch bags, but it had meant the world to her to have some connection. With someone.

As time went on, over lunch every day, the two outcasts found affinity in silly things like love of art and music, philosophical discussions and spirited arguments over the best jellybean flavors.

For a long while, Jax had been the only one who seemed to understand. At least, she'd thought he'd understood her.

But then, he joined the football team, and he was suddenly popular, and she receded into the shadows again, a ghost in her own life. Suddenly he didn't meet her eye in the hall anymore. Suddenly he had a new lunch crew. And suddenly she was alone again.

Well, not totally alone. She'd made some other friends by then, other misfits like his sister Sheida who was too smart for Coho High, and Ben Sherrod who was an outcast too, and Ian MacMurphy and the yearbook team. But even with these new friends, Natalie felt the loss of Jax's friendship to her core.

That kiss in the gym, behind the bleachers, had been the killing blow of their relationship but, honestly, it had begun to fade long before then.

Celeste reached out and touched her hand. "Natalie. You should go to bed."

Nat blinked. "What?"

"You're practically falling asleep right here at the table. Come on. Let's get you and Pepe upstairs."

"But Amy? The boys?" She'd hoped to see them tonight. If even for a moment.

Her sister chuckled. "They're probably in bed already. It's past nine and Amy gets up at 0-dark-thirty. You can stop by and see them tomorrow."

Oh. Right. Nat was used to all-hours living. She needed to remember that when people lived in small towns, they had small schedules. "How's Amy's bakery doing?"

Celeste shrugged. "It's the only bakery in town." She stood and collected the plates and trash. "Come on. You're tired. You go to bed. I'll clean up."

And yeah. Celeste was, as usual, exactly right. Natalie was asleep almost the moment her head hit the pillow. There was barely a moment to reflect on her unexpected altercation with Jax—which was a blessing.

He was nothing to her now but an artifact from a wounded past.

She'd moved on.

No doubt he had, too.

Chapter Two

Natalie woke up early the next morning. Usually when she had the chance to be a layabout in bed, she took it with gusto. But today, there was no nestling into the covers or slapping the alarm. Today she was wide-awake and ready to— *What?*

Checking in on Momma was first on her list, so after she dressed, fed Pepe and made sure to close him in her room—there would be time for him to wreak havoc on Momma's toilet paper rolls later—she headed down to the ground floor. Momma's room had always been upstairs, the master. It was hard to think of her being trapped on the ground floor. Thank God she was still mobile—with the help of a walker—but stairs were a challenge for her, Celeste said. At least for now.

It was hard to think of her like that—limited. Momma

had been a force of nature all Nat's life. Opinionated, demanding and usually right. Like all military wives, she'd been the general and commander of the family unit. But now... While Nat understood this was going to be a new normal, that there would be adjustments and expectations were changing, it didn't make reconciling to it any easier.

Momma was still asleep—a low rumble greeted Natalie's peep into the room—and Nat didn't want to wake her again, so she decided to head straight over to Amy's house. Now that she was here, she was super excited to see her nephews. She was excited to see Amy too, but it was a cautious enthusiasm because, for some reason, she and Amy seemed to always butt heads.

She had Amy's address, so she plugged it into the GPS on her cell phone. It was a bit of a walk, but it was a beautiful day. Natalie tipped up her nose and drew in the slight hint of brine from the sea. The gulls wheeled overhead, and a slight breeze riffled her hair. She'd forgotten how much she loved being on the coast. How much she appreciated the cool sea air. Though Los Angeles was also on the coast, it was a huge sprawling city and most people never even saw the ocean. It was a bustling place too, invigorating even, but despite living around so many people, she'd often felt alone. Here, walking along the sun dappled sidewalk beneath the maples, she truly was alone, but didn't feel it at all.

To her surprise, there was something just...homey about being back. She tried not to think about it too much, because she was just here for a visit. It wouldn't do to become attached to things. As soon as her show came out of hiatus, she and Pepe would be on their way back to that one-bedroom condo in the Hollywood Hills. It was much better to remember what kind of small town this was. It was better to remember why she'd left.

It wasn't hard to do.

Still, her heart warmed a little as she passed by the pier and the old man fishing there lifted a hand and smiled. She waved back before she could remember to stop herself.

Amy's house was in a part of town that used to be considered the wrong side of the tracks, even though trains loaded with timber had stopped running to Coho Cove long ago—even before Natalie had moved here. It was a sturdy, three-story brick structure with a white-washed exterior. Natalie's lips quirked up as she took in the beautiful garden. Yep. This was where Amy lived. Amy had always had a green thumb. Nat, on the other hand, could kill a philodendron with a glance.

The white picket fence was a lovely touch. Nat pushed it open and made her way up the stairs to the porch and rang the bell. There was a thudding response as someone pounded down the stairs to open the door, but Nat couldn't tell who it was through the beveled glass window. One of the boys, maybe? Amy wasn't much of a stair-thumper.

Her curiosity was horrifyingly satisfied when the door swung open to reveal—*egad*—a bare male chest. Very bare. Very male. He wore a pair of heather gray sweatpants that hugged his hips in an alluring fashion, but low enough to make a girl wonder if they might, at any moment, slip off.

It took a minute for her to wrench her gaze from this panoply to his face.

Her gut lurched.

Jax.

He was standing in Amy's foyer, half naked and scrubbing his hair with one of Amy's towels. Even though he had a plaid shirt in his hand, the implication could not be ignored. Natalie's widowed sister and her long-time crush were a…thing.

She had no idea why she wanted to sink to the ground and weep.

Or, maybe she did.

For a minute, Jax couldn't speak. He could only stare at Natalie in shock. He'd just been thinking about her, after all. Well, thinking about the dream he'd had about her—one that had haunted him for years.

This one had been different, though. It had left him with a tantalizing feeling that there might be hope of redemption. But that kind of hope was a dangerous thing to trust. The dream had clearly been informed by running into her last night at Smokey's. And the fact that he'd fallen asleep thinking about her and how he might possibly orchestrate an appropriate apology.

Now that the moment was here, his throat closed up and his brain switched off. He'd played through this so many times in his mind. He had no idea why he was paralyzed. He had no idea why fear filled him the way it did.

Well, damn it. He did. He was afraid of how she would react. Stupid and cowardly of him, but there it was. She'd never been a vindictive type. Even now, she smiled at him, and it seemed sincere. Was it possible that she'd forgiven him? Was it possible she didn't even remember that kiss?

Hmm. He didn't like that idea at all.

Was it possible that—

"Ahem."

Oh, crap. He should say something. He really should. Shouldn't he?

"Ah, Natalie."

She nodded. "Jax." And then, when he didn't say anything more, because, frankly, he was a dumbass, she added, "Is Amy here?"

He looped his towel around his neck and opened the door wider. "She's at the bakery. She'll be back in a bit. Um, come in. I was just about to make breakfast for the boys."

"Ah."

He had no idea what she meant by that *ah*, but it hardly mattered. She said nothing else as she followed him thorough the wide hallway to the kitchen at the back of the house. He quickly lost the towel and pulled on his shirt. Not that she made him feel exposed—but she kind of did.

"Coffee?" he asked, as it seemed a logical thing to say. She nodded and he poured them each a mug. Then they both sat at the kitchen table and stared into the dark brew for far too long.

She finally cleared her throat and murmured, "Good coffee."

"Thanks," he responded, though he hadn't made it.

Damn. Why was she so hard to talk to? She hadn't used to be hard to talk to. There had once been a time when they'd been on the same wavelength. They'd both been social outcasts, both had a slightly nerdy sense of humor, both never felt at home in this town. That had all changed when he'd started playing football, when all of a sudden he'd become...popular. Everything had changed between them, too, and he had no idea why.

But he certainly knew why things were awkward now. It only made sense for him to bring it up, to apologize and put it to rest once and for all. He sucked in a deep breath and prepared for the inevitable. What was the worst thing that could happen? He could apologize and she could tell him to stuff it? He certainly couldn't blame her for that. At least he, then, would be at peace knowing he had done the right thing. Wouldn't he?

A simple apology shouldn't be so hard. Should it?

He cleared this throat. She lifted her head. Their gazes clashed.

I'm sorry. It was easy to say. Two little words...

But before he could get a word out, much less two, the house shook around them.

Oh, not an earthquake—which would probably have been worlds less destructive. Nope. Amy's boys had woken up and were making their way down the stairs. Or perhaps it was a herd of rhinos...

Nope. First Georgie and then John J came barreling into the kitchen. Georgie, the oldest at six-almost-seven, skidded to a halt. His eyes lit up and he bellowed at a decibel that only a six-almost-seven-year-old could reach. "Aunt Nat!"

John J, who didn't stop in time and plowed into Georgie, screeched. "Auntie Nat! Auntie Nat!"

Both boys swarmed her, chanting, "You're here! You're here!"

It was kind of fun watching her deal with this onslaught, answering their patter of questions—*Yes, I brought you presents. No, they are at Grandma's house. No, Mickey Mouse did not come with me. Yes, T-Rex is the coolest dinosaur.* The boys were overwhelming on a good day, but she didn't seem overwhelmed in the least. With John J on her lap in his Buzz Lightyear pajamas and Georgie by her side, they chatted and laughed and got reacquainted while Jax made pancakes.

Hardly a gourmet endeavor, but the boys didn't mind, especially when he made them mouse-cakes—three circles really, with a blackberry for a nose. One of the reasons he loved these boys—other than the fact that he'd been stationed with their father in Afghanistan and become close friends with him before he died—was that they were so easy to please.

Natalie, on the other hand…not so much. She wrinkled her nose as he set her plate in front of her. "A mouse?" she said, the teasing complaint clearly aimed at the boys. "You want me to eat a mouse for breakfast?"

Jax couldn't help grinning because, somehow, the boy's presence had cracked the ice between them, at least for the moment. "Yep."

"Come on, Auntie Nat," John J urged, waggling his syrup-dripping fork. "They're good."

Georgie nodded and added, with his mouth completely full, "It's not polite."

Nat snorted a laugh. Jax liked the way her eyes twinkled. "Not polite?"

"Mmm-hmm." Georgie swallowed and said, oh-so-primly, in a voice that might have been his mother's, "When someone goes to the trouble to make you food, you say thank you very much and at least try it."

John J nodded in agreement.

It was cute the way Natalie addressed her plate, first poking the mouse head with her fork, and, when it didn't move, she took a tentative bite. The boys stared at her, on bated breath, until she sighed and nodded. "Yes. It is good. I suppose." This last bit was accompanied by a leery glance in his direction, which made the boys howl with laughter.

For some reason, it made Jax grin.

Maybe because this was fun.

Maybe because his sense of impending doom and roiling regret had ebbed.

Maybe because she was grinning, too.

At any rate, it was…nice.

The boys finished their breakfast and hared off to get dressed, leaving Nat and Jax alone in the kitchen surrounded by an uncomfortable silence and mouse parts. Before either could rally an actual topic of conversation, Amy burst through the kitchen door from the garage. She gusted a sigh as she dropped a brown paper bag onto the table with a thud. "Good Lord. Why did I think it was a good idea to open a bakery?"

"Because you love carbs?" Nat suggested.

Amy whirled around, her face alight. "Oh my God. Nat. Are you here? Is it really you?"

"A hologram, actually," Nat said as Amy pulled her into a hug. How Nat. She excelled at snark. Jax had forgotten how much he missed her sharp wit and humor.

How much he missed her.

Amy's hug was warm. Nat didn't want it to end.

"Well," her sister said. "I don't care how you're here, as long as you're here."

"Thank you."

She tipped her head to the side and gave Nat the once-over. "You look great. What's different?"

"Um, my haircut?" Nat fluffed her short curls.

Amy smooshed up her face and shook her head. "No. That's not it." As usual, her attention quickly flicked to the next item on the agenda. "Are the boys up?" One would think the mess on the table would have answered that.

"Jax made us all pancakes," Nat said.

"Oh, thank you, Jax." Amy patted him on the shoulder.

He poured her a cup of coffee. A horribly domestic thing to do. "How'd it go?" he asked in an equally domestic tone. Nat wasn't quite sure why it made the mouse in her belly skitter.

Amy rolled her eyes, blew out a breath and collapsed into a chair. "I can't believe Henri quit." She turned to Natalie. "My best pastry chef."

"Your only pastry chef," Jax reminded her. This was Coho Cove after all. Probably not a lot of French pâtissiers floating around.

"Poof. Off to greener pastures. I was able to hire

another straight out of pastry school, but, well, what the hell are they teaching in pastry school these days? I have to hold her hand every moment. What's the point of hiring someone if it doesn't make life easier for me?"

Natalie, for her part, shook her head.

"She'll come along," Jax said soothingly. "Just give her some time."

Amy made a face at him. "You just say that because she's got the hots for you."

A flush crept up his cheeks. When his gaze met Nat's, he quickly looked away. "I can hardly help that," he muttered.

"Stop smiling at her, then," Amy said crisply. "She's an impressionable girl." Like the proverbial ping-pong ball, she turned back to Nat. "How long are you staying?"

Well, hell. What kind of question was that? Nat forced a laugh. "Come on. I just got here." This time, when she accidentally met Jax's gaze, it was her turn to look away.

"Well, I'm glad you're here," Amy said with a sigh. "It'll be good for Momma."

"How is she?" Nat asked, as Jax busied himself cleaning up the breakfast mess. Again, terribly domestic. It would be wise to simply accept the fact that Amy and Jax were an item and just deal with it. Trouble was, she really didn't want to, which was beyond idiotic because Jax had never been the guy for her, no matter how much her little angsty, teen heart had wanted it to be so.

Amy grabbed John J's plate before Jax could take it, and started eating leftover mouse. "Haven't you seen her?" Ugh. There was that sharp, judgy tone—often prevalent in her sister's observations—that made Nat want to curl up and hide. Instead, she sucked in a deep breath and forced a brilliant smile. Was it cowardly to avoid an unpleasant confrontation by keeping things light and avoiding deeper issues? Maybe. But with Amy, she'd found it to be the best course. She didn't want to spend her visit bickering with her sister.

"Well, I spoke to her a little bit, last night. But she was in bed. And she was still asleep this morning, so…"

Yes! The smile worked. The bomb was defused. Amy gusted a sigh. "She does sleep a lot. The doctor said it may help her heal." She shook her head. "I'm worried about Celeste too."

Natalie's brows furrowed. "She's been carrying a lot of the load."

"Humph." Amy crossed her arms. A familiar storm arose in her expression. "I'm carrying a load, too—"

"I know. I know." Crap. Nat knew that tone. She shot Jax a desperate glance, and then, when she realized whom she was seeking help from, she looked away. "I meant because she lives with Momma. It's twenty-four seven."

"And two boys and a bakery aren't twenty-four seven?"

"That's not what I—"

"Look, *I've* always been here if Celeste needs help." Amy's meaning was clear.

Natalie swallowed heavily. Acid rose in her throat at the implication. "And I've always been away? Is that what you're saying?"

"I'm not saying it," Amy said. What she didn't say, what was plain as day in her stance, was, *but it's true*.

"Hey," Jax said, apropos of nothing. Surely not to steer the conversation away from a dangerous snipe-infested bog. "Amy, were you able to get a sitter for tonight?"

Amy stilled. Her mutinous expression waned. A smile peeped out. "I did." Then she turned to Nat and gushed, "Oh, Nat. You have to come to Lizzie's party tonight."

Natalie swallowed, hard, and stared at her sister. "Lizzie who?" Surely not Lizzie-the-Gorgon-of-Coho-High?

"Lizzie Chisolm, of course." Amy beamed.

There was no *of course* about it. "You hate Lizzie Chisolm," Nat reminded her sister. "Didn't she draw a moustache on your face with indelible ink at Lynn's sleepover?"

"Oh, pish. That was long ago."

"Not that long."

"We were fifteen. Besides, Lizzie and I have made up. We're besties now."

"Besties?" They'd been cats in a yard fight. "I guess I have been gone for a while."

Amy shrugged. "We took Lamaze classes together when I was pregnant with John J. Both our husbands were overseas. That kind of thing creates a bond."

Natalie nodded and smiled, but inside, a sudden pain pricked at her. She should have been here to take Amy to Lamaze classes. She could have been.

Except she wasn't.

She chose that moment to accidentally glance at Jax, so she saw his sympathetic expression. It looked like... pity. She immediately tightened her spine and threw back her shoulders and brightened her smile. Of all people, he was the last one she wanted to suspect that she had missed her family. She'd missed them terribly, despite her determination to pretend otherwise. Even to herself. Being here with them, now, only served to remind her how much.

Jax left a few moments later, claiming he had to get to work. It was only a small consolation that he just left, that she didn't have to watch him kiss her sister good-bye. That would have been misery.

For some annoying reason, that interaction with Natalie at breakfast stuck with Jax all day, souring his mood and causing irritating mistakes in his work. At one point, he just threw down the chisel and walked away.

Fortunately, he only walked as far as the coffeepot in the kitchenette, which was at the far end of his studio. He pulled down his mask and took a deep draw of the brew in his mug. It was cold and bitter, but that was what he needed.

Something, anything, to get back in the groove.

He loved creating art in wood—everything from huge, humble logs to delicate driftwood. It was the true joy of his life to be able to make something natural, organic, beautiful with his own two hands. And, occasionally, with a chain saw. The fact that people wanted to *pay* for his art was just icing on the cake. It had begun as therapy to work through issues that had arisen during his time in the service, but now it was also a revenue stream—especially with the high-end clients who visited the Sherrod, his friend Ben's resort on the south beach.

His PTSD still haunted him, paralyzed him, blocked him from living the life he wanted, the life he could feel, hovering just out of reach. But he was getting better. And that gave him hope.

Usually when he worked, the ideas flowed effortlessly from his imagination into the wood. It was like magic. Like he and his tools were one. But not today.

Today his mind was elsewhere, as though he were fighting himself. Which was ridiculous, of course. He knew what he should do. He should just quit for the day and go fishing. Or go for a run on the beach. Or tackle those administrative tasks he saved for the muse's day off.

He was debating the options and trying to silence his workaholic conscience when someone knocked on the door of his shop-slash-residence. Though it was mostly shop—with a hot plate, small fridge, a room for sleep… and the aforementioned coffeepot. It was nothing fancy, but his muse didn't care much for fancy. His place was isolated, quiet, serene. Everything his soul needed to heal.

With a sigh, he brushed the sawdust from his long-sleeved shirt, propped his safety goggles onto the top of his head and opened the door.

It was hard not to break into a grin when he saw his buddy Ben Sherrod standing there with an enormous chunk of driftwood in his arms, cradling it like an over-fed baby. "Hey, Jax," he said. "I come bearing gifts."

"Wow." Jax took a moment to appreciate the worn curve of the piece, the jaunty thrust on one end and the mouth at the other. It was a salmon. He saw it hiding in there. "This is fantastic."

"Do you mind taking it, then?" Ben said with a grunt. "It's heavy."

"Oh, of course." Jax took the log and carried it over to his drying bench, where it would have to sit until it was dry enough to work.

"It washed up on the beach yesterday and I immediately thought of you." Ben was one of Jax's best procurers. A great deal of his friend's business was real estate development all over Washington state, so he always brought in interesting pieces of wood and logs. Once, he'd shown up with a load of burl wood—which was beautiful to work with, and nearly impossible to get anymore.

"Thanks. I appreciate it."

Ben meandered over to Jax's work in progress— a full-size representation of a Dryad in Summer, and drew his hand down her curves in appreciation. "This is beautiful. What is she? A mermaid?"

No, dammit!

Jax drew in a deep, calming breath. Not everyone had an artist's eye, after all. "She's a dryad." A *summer* dryad, thank you very much. He'd successfully captured her form emerging from the wood, but was struggling with her face.

"Nice. She'd look great in the foyer of the Sherrod."

Jax snorted a laugh, because Ben said that about all of his theme pieces. "I'll let you put in a bid on her," he joked, although it probably wasn't a joke. More than once his pieces had gone to auction.

"She'd have to wear a bra, though," Ben said. "I run a respectable establishment, after all."

He knew Ben was teasing, so he responded with simplicity. "Well, I'm not giving her a bra." The human form was beautiful in all its glorious diversity. Also, if he were being honest, sculpting naked was half the fun of the job. "Can I offer you something to drink?" He waved at the kitchenette. "Beer's cold. So's the coffee."

"Beer, please." With the ease of an old friend who'd been over many times, Ben tipped over the card table and brushed the sawdust onto the floor, did the same to one of the chairs and took a seat.

Jax handed him a beer and then, before he could sit as well, said, "Oh! I forgot. Amy sent some pastries over."

Ben barked a laugh. "Pastries with beer? Um… I think that's a hard pass."

"Naw, you'll like these." Jax popped the covered plate into the microwave. "They've got hot dogs in them."

It was funny, the way Ben raised a brow. "Hot dogs? In pastry?"

Jax barked a laugh. "Ah, but you forget. Amy has *boys*. She knows what boys like." Thirty seconds later, Jax set the plate on the table and lifted the cover with a flourish. "Voilà."

He got comfy as Ben tentatively picked up a pastry—

a little hand pie, actually—and took a nibble. "Mmm," he said.

"Good, right?" Jax grabbed one as well. And damn, it was tasty. But then, it had been a long time since breakfast, and he was hungry.

They ate in silence, the only sounds their murmurs of appreciation, slurps on their beers and the occasional belch. It was a comfortable silence, the kind between friends who knew they didn't have to talk if they didn't want to.

Jax took a moment to appreciate the value of having a friend like that. It was soothing, having a buddy who *saw* him. They were few and far between.

Ben had always been a steadfast support in Jax's life. They'd both been social outcasts in elementary and middle school—Jax because of his father and Ben because of his. Hardly for equal reasons, though. Ben's dad was a gazillionaire, which made people uncomfortable, and Jax's dad hailed from the nearby North Chinook village, their ancestral lands, which also made people uncomfortable, but for a different reason entirely—especially since the tribe's Federal recognition had been revoked.

It had only made sense for the two outsiders to bond together way back then. They'd gone a step further and created a secret alliance back in junior high—Ben had named it that because he'd been a *Survivor* fan at the time. That bond held strong, even after Jax gained some popularity when his body filled out and he discovered a gift for playing football. Although that fleeting popularity had gone to his head for a minute, and he'd aligned with people like Baxter Vance and his minions... Ben had remained a loyal friend.

When Jax returned home from the service, battered and in pieces, Ben had been there for him. Again. Still. No matter what. But nearly everyone else—all the people who had meant so much to him in high school, those whose opinions had had a hand in shaping his life and identity for a time—had dissolved away like sugar in the rain when he'd needed them.

But Ben had been stalwart, strong, supportive. Even though he'd been going through his own hell as well.

Their camaraderie was maybe even stronger now.

"How's Quinn doing?" Jax asked when he finished munching.

"She's good."

"Is she, ah, talking yet?"

Ben shook his head. Ben's daughter was five, and had been in the car during the wreck that had killed her mother. She hadn't said a word since. "Her nurse says she's showing more emotion. That's a good thing. I guess."

Jax nodded. "Just gotta give it time." That was what the therapists said, anyway.

"Yep." Ben lifted his beer, but it was a dour toast.

"So...how are you doing?" Jax asked. It had been over a year since Ben's wife, Violetta, had died, but his buddy played his cards close to the chest. It was hard to see if he was still suffering.

His heavy sigh was a testament to that. "I'm fine. Thanks."

"Just fine?"

"Fine enough."

"Okay."

"Okay."

It was logical to assume Ben's glower meant, more or less, *drop it*. So, he did. Searching for another topic took a second, though, and Jax had no idea why, when he opened his mouth, he said, "Hey, have you heard? Natalie Tuttle's back in town." And then, "Do you remember Natalie?"

Ben snorted a laugh, perhaps in relief that the subject had turned from him and his pain. "I *should* remember her."

A slurry of magma surged in Jax's gut at Ben's tone. He had no idea why. Heck, Ben and Natalie would be great together. Perfect together. In fact—

"I had a crush on her sister, remember?"

Of course. Of course, he remembered.

It annoyed him that he had to remind himself to remember what mattered to Ben, though. Because his own self-interests tried to dominate his thoughts. It was a natural response, his therapist told him, when the mind was stuck in survival mode due to trauma. It was a hard pattern to break, but he was trying.

"Celeste." He shot a grin at his buddy. Unlike her sisters, Celeste was quiet and no-nonsense, and just got things done with no drama. "She's a sweetheart."

Ben grinned, but it was more of a grimace. "She hates me."

"I can't imagine that."

"Hah." Ben grabbed another pastry. "I'm the beast who built that *revolting resort* on the Point. She's the woman who glared at me through a thousand planning commission meetings. The environmental impact reviews were particularly uncomfortable."

"I can't imagine Celeste glaring at anyone."

"Try building a resort on the Point in Coho Cove." Ben sipped his beer. "I heard you're staying at Amy's now," he said apropos of nothing.

They hadn't been talking about Amy—they'd been talking about Celeste—but whatever. "Yep." Jax swirled his beer. "She's training a new baker and needs to be on-site super early. She doesn't want to leave the boys at home alone first thing in the morning, or wake them up to take them in with her." And she could hardly take them to her mother's now—especially since Pearl was recuperating and their housekeeper was recovering from a broken hip. "Just makes sense for me to sleep there."

Ben made a face. "She doesn't want the boys home alone? Can you blame her?"

They both laughed. They both volunteered in a local mentoring project for boys who'd lost a parent, chaperoning camping trips with Georgie and John J, and were fully aware that Amy was raising arsonists. "In exchange for sleeping over and being there when the boys wake up, she's paying me off in food."

"Sounds like a great deal. Amy gets some much-needed support, and you get out of the Batcave."

Jax grinned and held his pastry aloft. "It's not bad." It was true. It *had* been good for him, too, forcing him to leave the safety of his self-imposed prison and interact with other humans when his soul just wanted to run away and hide. And the boys… They challenged him, entertained him, exasperated him, revived him. It was impossible to be self-absorbed and maudlin in their presence. So, yes. It had been a good arrangement.

And today, there'd been another benefit. One he had never expected. Because he'd been there this morning, he'd seen *her* again. Talked to her again—

Ben must have caught his expression. "What the heck are you thinking?" he asked on a laugh.

"Huh? Oh, nothing."

"Hah! I call BS." He so often did. It was one of the things he appreciated about Ben. Even though it was irritating. Or because it was.

"Okay. All right. It's Natalie."

Ben snorted. "I figured you brought her up for a reason."

"She's back in town."

"So you said."

They sat silently for a minute, Jax looking for words and Ben being patient. "Do you remember Senior Skip Day?" he finally asked.

Ben shook his head, probably in an attempt to keep up with Jax's pivot. "I remember spending it in detention."

"Right." They'd been caught, a whole clowder of them, over at Sorry Beach, having a non-sanctioned party. They'd been rounded up—nearly the entire senior class—and herded into the gym for detention. God, they'd been young. "I, ah, kissed Natalie behind the bleachers that day."

Ben's look was wry. "I know that. Everyone knows that. I'm surprised it wasn't in the yearbook."

Jax made a frustrated sound. "I didn't mean it the way it happened."

"You didn't mean to kiss her? Or you didn't mean to kiss her behind the bleachers?"

"Neither! Damn it. Baxter and Cubby bet me I wouldn't kiss her—"

"You kissed her on a bet?"

"Oh, wait, my friend. It gets worse." His gut churned as he thought about it.

"Yikes."

"Yeah. So, there we were in this clinch under the bleachers, and her eyes were wide, and she was staring at me and…"

"Dude. You can't just trail off like that."

"I kissed her…" It had been an excruciatingly sweet kiss. He'd always wondered what might have happened, what could have happened between them if things had ended differently.

"And?" Ben prompted.

Jax raked his hand through his hair. "Apparently, Baxter and Cubby and Sharon and Lizzie—the whole gang—"

"The *popular* kids." There was hardly any vitriol in Ben's tone even though he'd been victim to their cruel pranks as well.

"Yeah. Anyway, they were all around the corner, watching. And when I kissed her…"

"What?"

"They all ran over and started laughing and saying

things—horrible things—to her. Then Cubby slapped me on the shoulder and said good job for kissing the dog, and they all started woofing."

Ben upended his beer. "They were the worst."

"Total jerks. But the thing is… I was kind of a jerk, too. I mean, I had been. I'd tried to be like them… Certainly enough for her to assume I'd been in on the joke. I hadn't been. But, oh, man, the look in her eyes when she stepped away, took it all in, saw them laughing at her… I honestly, truly didn't know what they had in mind when they goaded me to kiss her…"

"Who knows if they even planned it," Ben said on a snort. "Back then, they all had a kind of knee-jerk mentality. With the emphasis on *jerk*. They'd take any opportunity to bully someone they considered a lesser soul."

"I know. I just hate that I was a part of it."

"And now she's back." Leave it to Ben to work it all out.

"Now she's back."

"What are you going to do?"

What? Anything? Nothing? "I have no idea."

"What do you *want* to do?"

"I want to take it all back—"

"In this reality, Jax. What do you want to do?"

It took a minute to get the words out, because something inside him was holding them back in. But finally, they released in a rush. "I want to apologize. I want her to forgive me. I want it to be over. I want to be free."

"Wow. This really has haunted you."

He wasn't sure why, but it had. For too long.

"Then there's only one thing to do." Ben grabbed the last pastry and popped it into his mouth. "As you said. Apologize. Just do it."

"But…"

Ben blew out a sigh. "But what?"

"But what if she doesn't accept? What if I dredge all that pain back up? What if—"

"What if you explain yourself, and tell her you are deeply, sincerely sorry for any pain you might have caused when you were in the throes of hormonal chaos, and see what she says?"

What if? "It would be nice not to have that horrible feeling whenever I think of her."

"I imagine it would be nice for her, too, to let it go. I mean, if she still remembers and all."

"Do you think she still remembers?" It was a foolish, hopeful and foolishly hopeful question. Of course, she remembered. He'd seen it in her eyes. She'd been carrying this weight as long as he had. He owed it to them both to address it. No matter how it played out. It was the right thing to do.

In response, Ben took a shot across the room, dunking his beer can in the trash with a *thunk*. "Just do it," he said. "You'll feel better."

Jax nodded. He felt better now, as though working through this thorny issue this had lifted a weight of some kind. Yep, it might not be perfect or easy or fun, but he owed it to her, and he owed it to himself, to suck it up and say sorry.

Oddly enough, after Ben left and Jax went back to work, he was taken with a familiar ease, moving the chisel with gentle precision, as though some higher power was guiding his hand.

He didn't stop until he finished his dryad's face, and wouldn't you know it, she looked suspiciously like Natalie Tuttle.

Chapter Three

When Natalie returned from Amy's, Celeste asked if she could pick Momma up from physical therapy at the Elder House on the nearby tribal lands. Celeste worked there as a nurse, and had dropped Momma off in the morning, but she had a Coho Days committee meeting across town that afternoon. Nat didn't bat an eye because Celeste had always loved being active in the community; she especially enjoyed coordinating community events. Besides, it was a chance to help out—the reason she'd come—and it was a great excuse to tool around town in the daylight. Most of all, her old friend Sheida also worked there and Nat was excited to see her again.

When the GPS deposited Nat in the parking lot of the *new* Elder House, she was surprised. It was a gleaming, sprawling, multi-winged longhouse lying low to the ground, with big bright windows balancing the space and lifting it up. It seemed to blend with the natural surroundings in a way that enhanced the beauty of the shoreline without dominating it. It was, in a word, beautiful. She barely remembered the old Elder House, but it was certainly not this.

As she made her way to the oversize front doors, they opened on a mechanical whine, and a slender, stylishly dressed woman stepped out to greet her with a beaming smile. Her heart took a leap as she recognized Sheida Stringfellow. At once, Nat was flooded with warmth and memories.

Though they'd stayed in touch after Natalie left, and even gone on a few trips together, it had been a while since they'd seen each other. Far too long.

Sheida had graduated from high school with honors—a year early—and then gone on to the University of Washington, where she'd graduated in record time with a major in psychology and had then gone on to earn several master's degrees. She was Celeste's boss at the community center-slash-retirement home for tribal elders. Seeing her now, that welcoming smile, that energy only Sheida radiated in exactly that way, was like a rain shower of remembrance. Emotion, warm and resonant, welled.

"Sheida!"

"Welcome, Nat!" she said with an enormous, enveloping hug. Sheida did a lot of things with a hug. She always had. "Finally, you're back. Good glory, I've missed you," she said as she hugged Nat again. And again, for good measure. "So," she said, once she got all the hugging out of her system. "How are you?"

"I'm great." Funnily enough, she was. She felt...really good. Maybe it was spending the morning with the boys, or seeing Sheida again, or all the hugging, but she felt...great.

"All good with the job?"

"Love the job."

"And are you seeing anyone?"

Nat's smile froze. It was a normal question from a friend after a couple years apart. She just wasn't sure how to answer. So, she went with a vague, "I'm dating." Which was true. Kind of.

"Ah. Anything serious?"

She thought of Carl, then barked a laugh. "Not really. No." She and Carl enjoyed each other's company, but it was hardly serious.

She was about to return the lob, but before she could, Sheida turned to the building behind her, threw out her arms and said, "What do you think of my baby?"

Nat blinked. "Your baby?"

She laughed at Nat's expression and waved at the building again. "The Elder House. Celeste did mention that I'm the queen here, right?"

"Not in those exact words—" They both chuckled. "But honestly, this place is not what I expected."

"A double-wide on the beach?"

"Kinda?"

Sheida nodded. "Hmm. Well, we *were* close to that at the old tribal elders' building. It's now the Lodge House."

Nat blinked. "What is that?"

"Oh." Sheida rolled her eyes. "A place for the guys

to drink beer, play pool and watch sports on ginormous TVs. Oh, and give each other awards banquets."

"Nice."

She shrugged. "Keeps them out of trouble. But the new Elder House is so much more. I can't wait to give you a tour."

It looked fantastic. "How did the tribe afford all this?" As an unrecognized tribe, this small community didn't have access to the resources or affiliations that some of the other local tribes enjoyed. Funding for social services had always been a challenge.

Sheida smiled. She leaned in and whispered, "We have a secret angel." At Nat's quirked brow, she added, "Someone who saw a need in the community, had extra money, asked what we wanted and gifted it to us. *Us* being *me*, I suppose, because I was the one who he— *or she*—" she hastily added "—consulted with on the project."

"Does that make you a tribe elder?" It was supposed to be a jokey question, because Sheida was anything but old.

Her response was definitive. "Yes." And when she read Nat's expression, she grinned. "Being an elder in the community is a state of mind, honey, not a number as arbitrary as age. You become an elder when you decide to give back to your tribe. At least, that's what we try to teach the kids here. Come. Let me give you a tour," she said in a tone that made clear a tour would be given. She linked her arm with Nat's and tugged her into a foyer sporting a reception desk, a spattering of comfortable furniture and the occasional potted plant.

They didn't get far before a tiny voice called out, "Miss? Oh, miss?"

Sheida turned and smiled at a white-haired woman in a paint spattered smock who had emerged from the Art Room. "Yes, Ms. Ida. What is it?"

Ms. Ida's forehead accordioned. "Someone's been stealing the toilet paper from the community bathroom again."

When Ms. Ida leaned around Sheida to eye Nat suspiciously, she swallowed the urge to deny it was her.

"I'll have Henry tend to it, Ms. Ida. You go on back to pottery class." And, when the older woman didn't budge, thank you very much, Sheida added, "You don't want to miss anything."

Ms. Ida frowned and grumbled, "Well, all right," before heading down the hall, but not without another long hard look at the size and shape of Nat's bag.

Once they were alone, Sheida took Nat's arm again and relaunched the tour. "She is a dear, but— Oh, Henry," she called to a young man in overalls who emerged from a door behind the reception desk.

He came over at once. "Yes, Ms. Stringfellow?"

"Henry, Angry Bear has been stealing TP again. Can you restock the bathroom, please?"

"Sure thing, Ms. Stringfellow," Henry said with a salute, and headed off to comply.

Natalie stifled a chuckle. "So, you have a resident named Angry Bear?"

Sheida grinned. "It's a code name. So we don't hurt his feelings. But he's very grumpy," she added in her defense, though she needed none.

"And a klepto, apparently."

"Only with toilet paper."

"Good to know." It was hard to tamp down her smile. "Gosh, Sheida. I love the energy of this place. And how hard you work to make people happy."

She shook her head. "Well, you can't make people happy. People are happy or unhappy. Whatever they want to be. It's a choice. I just try to make it easy for them to choose happy."

"What a nice way to spend your life."

"Aw, thanks. I think so. Come on. So much to see." She really wanted to give that tour. Like, *really* wanted to. So, Nat let her. "The residence is here on the right." The "right" being a hall with doors all along it branching to the east. "Most are apartments, but there are a couple studios. There's a day room, dining room, gym, sauna, spa, med office…" She waved her hand, pulling Nat along behind her.

"That's where Celeste works?"

Sheida nodded. "Mostly. Though we all agree to help where it's needed. Sometimes she applies Band-Aids and snuggles at the day care."

"Aw, I bet she'd like that." Celeste loved children. Then, "Wait, there's a day care?"

"Cradle to grave, baby. Cradle to grave." Sheida grinned and headed down the left wing. "Day care is over here, far enough away from the senior day room, so we don't get complaints about the noise." She waggled her brows and added, "From the toddlers."

"Of course."

They headed down the west wing hallway, which

Sheida explained was the Community Center portion of the facility, passing meeting rooms, a library and a door marked Cattery in Progress. At the end of that hall, Sheida paused before a large window looking in on a room on the other side of the glass, painted in hard-core primary colors, splattered with very happy—possibly manic—cartoon critters and filled with soft furniture and pillows. "This is the Menagerie."

"Why do you call it the Menagerie?" Nat asked.

"Oh. Just wait." Sheida leaned against the wall and focused on the room.

"What—?"

"Just wait. Recess is almost over."

Indeed, in mere moments, the door flew open wide and a herd—an actual herd—of ankle biters swarmed in, yelling and hollering and whooping with the energy only the freshest souls seemed to possess. It was a total chaos of joy and unbridled youth, pleasantly muted.

"Ahhh." Sheida sighed. "This view always lifts me up."

"I'm surprised I can barely hear them." Indeed, after that initial explosion of enthusiasm, the caregivers followed, more sedately. One of them clapped and bellowed. "Okay. Snack time. Settle. Settle," but even that was at a reasonable decibel.

"Our angel did that." Sheida sighed again. "Upgraded the enclosure without us knowing, or even asking, for it. He added special sound-dampening glass. Oh. Whenever I think of it, I just want to kiss him on the mouth."

"Who is he, your angel?" Ooh. She was dying to know.

Sheida paled. "Did I say it was a man?"

"You said *he*."

"I'm not supposed to say. Don't ask. It's a secret." She locked her lips and threw away the imaginary key. "Anyway, this is where we're going."

She tugged Nat around the glass menagerie into a large sunroom speckled with tables, couches, overstuffed bookshelves, game tables and whatnot. It was in use, but it was a gentle use, tribe members of all ages reading, playing cards or sitting in rocking chairs, gazing out a bank of floor-to-ceiling windows facing the vastness of the Pacific. The tide was on its way in, so there were miles of ripples dancing over the flats, making their way back from deep water. The sky above was blue and gray and tufted with fat clouds. The sun shafted through in shards, bringing a warmth that went beyond physical comfort. It was, simply said, beautiful.

This was art. By an incomparable artist.

Sounds were soft, soothing. The murmur of conversation, the click of a pool ball, the rap of an old man's knuckles on his armchair, in time to a tune only he could hear; he sat in a corner designated by a brightly painted sign that said Silent Disco. The light on his headphones was blue, which probably had some hidden meaning as the woman next to him was tapping her fingers, eyes closed, to the beat of something green.

As for the smells, pine cleaner tangled with the fresh hint of sage and...was that—? Nat's nostril twitched. "Coffee?"

"Yep. Hi, Lauren." Sheida sketched a wave to the barista behind a mahogany counter abusing a sterling pitcher with a steam cleaner. "Hon, have you seen Pearl?"

Lauren thrust her thumb toward the day care's side entrance, a door Nat hadn't noticed yet. "She's with the babies." Then they both laughed as though someone had told a joke.

"Your mom loves the babies," Sheida explained when she noticed Nat's blank look. "Do you want to go to the nursery?"

Not really. At least, she didn't have a burning desire. But Sheida's expression had a whisper of *please* in it, so she nodded. "Sure."

"Here you go." Lauren set two to-go cups on the counter, even though no one had ordered coffee. "It's that mushroom blend you like," she said to Sheida, who gave a mini moan of ecstasy.

"I love every one of your corpuscles," Sheida said to Lauren, grabbing a cup for herself and handing one to Nat.

Who wrinkled her nose. "Mushroom. Coffee." It bore repeating. "Seriously. You're going to make me drink mushroom coffee?"

"I'm not going to make you do anything. Drink it or don't drink it. Besides, who am I to tell you what to do to offset the neurological degradation of aging, or the nootropic properties of regular everyday mushrooms— not even the fun ones? Who am I to… Oh. Right. I'm a doctor—"

"Only of psychology."

"And a nurse. And also…" She paused for smirk purposes. "I got a certificate in herbal healing *on the internet*." This last bit she said with all the pomp and pride with which one might say, "I went to *Hav-ahd*," though it was clear she was teasing "Now, hush. Here we are." She stopped at a closed door, and they both peered through the tiny window at a room painted in soft pastels with bold, simple black-and-white prints hung low on the wall.

It was a surprise to Natalie when she realized *why* the paintings were at crib level—which was silly, really, because, upon reflection, it was so logical. The art was, simply, for the babies.

White cribs marched along one wall, separated by matching changing stations. The other side of the room was a soft mat crawl space filled with toys, and baskets of toys, and, also, more toys. There were rocking chairs posted at all four corners of the room. It was a beautifully designed space filled with color and life.

Then, over by the window, something caught her eye. The eye is drawn to familiarity, they say, so it only made sense that the first person her eyes lit on in that room was, in fact, her mother, sitting in one of the rockers, holding a baby.

What hit her, and hit her hard, was that this was not the Pearl Tuttle she'd expected. For one thing, her eyes were alight, shining with a pure emanation of joy as she stared down at the little bundle in her arms murmuring sweet nothings. Of course, Nat couldn't hear what she was saying to that bundle—on account of the angel with a fetish for soundproofing things—but it must have been sweet.

The baby was enraptured. In awe. He/She/It stared up at this woman Natalie had a hard time recognizing, with wide eyes, faith and an open heart.

And Momma?

Same. She was all in.

It was a beautiful thing to see.

The lines she'd laboriously carved into her face—through decades of frowning, that world of worry she liked to carry on her shoulders—all gone. Staring down at that innocent babe and gurgling nonsense to someone who totally understood nonsense, she seemed to be the purest form of herself Nat had ever experienced.

Something of extreme comfort, the warmest, purest hug, suffused her as she soaked in the sight of her mother, the woman she barely knew now, beaming with love.

"Why are you smiling like that?" Sheida asked musingly.

"Never mind. It's nothing." Nat took a sip of her coffee, but the smile remained.

Sheida sighed deeply and mournfully and then fell silent, staring off into space in a very deliberate, dare we say passive-aggressive, way. As she did. Still, apparently.

That thought made Nat's lips kick up. "What?" she asked.

Sheida glanced her way, eyes wide and lashes aflutter. "What, what?"

Seriously? "What was that sigh for?"

"Did I sigh?" She knew she had, so Nat assumed the question was rhetorical and fluttered her lashes right back—speaking without words the way old friends do. "Fine." Sheida heaved—yet another—sigh. "It's just, you still do that thing, Nat."

That thing? A couple more lash-bats ensued as she waited for Sheida to continue. Because she would.

"You always used to say *nothing* when I'd ask you any question about your emotional state. And you're still doing it."

"Maybe I don't want to talk about my emotional state."

"I understand. Your family isn't exactly easy." She completely ignored Nat's snort. "But you had such a happy look on your face. I was just wondering what you were thinking."

"Well, look at her." Nat nodded to Momma.

"Mmm-hmm. What do *you* see?"

Nat shot her a frown. "Don't psychoanalyze me, please."

"Don't assume everything is about you, please. I'm just wondering. What are you seeing there?"

Nat shrugged. Struggled to find words. "Mother and child."

"Hmm."

"Don't *hmm* me."

"I can't help it. Years of training."

Fine. Whatever. "Just look at her." Pearl Tuttle. Prickly, persnickety, perfection-preferring military Momma. But here, now, helplessly, hopelessly in love. With a tiny face and a button nose and those impossibly small fingers curling around Momma's as though it were a lifeline. An unexpected realization danced into her head, partnered by a lightness in her heart.

"She must have loved me like that, *glowed* like that once, with me in her arms. Wouldn't you think?"

Sheida thought about it for a minute. "Yeah. Probably." And then she spurted a laugh when Nat whipped around in playful outrage at that *probably*.

"Why do I feel jealous of that baby?" She asked herself, but it came out loud, which caused Sheida to assume she wanted some clinical response.

"Well—"

"You don't have to answer."

"I was going to say, sometimes, the elders come down here just to hold a baby for a little while. There's something very grounding about it. You remember what it means to be alive and how special life is. How fragile we are and mostly, how flipping fast it flies by. We forget sometimes. I think it's healing, too, although the clinical findings are more experiential than—"

"You can stop talking now," Nat said and Sheida laughed and pulled her into a hard hug—the ferocity of which nearly spilled Nat's precious mushroom coffee.

"Have I mentioned how much I've missed you?"

"Yes." The hug lasted a long time. It kept on going until Nat returned it. But it made her feel better—which was weird because usually getting emotional made Nat feel uncomfortable.

Whatever. Sheida was good at it. Sheida was good at everything.

Momma looked up just then and their eyes met, and she smiled. All thoughts of Sheida and her wily ways fled. Momma hadn't smiled at her like that in a while. As though she *saw* her.

And actually *liked* her.

Her heart gave a hard thud.

Sheida opened the door and wafts of Mozart and baby powder floated out on the escaping air. "Hey, Pearl. How are you doing?" She took Momma's hand for a quick squeeze.

"Oh, fine. I'm just fine." Her attention barely lifted from that beautiful baby face.

"Natalie is here to take you home, hon."

Momma's frown lines surfaced. Natalie's gut clenched. She had to remind herself the scowl wasn't for her—Momma just didn't want to leave yet. Probably.

"I can bring you back tomorrow, if you like," she said, in an attempt to banish the cloud lowering over her.

And it worked. Momma's smile blossomed. "Really?"

"Really." Why hadn't it been this easy to please Momma before?

Sheida bent down to take the baby and Momma let it go, but with obvious reluctance. "I'll see you tomorrow, sweet Nattynatnat," she said in a singsongy voice Nat remembered from oh so long long ago, and a shiver scudded through her gut.

Because Nattynatnat was Momma called *her* when she was little.

Sheida walked Natalie and Momma to the parking lot, subtly supervising Momma's movements with her walker on the uneven asphalt. Nat tried not to notice how unsteady she seemed now, but it was hard to miss. Especially when Sheida had to help Momma into Nat's car.

"See you both soon," Sheida said before she closed

the passenger door. It wasn't a suggestion. More like a command.

Nat smiled. "I'm looking forward to it." Then with a deep breath, she slipped into the driver's seat, preternaturally aware that this was the first time she and Momma had been alone together in…years.

"Momma." Somehow, she choked out the word. Somehow, she smiled at her mother. "I don't know if I mentioned it last night, but it's so good to see you."

Momma, being Momma, grunted and waved her good hand in a depreciating manner. "I look like hell." Just as they'd been the night before, her words were a bit garbled, as though she'd had a bit too much to drink at a party. One thing about Momma, she'd always been exquisitely put together. It was strange seeing her with no makeup, no jewelry, and her hair—speckled now with a wash of gray—merely pulled back in a band. Somehow the simplicity of her presence made her seem even more delicate, frailer than ever.

Nat started the car and pulled out of the lot. "Well, you look wonderful, Momma. A sight for sore eyes." Yeah. Despite everything, it was lovely to see her. Even as she was. It was certainly better than the alternative. Many people didn't survive strokes at all. Pearl Tuttle, though? She was too stubborn to let something like a subdural hematoma take her down. She'd always been the strength of the family, the backbone. Through thirty-odd moves she'd managed Colonel Tuttle's entertaining—practically a commandment among military officers—and overseen the endless merry-go-round of moving, at the same time keeping track of their household goods, the family accounts and four rambunctious children. And still, some-how, she'd always made Christmas special. No matter where they were in the world, Momma made it home.

"It only took a stroke," Momma muttered to the closed window.

Nat shook her head. "I beg your pardon?"

Momma caught her gaze and held it; the slightly over-wide left eye ruined the perfect symmetry of her face. "For you to come home."

Oh. Right. Nat forced a smile. "I'm on hiatus."

Momma sniffed. "You've been on hiatus before."

Oh, good glory. She should have expected it, this guilt trip. It was, after all, family fare at the Tuttle house.

There was nothing for it. Only one thing to do. "I'm sorry for not visiting, Momma. I have missed you."

Another sniff. And then, after a while, "I've seen your show."

Hardly *her* show. She dressed the sets. "Did you like it?"

A shoulder lifted. "That one man is attractive."

"Devon Donovan?" A wild guess. He was the show's heartthrob.

"Dark hair. Tall?"

"Mmm-hmm."

"I don't like his language, though."

"Momma," Nat said on a laugh. "I don't write the dialogue."

This earned her a familiar glance, one that said *only losers make excuses*.

It would be best to turn the topic. She sucked in a

breath and said cheerily, "I saw the boys this morning. I can't believe how much they've grown."

"Children do that when you're not looking…" It was hard to tell by her tone if she was referring to Amy's kids or her own, but it hardly mattered. Momma found the button to roll down the window. She put her nose in the breeze, effectively ending any conversation until they got home, and Nat walked her through the front door. Then, of course, she had something to say.

She stopped short, teetering on her walker, and sniffed. "I smell urine."

Nat blinked. "Urine?"

Thankfully, Celeste breezed into the living room with a bowl of tomato soup. "There you are!" she said cheerily. "Momma, I've got your lunch." She set the bowl on the side table, then settled Momma into her chair beside it. Then she bent down to make eye contact. "Momma, make sure you eat this." She turned to Natalie. "It's hard, sometimes, getting her to eat."

Momma snorted. "Don't talk about me as though I'm not here."

"Sorry, Momma."

"Why do I smell urine?"

Celeste patted her shoulder. "It's probably the litter box. Natalie brought her cat."

Momma's face twisted up, even more. "I hate cats."

Natalie frowned at her sister. She'd been planning to mention Pepe. She just hadn't gotten around to it yet. "How on earth could you smell the litterbox from here?" It was way up in her room on the third floor.

Celeste's expression was only slightly repentant. "She's very sensitive to smells now."

Momma sighed and picked up her spoon. "It's my superpower."

"I'll go change it. Get some baking soda or something…"

"Don't worry about it. I'll get some air fresheners at the store." Celeste offered a too-cheerful smile. "I think it will be good for us all to have Pepe here."

Momma rumpled her face. "Who the hell is Pepe?"

"Pepe's my cat, Momma. I'd like to let him out of my room, if you don't mind."

"Does he smell like urine?"

"I'm very sure he doesn't. I'll make sure he doesn't."

"All right. Fine." She waved her hand again, this time in dismissal. She found the remote and waggled it aggressively. "Go. Come back after my show."

Celeste took Nat's arm. "Come on. Let's find some baking soda in the kitchen." And Natalie followed, her mood dark and desultory.

Once they were alone, she dropped into a chair at the battered old table that had followed them around the world and shook her head; her mind spun.

"Are you okay?" Celeste asked.

Nat shook her head. "It's just…well, I guess I wasn't expecting her to be so…different."

Celeste shrugged and grabbed two cold sodas from the fridge. "The doctor says it happens sometimes after a stroke. People's personalities can change. Mood swings. Aggression sometimes." And then, when Nat didn't respond, "It's gotta be hard for her too."

"Oh, God." This was all overwhelming. Emotional. Painful. "She's not Momma anymore."

Celeste sat as well. "She absolutely *is* Momma. Just without…"

"What?"

"Filters?"

Momma had always been elegant and proper. Speaking in a low, modulated, soothing voice. Never breaching unpleasant topics. Never saying what needed to be said in favor of dancing around it.

It was as though this stroke had wiped away a veneer, one that had stalwartly kept everything in perfect order. One that did not allow for emotion. Like Dad, she'd always soldiered on with grace. No matter what.

"She's getting older, too," Celeste continued. "Older people often just say what they think."

"I suppose." Natalie stared at the logo on her soda can for no reason other than to stare at something. Suddenly this visit had become eminently more painful. More painful than she could have imagined. For the first time since she'd received the news of Momma's stroke, the truth hit home and hit home hard. Nothing would be the same. Not ever again.

Chapter Four

Jax was sanding his newest creation and still trying to decide how to approach Natalie when the alarm on his cell phone buzzed with the warning that it was time for him to clean up for supper. He'd had to set it, on account of the fact that he always forgot to stop working to eat, and Amy got annoyed when he missed supper. It was, in her opinion, the most important meal for a family. A time to "sit around a table and have a civilized conversation," she'd said more than once.

The fact that she considered him family warmed his heart.

Not that he didn't have a perfectly fine family in Sheida and Pops. But he'd discovered, a man cannot have too much family. Amy and the boys filled a hole in his soul that no one else could. So, if Amy Tolliver wanted him at the supper table at 6:00 p.m. with hands washed and heart open, he tried to comply.

Jax had met George Tolliver in Afghanistan when they just happened to sit near each other one night in the mess hall to watch a Seahawks game being streamed all the way across the world, from a place they both called home.

The ubiquitous so-where-you-from conversation during commercials had revealed their connection to Coho Cove. It was Jax's hometown and George's wife was from there, too. And, wouldn't you know it, Amy Tuttle was his wife.

He and George had bonded. And, damn, George had been a great guy.

It had been Jax's honor and his most sincere regret to accompany his body home after he'd been killed.

That meeting with Amy, to pass on her husband's remains and hand her a folded flag, had been the hardest thing he'd ever done. And he'd done a lot of hard things. Still, the meeting with Georgie and John J—those two precious, fatherless little boys he'd felt he already knew from all the stories and videos and Zoombombs— Well, hell. That had devastated him.

As much as a part of him had wanted to curl up and die because his own life had been shattered, he knew he owed his friend something better. So, he'd adopted George's sons as his own. In a spiritual sense.

And Amy let him.

Where he might have been a glorified babysitter for her, she'd been sharing something he'd needed desperately.

A restored faith in humanity, maybe.

Laughter, definitely.

A chance to be important to someone, absolutely.

So, even though she sometimes irritated him, and she constantly tried to "fix" him, he allowed it. And though he'd never admit it, he sometimes liked it. If that meant setting an alarm to have supper together, it was a small price to pay.

As he stepped through the mudroom into Amy's kitchen, the scent of chicken and dumplings simmering in a pot on the stove hit him hard and his stomach growled. It had been a long time since lunch.

That was another thing he appreciated about his arrangement with Amy. She provided the niceties he couldn't be bothered to provide for himself. His therapist told him this kind of self-care denial was part of his lingering depression, so he actively looked for ways to fight back against that nebulous darkness. Awareness was only step one. He knew he had to challenge his inclination to isolate himself from the world. Thank God, Amy and the boys made it easy.

"Smells great," he said as he hooked his hat on the rack by the door beneath a sign that said Family Gathers Here.

Amy turned from her investigation of the fridge and frowned. "You're late."

"Not very."

She looked him up and down. "At least you showered."

Jax bit back a grin. Sometimes he wondered if Amy had adopted *him*, too. He rolled up his sleeves and finished setting the table as Amy ladled out thick redolent chicken stew into clunky bowls. *"Boys!"* she bellowed without warning. Jax, still used to the afternoon quiet of his studio, only jerked a little. *"Supper!"*

A pounding of footfalls shook the house as the boys raced each other down the stairs. They exploded into the kitchen in a bundle of fresh-faced innocence and mischief.

"Dinner!" Georgie announced as he noisily took his seat.

John J, as always, was more sedate. But not by much. "Chicken dinner," he sang, doing a little dance. Chicken and dumplings were his favorite. Jax didn't mind it, either.

"Sit down, John J," Amy said as she set the bowls on the table. Jax grabbed the salad bowl and breadbasket and joined them all at the well-used kitchen table.

After John J's prayer, thanking the chicken for its sacrifice—a habit he'd picked up after the visit to a local petting zoo—they all dug in. And damn. It was good.

Warm and creamy and filling. Amy's dumplings were like air, yet still soaked with broth on the bottom. "Mmm." All he could manage. But no one minded the lack of conversation. Not at the moment.

First bites, he reflected, were always the best bites.

"Oh, Jax," Amy said after she'd sated her initial hunger. "Just so you know, the boys are spending the night at Dylan's, so you don't need to stay over tonight if you don't want to."

"Sleepover?" he waggled his brows at the boys. "Fun."

Amy's smile was blinding. "Fun for me, too. I'm taking Nat to Lizzie's party."

Jax's heart skipped a beat. Just at the sound of her name. "Uh, Nat's going to Lizzie's party?" That did not seem like the Nat he once knew.

"She's going." Amy's grin was wicked. "She just doesn't know it yet."

That sounded unpleasant—for Natalie. Jax grimaced at the memories. Lizzie had been horrible to her back in the day. Even *he* had noticed, and he'd been a selfish jerk back then. Jax wondered if Amy knew just how beastly Lizzie had been to her sister.

Amy, being Amy, soldiered on without concern for trampled feelings. "Nat needs to reconnect with her high school friends."

"Does she?" Navigating those shark-infested waters was hard for him right now. He could only imagine how Nat felt about it. Also, Lizzie hadn't been her friend.

Seemingly oblivious to his concerns, Amy scooped another serving onto his plate. "She needs to see that they were just kids back then. She needs to see we've evolved." Amy didn't catch her own Freudian *we*, but Jax did. It was possible that Amy blamed herself for Nat leaving and never coming back—their relationship had always been rocky. He recognized the sentiment because he felt the same way.

"She was never much of a party person," he reminded her gently.

Amy frowned. "She went to the Emmys. Put on a fancy dress and jewelry and make up. I saw the photo on her Instagram. She did it once. She can do it again. Besides, Lizzie specifically asked me to bring her."

"Why?" Again, Lizzie had been horrible to Natalie. Just awful. Maybe she wanted to apologize, too?

Amy sniffed. "Lizzie's a fan of the show." *Ah.* And having Nat come to her party was like having a celebrity there by proxy. Yeah, that sounded like Lizzie. Then and now. "I know you don't like to socialize, Jax," she said, continuing to trample on feelings, "but you should come, too. Susan will be there."

Susan? It took his brain a minute to connect with Susan Warren, a very lovely, pleasant person he'd neither seen nor thought of in months. How was *she* relevant to this conversation?

He didn't need to ask. That was one of the benefits of communicating with Amy. You never had to ask her what she meant because she would tell you. Whether you wanted to know or not. "Susan has a crush on you."

Oh, God. His stomach cramped up a little. Not that there was anything wrong with Susan or the thought of Susan being interested in more than they had now— which was, basically, never seeing each other. He just wasn't ready for a relationship. Certainly not with a woman who wasn't inclined to *see* him. It had been that way with his ex-wife Melissa.

Their relationship had worked, as long as he played the role she expected. When he needed to make changes, when he started to choose who he was over who she wanted him to be, everything had fallen apart.

She hadn't wanted *him*.

She'd wanted only her *idea of him*.

She hadn't even *seen* him.

With everything else that had been going on at the time—the sleepless nights, the horrible nightmares, the sense of being trapped, the guilt for wanting to be true to himself—the weight of her expectations had been too much, and their marriage had ended.

He tried not to be resentful that he hadn't been enough for her as he stood, but it still ate at him that he simply wasn't enough for her. At the time, that resentment had simply fed his overwhelming desire to just walk away from the world. Which he had.

"For pity's sake, Jax." Amy leaned forward to fix him with that expression—the one that warned him he was about to get one of her handy-dandy advice lectures. "You cannot be a hermit forever."

He forced a smile. "Why not?"

"It's not healthy."

Sometimes it was.

"What's a hermit?" Georgie asked.

Amy tipped up her nose. "A hermit is a man who doesn't like people."

"I like people." A grumble.

"Do you?" Her stare was unflinching.

Jax shrugged. "I like *some* people."

"Sometimes I don't like Dylan," John J said, referring to one of the boys' playmates. "Am I a hermit?"

"No, sweetie." Amy reached over and ruffled his hair. "A hermit also lives in a hut on the beach and hoards driftwood."

"It's not hoarding. It's drying." He couldn't believe he had to explain this to her again. Seasoned wood worked better. "Besides," he added, for the boys' benefit, "I am working on trying to be more social. Hermits don't try."

Amy frowned and shook her head. "You're so good with the boys," she said apropos of nothing. "You should have kids."

"Wait. How did we get from me being more social to me having kids?" It was like that with Amy, sometimes. Feeling as though you missed a paragraph in the story.

She sighed. "I'm just trying to help."

She was. He knew it. And he adored her for it.

She just wasn't very good at it.

"Maybe I should go to the party," he said before thinking.

She gawped at him. "What? Like *in person*?"

Nat would be there. Maybe he could find a moment to talk to her… "Why not?"

"Jax!" He noticed that she was beaming at him. "I'm so proud of you."

"I— What?"

"You just suggested being sociable. I didn't even have to nag you."

Well, technically she had nagged, hadn't she? But it didn't matter. The seed had been planted, there in Jax's head. This party might be the opportunity he needed to get Nat alone, and finally put his guilt regarding that day in the gym to rest forever.

Natalie was still musing over the changes in Momma by suppertime. Part of it was the stroke, no doubt, and part of it was just aging—but there was something else. Something she couldn't put her finger on.

It nagged at her as the three of them—Momma, Celeste and Natalie—sat around the too-large table for supper. Funny, though, how they still left Dad's chair empty for him. And Nate's. As though, at any moment, they might push through the door in a flurry of laughter and male energy.

It was hard for Nat, still, after all this time, when she had to remember they were both gone. It didn't paralyze her as it had in the past, especially losing Nate, but the pain remained, an artifact of grief.

"So," Celeste said with a gust as she swirled the wine in her glass. "I hear you're going to Lizzie's party tonight."

Nat choked on her soup. "Who told you that?"

"Amy."

Awesome.

Natalie had no intention of attending Lizzie Chisolm's party—even though her name wasn't Chisolm anymore. Amy might have made peace with the girl Lizzie had been, but Natalie still remembered everything—viscerally. Most especially the time Lizzie and her friends had chased her around the locker room spraying her with deodorant. Or sidled past her in the lunchroom making snorting noises.

And most especially, she remembered Lizzie's smirk after Jax's kiss, which had been a joke to everyone, apparently. Everyone but Natalie.

Yeah, the last thing Natalie wanted to do was see her again. Much less step into her home. She would have married some rich guy. She would live in one of the fancy houses on the hill. Or the newer ones they'd built close to the beach. She would belong to the country club at the new resort on the Point. It was all too banal to contemplate.

No doubt Amy had made up her mind that Natalie was going to attend said party, and she'd roped in Celeste as an accomplice. They probably thought Nat would go to this party, see how wonderful and grown up her tormentors had become, and be magically transformed into someone who wanted to move back to town. Not. Likely.

For some reason, the topic captured Momma's attention. She stopped sipping her soup long enough to glance up and offer a crooked smile. "Good. I'm glad you're trying to fit in."

Nat glared at Celeste, who grinned widely.

Fit in? Seriously? She crumpled her napkin. "Actually, I was thinking about staying home tonight. Momma. With you."

Momma—the decorous and demure maven of military hostess fame—snorted, soup as her spittle. "I'm tired. You go."

"Momma, I really don't want to go to the party Amy and Celeste can go. I'll stay here."

Celeste snorted. "I'm not going." And, when Nat frowned at her, she shrugged. "I wasn't invited. Lizzie was never in my circle of friends."

"Ugh. But *I* have to go?" How was that fair?

"She always was antisocial," Momma announced to no one. And everyone.

Nat tried, with everything in her, not to roll her eyes. "I'm not antisocial. I just don't like *those* people."

Momma sent her a look. "I don't like *any* people and you never heard me complain."

"Momma." Celeste reached out to pat her hand. "You love people."

Momma snatched her hand back. "I love my children. Everyone else can go hang."

This revelation appeared to be a shock to Celeste as well. "I thought you loved people. All those parties you and Dad threw—"

"All for your father." She lapsed into silence for a minute, probably thinking about Dad, and then, "What was I saying? What was my point? Oh. Yes." She turned to Nat and shook a finger, which was never a good thing with Momma. "Whether you like them or not, other people matter. Figure out a way to get along. I did."

"It's going to be a miserable party," Nat insisted. A last-ditch attempt to cry off.

Momma poked her mashed potatoes as though they had offended her. "I expect a full report in the morning." And, no doubt, she did.

Nat's fate was sealed when—before dessert even—Amy showed up and plowed through the rest of her excuses, forced her to change into something acceptable, and then dragged her—kicking and screaming, or at least metaphorically so—to the car. At least, Amy's *live-in boyfriend* was nowhere to be seen. That would have been difficult to stomach indeed.

The only saving grace was the fact that Coho Cove was a small town and if she had to escape, if she really needed to, she could always walk home.

* * *

As he stepped into Lizzie's grand foyer, Jax struggled to calm the churning in his belly. Of all the things he could be doing on a beautiful night, this was the last on his list. For so many reasons.

As a kid, he'd always resented the people in the big houses, the ones with money and arrogance and little respect for the tribe who'd lived on this land for centuries. His father had counseled him to be openhearted and tolerant of everyone, which was ironic because none of the people in the big houses were ever openhearted and tolerant with Pops. They'd always treated him as a servant rather than as a fellow citizen.

Aside from that, being around a lot of people was triggering for him. A lot of people meant unexpected noises, movements he couldn't track, and of course, well, people. Jax had always been something of a loner, but after his intense experiences in a hostile war zone, his introversion had become something else. As though the fear and paranoia—and the nightmares—had attached itself to him and followed him home.

Therapy, and of course his art, had helped him control and express some of the trauma. He was getting better at managing his feelings when he wasn't in the safety of his haven, but it wasn't easy.

If it weren't for his hope of seeing Nat, he would not be here, surrounded by all this chaotic energy. Even the music was too loud for his sensibilities. He stationed himself with his back against a wall in a shadowed corner and scanned the room. The other people milling in Lizzie's spotless, minimalist great room were a who's who of Coho Cove, but that was hardly saying anything. He'd known most of these people his entire life and he figured they'd already had just about every conversation there was to have.

Fortunately, he wasn't here to talk to them. He was lurking on the sidelines for one reason and one reason only. Nat would be here. He would finally have the chance to force her to listen to his apology so he could scrub this unpleasant feeling from his soul. It was weird how some things just…clung. Often stupid little things, but it didn't matter.

He thought about getting a drink, but Lola Cheswick and Sherill Scanlon were over by the bar. It should be no surprise Lizzie had invited them since the three of them had been the cheerleading squad in high school. They were all married now, but life had worn on them. They didn't seem happy.

On the other side of the social pendulum, Angel Goulden, Gwen Deveney and Clara Pearson had their heads together by the fireplace, probably talking business. They owned three of the most popular shops in town—at least during the tourist season. Gwen ran a new age shop that sold crystals and books about healing and the like, Angel managed an upscale art gallery, and Clara's shop sold soap or something. The only reason he knew all this was because his sister, Sheida, was friends with them and she had a tendency to chatter. Also, Angel carried some of his work in her gallery on commission.

In counterpoint, the other corner was like a bad replay of a high school huddle with Baxter Vance and the aging members of the football team reliving their glory days. When Baxter saw him, he waved Jax over, but Jax merely responded with a distant raised hand.

He did consider heading for another knot containing what he termed the adults in the room. Anthony Skinner was the current mayor—also a Kiwanian, Lion, and the President of Coho Cove Historical Society, but Jax knew him from volunteer firefighter training. He was talking to Vic Walton, who'd bought the burger joint when it went belly up and opened a very classy bar in its place. Luke Larsen, another VFF buddy, hovered on the edges. Yep. That was a group he could kill time with until Natalie showed up. If she did.

But before he could make his way to that most preferable clump, Susan Warren emerged from the kitchen with a platter, caught his eye and headed his way. "Jaxon Stringfellow. What a surprise," she said on a laugh. Susan was a pretty woman, and a nice person with a kind face. Amy said she had a crush on him, but if she did, she never did or said anything overt. Which was a relief. Especially at the moment. He had no desire to dodge her attention. "How on earth did Lizzie get you to leave your hut?"

Not a hut.

"Hi, Susan." He surveyed the offerings on her tray and selected a bacon-wrapped scallop. "It's an art studio."

Her dimples blossomed. "Yes, well, you never leave."

"I leave." He did. On occasion.

She thrust the tray at him. "Take another. You need to eat. You're too skinny."

He chuckled at her insult. "Thank you?"

She winked at him and turned to saunter through Lizzie's blindingly white living room to offer canapés to other guests.

Sheida sidled up, right in Susan's wake. She leaned against him and handed him a beer. With her at his side, he un-tensed. A little. "Susan's cute," she purred.

"Mmm-hmm."

"And single."

"Mmm-hmm."

"You should ask her out."

His gut clenched. "Nope."

"You shouldn't spend so much time alone. You should go on a date once in a while."

He pulled back and studied her. "You have no idea how much I date. Or not."

She blew out a breath, causing her bangs to fluff. "Everyone in town knows how much you date, Jaxon. Which is, never. It's shameful to waste a perfectly good bachelor. Especially in a town this small."

He took a swig of his beer. "Okay. Let's talk about *your* sex life."

She might have blushed. But she didn't falter. She never did. "Did you hear? Natalie Tuttle's back in town."

"I did."

She frowned and smacked him on the arm. "You knew? And you didn't tell me? You're fired."

He had to chuckle. "You can't fire your brother."

"I'm not so sure about that." She waggled her brows. "Hey, any word from Pops?" Their father, Alexander Stringfellow, was something of a snowbird who spent spring in the Southwest rockhounding. He would go off for months, and then, when the weather turned too warm, he would come back with loads of precious and semiprecious stones, which he then polished, shaped and sold. He'd always been creative—Jax's woodworking studio had been Pops's playground before arthritis made it too difficult for him to manage some of the tools. Jax had learned the basics of wood sculpting at his father's knee.

He shook his head. "He hasn't called." When Pops was *on the hunt*, he was terrible at keeping in touch.

Sheida sighed. "If he would just send a text once in a while…"

Jax chuckled, because they'd had this conversation a million times before. Pops would do what Pops would do. He often reminded them—when they complained about his unwillingness to carry a phone—that they were all adults. Which was his way of saying, basically, that he would do as he pleased. And he did.

Jax couldn't complain, because when he'd returned home and decided to sequester himself from the world, Pops's response had been unconditional support. He'd always been a great listener, and wise beyond his years. He'd even given Jax his woodworking studio and most of his tools.

So, as much as Jax wanted to hear from him occasionally, to know that he was safe, he had to respect his father's independence. It was, he was learning, quite a challenge. As his father aged, he valued his independence even more.

After a moment of silence, Sheida sighed heavily. "Is it me, or is this room exceedingly bright?"

"It's very white." The walls were white. The trim was white. Even the sofa was white.

"I noticed. It's giving me a headache."

He grinned. "Excellent excuse, when I'm the one who needs to sneak out. Thanks, sis."

She made a face. "You can't sneak out. This is your only social life."

"I—"

"Don't tell me. You're in love with your chunks of wood. Not the same as a real woman."

"Come on." He waved around the room. "These women? Who am I going to date?"

"Susan is cute."

"The ink on her divorce is barely dry, besides—"

Someone walked into the room just then. A mere flash in his peripheral vision but she caught his attention. It locked on her. His brain seized. His pulse launched into a panicked patter. Suddenly he could not…do…word things. With words.

"Besides what?" Sheida asked. When he didn't answer, she turned and looked at where he was staring, and huffed a laugh. "Will you look at that. Amy brought Natalie after all. We should go over and say hi."

"You go. I'll come later," he murmured and then, like an idiot, or the coward that he was, he ducked into the bathroom until his heartbeat calmed. When he came out, Amy and Sheida were chatting away, but Natalie was nowhere to be seen.

She'd fled.

Damn it all anyway.

He'd missed his chance.

There was no reason for Natalie's stomach to clench the way it did when she walked into Lizzie's great room. Oh sure, all the heads turned when she entered, the eyes of all her old enemies zeroed in on her once again.

Baxter and his buddies caught her attention first, and then she spotted the cheerleaders by the bar, and her blood went cold. It took some effort, but she tipped up her chin, gritted her teeth in a smile, and followed Amy to the bar. Though it was mis-stating things to say she followed Amy when Amy had hold of her arm in a death grip.

"Be social," she muttered as they approached. Nat's heart gave a hard thump as a horde of hot memories whipped through her. It was Natalie's worst nightmare. Sherill Scanlon and Lola Cheswick. Standing there. Together. High school angst in stereo. Amy—the traitor— smiled at them both. "Hey, Sherill. Lola. Where's Lizzie?"

"Hi, Amy," Lola said. She was still perfect, still gorgeous. Still managed to look down at everyone, even though she wasn't tall. "She's on the patio, I think." Many of the guests had gathered out there as it was a mild evening. She turned her attention to Nat. "Oh, my. Is this Natalie? I'd heard you were back. Goodness, I barely recognized you." Lola then strafed her with an assessing glance, as though calculating her fitness for further attention. It made the little hairs on Nat's nape prickle. They prickled even more at Lola's smile. "I see you've slimmed down," she said. "Good for you."

Something akin to rage washed through Nat at the personal and highly inappropriate comment, but only for a second. Back in high school, Nat would have killed for any hint of approval from the cheerleaders, and would have wilted at the slightest criticism. But— after having lived in the truly shark infested waters of Hollywood, after scrabbling to find and hold her own place in a very competitive world, after realizing her value was about so much more than looks—she'd changed. She hadn't realized just how much until now. Lola's backhanded half-compliment landed flat, painting her as petty and small, as she always had been.

It was a funny thing, realizing the lion you always feared was more of a bad-tempered house cat.

The thought made Natalie want to laugh. It was easy, then, to smile and nod and graciously say, "Thanks." Because the truth was, it didn't matter what Lola thought of her, and it never really had.

Still, she did not want to hang out here, especially when she saw Baxter heading their way. She'd rather be alone than with those three. In fact, alone sounded pretty good at the moment.

So, she pretended to scan the crowd. "Oh hey," she said, using an old ploy from way too many work parties. "I think I see a friend. Excuse me, won't you?" And she slipped out of Lizzie's sliding glass doors and onto the patio. She dared a glance back and yes, Amy was frowning at her, but Nat didn't stop.

She hadn't wanted to come to this stupid party anyway, but she wasn't too proud to snag a couple of

Lizzie's beers and make her way past the partiers on the patio, away from the cacophony and down to the beach.

She found a nice, deserted place to sit on a mound of sand and stared out at the moon dancing on the water. She could hear the whoosh of waves, feel the breeze and, if she closed her eyes, embrace the peace of the moment.

This part of Coho Cove, she liked. Really liked. If she lived here, she'd have a house by the beach, or at least with a view of the ocean. Not a huge one like Lizzie, though. A cabin maybe? Something small and cozy with a firepit and—

"Hey."

Natalie's heart jumped at the sound of Jax's voice. Apparently skulking off into the shadows to avoid people didn't work quite as well as it had in high school. It took everything in her to hold back a maudlin sigh. The evening had been uncomfortable enough already.

He gestured toward her. "May I?"

Was he serious? *This is my dune. Go find your own.* But of course, she couldn't say that. Out loud. "Sure." She scooched over. A bit. When he dropped into the sand, with a beer-scented huff, he was hard to ignore. But then, he always had been.

Although he had been physically perfect then, now, somehow, he was even sexier. Taller, muscular, so beautifully brown—as though he spent hours in the sun. His face had firmed as well, though his eyes—dark pools of soothing amber—and his slightly crooked smile hadn't changed much at all. The only thing she didn't care for in this grown-up iteration of him was his short, stubby hair. It was a military cut—she recognized it because she'd been surrounded by the military crew cuts her whole life. One of the things she'd most adored about him when he was young was his long hair. Dark and thick, back then it had flowed around him like a lion's mane. It had been a signal that he wasn't like the others. That he was different.

But now his hair was a reminder to her that he wasn't different at all. And he never had been. Now his brutally short cut was enough for her to cling to as a reminder that his charisma, his allure—or at least the allure she had always imagined—wasn't real.

Or, at the very least, wasn't for her.

It was a damn shame, because he was undeniably hot.

Other men didn't emanate this much heat, did they? Or maybe the heat generation was a result of her thrumming pulse. Or her discomfort around him. At any rate, an uncomfortable flush climbed up her cheeks. Though, if she was being honest, it wasn't the heat alone that made him stand out to her. In truth, she didn't really know what it was, or why she always felt off-center around him. She always had.

They sat there side by side in silence for a while. She stared out at the invisible waves, wondering how long she had to stay before she could make her excuses, wipe the sand off her butt, and leave.

"So, Nat. How is your visit going?" he asked after a bit.

She glanced over at him, parsing out which truth to tell. She could tell him how it had shocked her to see Momma diminished and frail. She could share that she had been gobsmacked to realize that he was living at Amy's. That the boys were so much bigger than the last time she'd seen them. That it had surprised her to see Sheida in her element running the Elder House like an actual grown up. That it nagged at her that she'd missed so much by staying away. Instead, she forced a smile and said, "It's been great."

"It's gotta be strange, coming back after so long. I know it was for me. Did you know I left for a while too?"

"I did. Army?"

"Four years."

"Wow." What was there to say after all? He didn't elaborate, and she let the silence grow between them again, simply because she couldn't think of anything to say.

He broke the awkward pause with a non sequitur. "You know, Natalie, I...never really felt like I belonged here," he said.

She glanced at him for clarity, because she didn't understand the sideways jog. He wasn't looking at the ocean. He was looking at her. "On this beach?"

He chuckled. It warmed her. "In this town. I never felt like I belonged."

She nodded. "Neither did I."

He met her gaze solemnly, as though he were telling her his deepest, darkest secret. She shivered, but it was probably the snap of the breeze. "I always had one foot in each world, but somehow, didn't belong in either."

Unsure how to respond, she nodded. Because she and Sheida had been friends, she knew he'd split his youth between his mom here in town and his father, who lived in the nearby tribal village, but she had no real frame of reference. She imagined the two worlds would be difficult to reconcile.

"I tried really hard to belong, Nat." Was his possible that his expression became more intense?

"Why are you telling me this?" She meant to sound cool and confident, but the words whooshed out and the wind snatched them away. Somehow, he heard her.

"I'm trying to explain something to you."

She stared at him. "Ah... You don't need to explain anything to me."

"Yes. I do." The tenor of his tone gave her shivers. "I want you to understand." This, nearly a plea.

"All right, fine." The maudlin sigh finally escaped. Still, he was gracious and ignored it.

"Thank you." He rubbed his day beard and his brow rumpled. "Where was I again?"

"Foot in each world. Tried to belong..." Yeah. That was the gist.

"Oh. Right." It seemed her attention burned him. He looked away. "I was a jerk sometimes, you know, when I was a kid. I..." He forced his gaze back to hers. "I wanted to apologize. You know. For that..." Apparently, he couldn't say the word *kiss*. "For what happened on Senior Skip Day."

She stared at him. She'd never expected him to even address that thing with her, much less apologize.

Apologize.

How did that even feel? She thought about it for a minute.

Better. Yeah. Definitely better. It didn't fix anything, but somehow that didn't matter. Because it felt…better.

"Do you think you can forgive me?" he asked, so, so softly. And then, when she didn't—couldn't—respond, "Nat?"

How was she supposed to respond? As though that one memory had not influenced her entire adult life? As though her crush on him had not haunted her?

As though that kiss had not changed her. . .

As though the laughter and the pig-snorts and the catcalls from his friends had not crushed her budding sexual confidence into the dirt . . .

It was that damn politeness gene. How awesome would it be to say what you thought once in a while? What was honestly on your mind, in your gut?

Instead, she said, simply, "That was a long time ago. I've gotten past it."

Liar.

Still, when relief washed over his face, when his tension melted and his entire body seemed to relax, she was glad she'd fibbed a little.

If he was big enough to apologize for something that happened so long ago, she could be big enough to release him from the guilt.

What surprised her was just how relieved he seemed. His face broke into a great grin and he exhaled a long, heavy breath. "Oh, thank God. It was a long time ago, I know, but…"

"Hmm?" she prompted when he didn't continue.

"Honestly, it's always bothered me."

"Bothered you?"

"I couldn't shake it. I was mortified every time I thought of it. Honestly Nat, the last thing I ever wanted was to hurt you."

She met his gaze. "But you did."

He dropped his head. "I did. I'm sorry. Can you find it in your heart to forgive me?"

She shrugged and turned back to focus on the water, even though the moon had ducked behind a cloud and the shore was invisible. Her heart leaped at his sincerity, at his contrition for that young, embarrassed girl. Something in her soul lifted. Lifted and soared. "I dunno," she said shooting him a dark glance. "That's a lot to ask."

He winced and compunction pierced her conscience. Still, she wagged a finger in his direction. "It's gonna cost you."

He sucked in a breath. Steadfastly met her gaze. "Okay."

Her heart thudded. Okay? *Okay?* She could ask for anything—anything—and she knew that he would give it to her without hesitation. It was a lovely feeling, having such power over him—power he'd freely given. It crossed her mind—ever so briefly—that she could even ask for another kiss, were she so inclined. Or brave enough. Which she wasn't, apparently.

After her stupid stomach stopped fluttering, she said, with an evil grin, "You, sir, are gonna have to go get me another beer."

Chapter Five

Jax stared at Natalie. She was so pretty like this, in the light of the moon and the stars. She was always pretty, but especially like this. Her mischievous grin warmed him to the cockles of his heart and, to his surprise, some of his other cockles. It was a feeling, a desire he hadn't had in years. That—that warmth swirling low in his belly—was unfamiliar, unexpected and inappropriate to the moment, and somehow still welcome.

But there was more. More to process. He hadn't expected, that when this weight lifted, he would feel so light. So…released. With a grin, he hopped to his feet. "Don't go anywhere. I'll be right back."

He returned with a selection of beers, because her ask had been so modest and he'd wanted to show her how much he appreciated her letting this go. She laughed when she saw him coming toward her on the uneven sand, juggling them all.

"Wow, you do deliver, don't you?"

"I try. Which do you prefer?" He laid them all out, like a beach beer sommelier, so she could inspect them. She took one without even looking, popped the top and took a drink.

"Ah, yes," she sighed. "A very good year."

Jax settled back onto the sand next to her, feeling terribly satisfied with the world. "You didn't stay at the party very long," he said after a moment.

"I don't especially care for parties."

"What? You? I thought you Hollywood TV types had all kinds of parties."

She snorted, but it was a delicate snort. "We do. But those are all for work, ergo, they don't count as actual parties." She took a drink, and then added, "Which I'm not fond of, either. Unless it's a party with all my friends."

"Isn't that how parties are supposed to be?"

"Perhaps. But they rarely are."

"True. Well, just so you know, everyone is looking for you."

"Me?"

He waggled his brow. "You're the new kid in town."

"Oh, stop. You're reminding me why I always hated this place."

Something in her tone caught at his heart. "You mentioned you never felt at home here either..." He hated the thought. "Why?"

She shrugged. "I should have, I suppose. All my sib-

lings did. They melted right in. Like they…belonged."
She said the word as though it were some foreign phrase
she was practicing; there was a strange, wistful glint in
her eye. He couldn't look away.

"And you…didn't?" he prompted when she didn't
elaborate.

"Not here."

"Did you ever feel that you belonged?"

She broke from her trance with a harsh laugh. "Once,
I did. My life was perfect then. I traveled the world,
lived in many exotic places. Heck, I even got to cel-
ebrate my tenth birthday in Paris when my dad was
stationed in Germany." A sigh. "But then, one day, everything changed. Dad was gone—just like that, in a
blink of an eye—and Momma brought us here, to live
with Grandma Opal. The big wide world became this
little town. I felt claustrophobic. Then after my brother
died… I felt totally alone. I couldn't wait to escape."

"We noticed, when you left forever right after graduation." He twirled his bottle. "That was hard on your
family, you know."

"Sometimes you have to do what you have to do."

"So, did you feel like you belonged in California?"
He wasn't sure why he needed to know so badly, or even
why he wanted to know. He wasn't sure why it was suddenly essential to know. But it was.

"I suppose."

"You suppose?"

"Well, there were more people like me there."

"Like you?"

She laughed. "I don't know how to explain it. People

are a little more open minded. They like moving forward rather than marking time. I guess."

"Well, Tony Skinner has proposed we erect a gazebo in the park in front of city hall," he said in a hopeful tone.

She realized he was teasing and gave a little laugh. "My, that is progressive."

He lay back, rested his head on his hands and stared up at the star-speckled sky. She did as well. "I dunno," he said. "In my travels, I've found that people are pretty much people. There are small-minded people everywhere."

"Thanks for the reassurance."

He grinned. "Let me finish. I was going to add that there are also rather wonderful people everywhere as well. You just have to find them."

She made a snorty noise. "You sound like my mother."

"Your mother is wise." When she groaned, he laughed. "All I'm saying is, this town has its jerks. Every town does. But it also has some pretty damn wonderful people. If you give them a chance."

She went up on an elbow and looked down on him—in a good way. He tried not to notice the swell of her breasts. A challenge, though, because they were right at eye level, and it wasn't that kind of conversation. "I'm only here for a visit," she said. "A short visit."

"I know. But…every moment you're here, you're here. You might as well enjoy yourself."

She plopped back down on the sand. He tried to ignore his regrets. He shouldn't have been looking at her breasts anyway. "Are you saying I should go back to the party and…" she shuddered "…mingle?"

"Not necessarily." This was pleasant. He was in no hurry for it to end. "But I think you'll find most of these people aren't who they used to be."

"I should probably warn you," she said. He couldn't help noticing that the mischievous smile was back. "I'm still a dork."

He had to laugh. "You were never a dork."

"I was the dork of the county."

"Have you forgotten about Mike Antonelli?"

They both chuckled. "He was an A/V nerd. That's different."

"How?"

"He had a bona fide thing to be nerdy about. I was just nerdy in general."

Jax sighed and said into the wind, "Well, I thought you were cute."

She froze. Her cheeks reddened in the moonlight. "Not me, surely."

"Definitely." She was especially cute now. So cute, in fact, that he had the sudden urge to lever up and over so he could taste her lips. He had no idea why the urge was so strong—their last kiss had been a nightmare, after all—but he wanted to.

He was halfway to working up the courage to do so when the most annoying thing happened.

"There you are!" his supposed best friend called from afar.

Jax sat up and turned to look. Yep. It was Ben, waving as he approached. There was no reason for that dance of acid in his gut. "Ben." Not a clipped and cold welcome. Not completely.

Without invitation, Ben joined them. "Wow," he said, surveying the beer selection. "Looks like you two are having your own private party."

To which you were not invited.

"Hey, Natalie. I heard you were here. You look great by the way."

She laughed, some light giggle that made more acid join the party in his midsection. "It's dark, Ben. You can't even see me." She stood, though, and hugged him.

Jax watched in silence, through gritted teeth. *He* hadn't gotten a hug.

"Right, well, everyone else told me how great you look, and you know what? I believe them. Let me look closer." He touched his forehead to hers. "Yep. Gorgeous."

"Hush." When Natalie sat down, so did Ben. Beside her. "So, how are you, Ben? It's been a long while."

"I'm good. Great, really. We just opened a hotel on the Point."

Jax felt the need to break in with…something. "By we, he means *he* did it."

"My company." Without asking, Ben took one of the beers Jax had brought for Natalie. And completely ignored his glare.

"Sherrod Building," she said with too much reverence. "I hear the company's grown since you took over. I even heard about you in LA."

"Woo-hoo. I guess I'm fancy now."

"Weren't you always?" she teased.

Ben chuckled. "But look at you. Famous TV show person."

She shrugged. "It's a job."

"I love the show. So, you design the sets?"

She shifted a little, straightened, morphed into her professional self, perhaps. "I'm the art director."

"So, you choose the furniture and stuff?"

Jax disliked the glimmer in Ben's eye, but he wasn't sure why.

"I do."

"And the paintings?"

"Everything."

"Oh, great." Ben scooted closer, leaned in intently. "You know that one scene where Scott tells Kristen he's a clone?"

"Mmm-hmm."

"Well, I am obsessed with the painting hanging over the fireplace. Do you know the one?"

Nat gave a little nod. "Of course. I chose that painting."

"Do you suppose it's for sale?"

Natalie laughed. "Probably. I can ask, if you want."

Ben's eyes lit up. He leaned a little closer. "Oh, would you? It would be perfect in the entryway at the resort."

"I will do that."

Ben grinned in a way that sent irritation sizzling through Jax's bowels. Or maybe it was the way Natalie was looking at *him*, or her smile, or the way she seemed to be leaning toward Ben as well. "Ben has a daughter," he blurted, for no reason whatsoever. Hell, if Nat and Ben had a connection, who was he to interfere?

"Really?" Damn it. A tactical error. Natalie's expression lit up like a Christmas tree. "Do you have a picture?"

"Do I have a picture?" Ben's chortle sent a shiver up Jax's spine. He whipped out his phone and the next five minutes or so consisted of Ben explaining what Quinn was doing in a picture of her doing it, and Natalie oohing and awing incessantly.

It made him grind his teeth a little. Jax wasn't sure why it bothered him so much that Nat and Ben were hitting it off. Ben was his friend. He'd be thrilled if his buddy finally found a woman he connected with.

Just not this woman.

Not that he had any claim on her. He certainly did not. But that knowledge didn't help at all.

It was almost a relief when Amy and Sheida hunted them down. They plopped down in the sand as well and drank the rest of Natalie's beers. All of them. But the conversation pivoted away from Ben and how adorable his daughter was to an in-depth critique of how relentlessly white Lizzie's house was.

The others were engrossed, but Jax was too busy wondering why Natalie had gone all stiff the moment the other two women arrived. No one else noticed or remarked upon it, but to him, it was a clear as day. He wondered if it was his sister or hers that caused her unease. Sheida had squealed and hugged Ben effusively when she'd seen him—those two had become close over the past few years—and then she'd sat down right next to him. And Nat had clammed up.

Indeed, after several minutes of jocularity between

Sheida and Ben, Nat stood and brushed off her slacks. "'Scuse me. I need to visit the ladies'," she said in what was a transparent attempt at escape.

Without thought or intention, he stood as well. "I'll walk you back."

Their gazes clashed. "I'm perfectly able to find the house." She pointed in the general direction of the party noises. "It's right there." He couldn't help noticing that her teasing tone had an edge to it.

He forced a carefree grin. "I need to go, too," he said, and before she could say a word, or reject him, he hooked his arm in hers and headed for the house.

"I'm okay, Jax," she said when they were out of earshot of the others. "Really."

"Mmm-hmm. And I know a prison break when I see one."

She stopped short and gaped at him and he saw in her expression her shock that he had, indeed, caught her out. "I... It... Okay. I needed to get away. In my normal life, I spend evenings alone in my condo with a cat who is disinclined to conversation. Maybe it's turned me into an introvert. Too many people and I start feeling fenced in."

"I get it."

"So, I don't need you to come with me. To the bathroom." Her lips kicked up at the inanity. Then her expression faded into sadness. He had no idea why. "You can go back to...the others."

"I wasn't done talking to you, actually."

Her mouth opened. Closed. Opened again. "I thought we, you know, worked all that out. It's behind us."

"Yes. And I am more than grateful for your charity—"

"It's hardly charity."

"I just feel a need to clarify something. If you don't mind."

She huffed a breath. Waved her hand. "Clarify away."

Well, hell. Now that she said *that*, the words crowding in his head all sounded stupid. How did one clarify a thing such as this? In the end, he decided to do it the old-fashioned way. He thrust out a hand, looked her in the eye and said, "Friends?"

She seemed a little surprised for a moment, or sad. He couldn't be sure, the expressions flickered by too quickly. But then she nodded and slid her palm against his. He had no idea why that touch sent a ripple of awareness through him. "All right," she said softly. "Friends."

"Good," he said resolutely. "Good."

And then he watched her walk back to Lizzie's house, without his help, wondering why he felt as though he'd missed out on something incredible.

Nat lay awake in bed that night with Pepe purring on her chest, thinking about that interaction with Jax. Over and over again.

He had apologized.

Apologized.

She had not seen that coming. She wasn't sure how to feel about it because it challenged emotions and beliefs she'd built around her reaction to that sordid event, and her identity—all based on things that had happened years ago. To different people, really.

Why was it so hard to release? To pivot? To let go of high school drama?

Why was she still angry?

It was silly that there was a part of her that still felt rejected by him. But it was there, deep down in the swirling sea of her teenage insecurities. And she knew what it was. Her inner child wailing, *How dare he want Amy and not me?*

For pity's sake. She was a grown woman. She'd kissed a boy—many boys—since high school. She'd even had sex with some of them. More than once. She even had a *boyfriend* at home—it was an on-again, off-again relationship of convenience, but a relationship, nonetheless. A grown-up relationship, even.

So why did the mere brush of *his* hand—or the memory of that simple, friendly handshake—make her go all hot and cold?

Oh. She knew.

Because there'd always been something about Jaxon Stringfellow. Something that made her heart perk up and take notice. Something that made her...want.

Something that made her vulnerable.

He'd been her first love. He'd probably always have a special place in her heart.

She should be glad he and Amy had found each other. Amy deserved a man like Jax. The boys deserved a father like Jax.

But honestly, how hard would it be to watch? Knowing that deep down inside she wanted him for herself? And, oh dear heaven, she did. Desperately.

She was glad they'd agreed to be friends. Of course,

she was. Maybe, in time, she'd be more comfortable with that.

Thank God this was just a short visit. Thank God she could control how many times she had to interact with him—with Amy at his side.

And if it got unbearable, she could always claim some work emergency—even though most of her crew was off in Barbados pickling their livers in rum, No one had to know it wasn't true.

Jax would probably know, though. He'd always been a little more aware of things than the other men she'd known. He'd honed right in on her escape attempt on the beach.

When she realized she was smiling at the memory, she forced herself to stop. She had to put Jaxon Stringfellow firmly on the friend-shelf, grit her teeth, make it through this visit and then go back to the life she had created for herself over the past seven years. It was a good life. A great life sometimes.

And there was Carl.

They'd worked together on several shows over the years and had become close, providing each other much-needed companionship in the isolation of location work. Both enjoyed concerts at the Hollywood Bowl and exploratory dining, and occasionally, he slept over.

But when she closed her eyes and tried to bring Carl's features into focus, for some reason, all she could see was Jax.

Her sister's *boyfriend*.

The best thing she could do would be to avoid both of them while she was here. Like the plague.

* * *

When Nat woke up the next morning, her bedroom door was open, and Pepe was missing.

Damn it. She'd been so careful to keep her cat in the room so she wouldn't have to listen to Momma complain about animal smells. She didn't even change out of her flannel jammies before thudding down two flights to wrangle the beast back into his attic prison.

As she came down the stairs and around the lintel, she stopped short at the sight of Momma, holding Pepe on her lap and stroking him idly as she spoke to someone on the sofa, just out of view.

He laughed, that mystery person, and a sizzle shafted through Natalie's gut as she recognized the timbre.

Jax.

Yikes. Jax was in the living room and Nat was in her flannel jammies with her hair poking up every which way.

Heat washed through her. Yes, he'd apologized to her last night, but her emotions were still raw. The thought of facing him still made her gut clench. It only made sense to sneak back upstairs before anyone saw her and—

"Well, good morning, Mary Sunshine," Amy chirped as she came in through the kitchen door carrying two steaming mugs.

Momma turned her head until she could see Natalie, lifted a brow and said, pointedly, "Good *afternoon*."

Well, hell. Too late to run. She decided, instead, to saunter. Into the room. As though it was perfectly normal to appear in the front room, occupied with company—a gentleman caller, if you will—in one's jam jams.

"I couldn't find Pepe," she said. And then, all casual, "Oh, hey, Jax." Damn, he looked handsome.

"Natalie." His voice was low, his gaze intensely on her. Until it wasn't.

Because Amy stepped between them to hand Jax one of her mugs. "Just the way you like it," she said. "No cream. No sugar. Boring."

"Thanks, Ames," he said on a chuckle. "You need to come up with a new coffee joke, by the way."

Ugh. He called her Ames. Nat ripped her gaze from him—and Amy, who might, at any moment, cuddle up against him—and focused it on Pepe. "There you are, you silly." But when she tried to take him from Momma's lap, to her surprise, her mother wouldn't let him go.

"He's fine," Momma said crisply, holding Pepe closer. For once, the beastie didn't resist. *Traitor.* "He likes it on my lap."

For his part, Pepe just gazed at Nat. His expression was clear. *Some people want to adore me*, it said. *You snooze, you lose.*

"Is Nat up?" Celeste called from the kitchen. She poked her head out the door and her face blossomed into a smile. "Good morning, hon! Did you have fun at the party? I want all the deets." She waltzed across the room and handed Nat a cup of coffee. It smelled divine. So did whatever was baking in the oven. Her tummy grumbled.

While she didn't want to share any deets with any-one about last night, especially not in present company, she did want that coffee. So, she said, "Lizzie's house is white."

Celeste's lips quirked. "I wasn't asking for an architectural review."

"It *is* very white," Jax said, and Nat tried not to glance his way in acknowledgement of his support, but she did anyway.

Amy plopped herself in the recliner by the fireplace and frowned. "She likes a blank canvas. Lots of people enjoy a minimalist approach to design." She didn't glance pointedly around the room, at the dust-gathering thingamabobs Momma hoarded, but she didn't have to. Amy was a serial purger and made no bones about the fact that she considered Momma's treasures clutter. Amy's house was always spotless—unless the boys were in the room, of course.

For her part, Nat didn't mention that in her line of work, the things on a set were chosen with care to make unspoken statements about the characters in the story. In Momma's case, she treasured the memories those trinkets represented and wanted them in full view—including a raft of family photos featuring the smiling faces of loved ones lost. Nat wasn't sure what those empty walls and shelves meant for Lizzie, not to mention the dearth of family pictures. She either wasn't sure who she really was, or didn't want others to see her truth, or—worst of all—she had no imagination at all.

"Well," she said instead, with a forced smile at her sister, "it was certainly a tidy house."

Amy nodded, as though Nat had agreed with her. She hadn't, but in the interest of keeping the peace during this—short—visit, she kept her opinions to herself. But personally, she'd found Lizzie's home sterile and cold.

"I'm hungry," Momma said. She frowned at Celeste. "When's brunch?"

"Soon, Momma. The strata has to cool." Nat swallowed a little drool. Celeste's strata was fantastic. "Jax, I'm done in the kitchen. Could you look at that garbage disposal now?"

He nodded and unfolded himself from the couch. Gosh, his shoulders were broad. Nat tried not to notice. His smile, however, was impossible to ignore. It sent a shiver down her spine. "Gotta sing for my supper," he said with a cocky salute before sauntering into the kitchen.

The moment he was out of sight, Amy turned to Celeste and whisper-hissed, "Why do you always do that?"

Celeste, unprepared for this ambush, crossed her arms. "Do what?"

"Ask Jax to *fix things*?"

"Because he's good at it."

"You know he will never say no when you ask for something, Celeste. You're taking advantage of his generosity. Hire a damn plumber."

Something cold trickled down Nat's back. Amy had never liked sharing. Especially with her sisters. Especially men.

"I should change," she said. It was a great excuse to duck out. She turned to Momma. "Can I have my cat?"

"No."

Of course not.

No one in her family seemed to like to share.

It wasn't until she'd changed, they'd demolished all the food, and were reveling in a carb high that she finally reclaimed her cat from Momma's hold—and only because Momma handed him over when she left to go to the restroom and didn't demand him back when she returned. As they all sat around the table, digesting, Nat nuzzled his fuzzy head. "This is why I love pets," she said as Pepe squirmed beneath the weight of her adoration. He usually did. "This face. This fuzzy face."

"I wish we could have had pets as kids," Celeste said wistfully.

Jax paused his efforts blotting up crumbs and glanced at her. "You didn't have any pets growing up?" he asked in astonishment.

Nat sighed. "We did."

"Once." Amy added. "I never recovered."

At Jax's glance, Nat explained. "We had a rabbit name Mister Bunnynose. Dad got overseas orders and since the quarantine requirement for pets was six months, well, we decided it wasn't fair to keep him—"

"*I* didn't decide that," Amy grumbled.

"You were a toddler," Celeste reminded her.

Amy didn't care to be reminded of things. She made a face. "Mom and Dad never liked animals."

Momma sniffed. "I love animals."

Celeste shook her head on a chuckle. "You *love* babies."

Nat nodded. Oh, she had. Always stopped when she saw one, loved on it a little, or longer if the baby was amenable to attention. But dogs? Cats? Mice? Anything with fleas? *Vermin.*

"Babies." Mom's gaze drifted off to somewhere else. "Babies are so precious."

"It's the way they smell," Celeste said. "Of innocence."

"Apparently you've not been smelling my babies," Amy said with a rare flash of humor.

Everyone laughed—they all knew Georgie and John J. Innocence was *not* their superpower.

"So, what happened to Mister Bunnyface?" Jax asked.

"Bunny*nose*," Nat corrected primly.

Amy gusted an F4-level sigh. "We had to re-home him."

"Someone else got Mr. Bunnynose," Celeste mourned.

"Well, good."

All heads swiveled to Jax, eyes wide with outrage. "What?" Amy squawked, because squawking was her role in this sordid play.

He grinned so wickedly it made prickles of delight slither up Nat's spine. "I'm just glad you didn't eat him."

If he only said it to make Amy squawk again, it worked.

All of a sudden Momma turned to Natalie and grabbed her hand. Eyes wide and expression intense, she said, "When are you and George going to give me a grandchild, Amy-Mamie?"

Nat's heart stalled. She shot a glance at Amy—Amy-Mamie—already knowing what she'd see. Pain etched her sister's face, as always happened when someone mentioned George. But this was something more.

"That's Nat, Momma," Amy said with a sharp edge to her voice. "I'm Amy-Mamie."

Momma looked at her and frowned. "I know who you are," she huffed.

"And you *have* grandchildren. Two of them—"

Nat sensed a building storm—Amy in a huff and all—so she asked, by way of turning the topic. "Where are the boys?"

"Ben has them," Jax said with a grin.

"Ben *Sherrod*?" Celeste's lips twisted.

"They're swimming with Quinn," Amy added in a defensive tone. But then, Amy's tone always seemed defensive lately.

Celeste's expression puckered more. "At that *resort*?"

Amy blew out a breath. Nat got a sense this was some ongoing conversation between them; it was littered with old innuendos and rusty outrage. "Well, they're not swimming in the riptide. The resort has the only kid-friendly pool in fifty miles, so yes. Why do you always criticize my parenting?"

"I'm not criticizing." Celeste sent her a look that was a little too polite. "I just don't like the idea of ruining this lovely community with a tourist trap that—"

And Nat tuned out. Knowing her sisters, and their tones, this would go on for a while. Celeste was the firstborn and Amy the baby—with Nat and Nate squished in the middle like the creme in an Oreo. They'd used to try to make peace between their sisters until she and her brother had realized it was pointless. Nate had always known the truth…it was better to just let them vent.

She reached for the lone surviving pastry that had

been silently taunting her from its platter, but Jax reached for it at the same time and their hands touched.

It was just a second. A hint of a touch. A flash of awareness she did not welcome.

His gaze met hers. His lips quirked, warmed.

Her belly tightened. Her breath caught. Her defenses rose—

He'd apologized, she reminded herself, again.

And yet again.

It took everything in her to smile back, and even then, it was a fake smile. "You have it," she said magnanimously.

"No, you." He waved the pastry in her direction.

She shook her head. "I'm not really hungry."

"Neither am I. You have it."

"No—"

"Oh, for pity's sake," Amy muttered. She took the last pastry, ripped it in half and tossed it—*tossed it*—in the general direction of their plates. "Just eat the damn thing."

Nat did smile at him then, and she laughed.

And he laughed back.

After brunch with the Tuttles, Jax headed to the Sherrod Resort to meet Ben, and to pick up the boys for Amy because she'd had to run back to the bakery and put out a fire. It was always a treat to visit the Sherrod, because it was a gorgeous place designed to make a man feel as though he was luxuriating in nature rather than in a cement-and-glass building sitting *in* nature.

Also, several of his pieces were prominently featured

throughout the public areas, and that always gave him a thrill. Especially if he happened to spot someone enjoying them.

"Jax!" Ben's assistant Char came around the reception desk with a smile when she saw him. Char was always perky and professional. Her long blond hair was curled around her ear, highlighting the com pod that all of Ben's management staff wore. "Mr. Sherrod's expecting you, but he's on a call at the moment. Would you like to wait in the bar?" Jax eyed the dark and gloomy cave, then glanced out at the beautiful pool deck splashed in sunshine.

"How about I just wait for him out there?"

"Perfect. I'll send someone out with a beverage. Any preference?"

Yeah, it was nice being pampered once in a while. "Anything soft and cold, thanks."

Char nodded and disappeared, and Jax headed out to the back of the resort where Ben and his crew had created a swimmer's paradise, including lap pools for the adults, water slides and a lazy river for the kids as well as an assortment of hot tubs. He found an unoccupied cabana and collapsed into a lounger and idly watched people swimming and playing and enjoying the day.

Summer was edging its way into season, so it wasn't hot, but there was a pleasant warmth that might accumulate on a man and tempt him to jump into a pool, so he was glad when his drink arrived, iced and beading with condensation. It surprised him with a pop of citrus, so he groaned a little and jabbed at the ice cubes with the straw in appreciation.

It was the little things that gave pleasure, he'd come to realize, after a life jammed full of big things.

Little things. Like Nat's smile this morning at brunch. Hell, just seeing her come down the stairs, all tousled and sleep-happy, had made something in his chest hum. He could only imagine what it would feel like to cuddle up beside sleep-happy Natty and—

He had to cut off the thought because it was wandering into dangerous territory.

Yes. He was attracted to Natalie Tuttle, and he always had been—more so now that he was grown and knew better what he liked and needed. And yes, he wanted to entertain the thoughts nudging at his consciousness. He wanted to embrace and wallow in them.

In her.

But he'd just made peace with her, and they were both still processing. No matter what the circumstances, apologizing to a woman for an ancient screwup and then immediately trying to jump her bones was not okay. It was not the kind of man he was, or wanted to be. And frankly, she deserved better.

Besides, he didn't even know if she was available or interested in him—or if he was just that jerk from high school she tried not to think about. Yeah. He saw it in her eyes. Sensed it in the hesitation of her smile. Felt it in his soul. She still saw him as a threat. How did a guy get around that?

He reminded himself it was a real relationship— a friendship—he wanted with her. But he was honest with himself enough to recognize that as a polite lie. He wanted more. So much more.

What a shame timing was against them. She'd be leaving as soon as her show started back up, Amy'd told him as much. She was only here to help out until Pearl's housekeeper was back on her feet, Celeste had said. Sheida had mentioned that Martha Jean might never be able to return to work after her fall, but that didn't mean Nat would be staying. She'd disappeared with no warning before. He wouldn't put it past her to do so again. And he could hardly blame her.

He'd left town right after high school as well. A lot of them had. Only some had returned to stay.

Yeah. As much as he was interested in exploring his attraction to Natalie, he'd been excruciatingly aware this morning that there was still some kind of wall between them, and he could hardly object. An apology was a good start, not a magic wand. If he wanted a friendship with her—or anything more—it would take time and effort to rebuild trust. A lot more time than they had.

"There you are. Sorry I'm late." Ben collapsed in the other lounger and loosened his tie. He looked incongruous in a pool lounger in a full suit, and somehow right at home. Too at home. He reached over and grabbed Jax's drink and drained it.

"Hey!"

"Quit your whining. Oscar's bringing us some cucumber water."

"I don't want cucumber water." Jax made a face. "No one likes cucumber water."

Oscar arrived just then with cucumber water, and Jax took it just to be polite, then asked, "Is there any more of that lemon stuff?" and gestured to the glass Ben had emptied.

"Sure." Oscar whisked the glass away then whisked himself off to find more. There was a lot of whisking here.

Ben took a deep draught of his cucumber water and sighed. "Nice day."

"Very nice." Nicer without cucumber water.

"So, you want to have lunch out here?"

"Naw," Jax said, watching a giggling pink bundle emerge from the slide and hit the water with a splash. He grinned when he realized it was Ben's daughter, Quinn. "I already ate."

Ben glowered at him. "We had a lunch date. Why did you already eat?"

"I got hijacked by Celeste Tuttle." He hadn't intended to make Ben flush but wasn't surprised that he did.

Ben looked away, but his tone belied his interest when he drawled, "Really?"

"Mmm-hmm. Her garbage disposal was making threatening noises, so she asked me to look at it and forced me to stay for brunch."

"You and Celeste?" A grumble.

"And Amy, and Pearl. And Natalie."

"The whole family?" Was that a pout? "And how's the disposal?"

"Fine." Oscar appeared with more lemonade and Jax happily traded the cucumber nonsense for it. "So, did you have fun at the party last night?" he asked by way of changing the topic.

Ben growled low in his throat. "You left right after Natalie left."

"Not an answer."

"An observation."

"Since she's the only reason I went, and since she and I had a chance to talk things over, yeah. I left." Like a rocket.

"How'd the talk go?"

Jax shrugged. "Fine." A good answer. A vague answer. A perfect answer because he wasn't really sure how it had gone, other than the fact that they'd agreed to be friends and they shook on it and then she smiled at him this morning.

"I see," Ben said in that aggravating tone he used when he thought he saw something.

"It's fine. We're fine."

"Hmm."

"Really. We're friends."

"Friends?"

"We shook on it."

"And you're okay with friendship?"

Why didn't Ben just shut up and drink his stupid cucumber water? "She is." Silence fell then and lasted until Jax shot a glance at Ben. "What?" he finally barked.

Ben shrugged. "I didn't say anything."

He didn't have to. They knew each other well enough for Jax to *smell* his condescension. "Just say it."

Ben heaved a sigh. "We're both adults, Jax. Both been married. Both gone through that grinder—" Jax's gut tightened at his reference to Melissa and their—

thankfully brief—union. It had been a bad match, all the way around. They'd both been overseas and far from home and lonely, and it had crumbled quickly after Jax's PTSD started rearing its howling head. Too much for her to deal with, she'd said. Between his symptoms and his healing attempts and the small town he intended to return to after his discharge, which she found a backwater, they hadn't had a chance.

"Your point?" he asked with a thread of irritation. Thinking of Melissa and how they ended it always made him grumpy.

"If you like Natalie, you know, *like that*, you should tell her. At least then you've tried."

"Mmm-hmm." It was way too soon for that kind of pronouncement...even if she was the first woman he'd been interested in, in that way, for longer than he could remember.

"Seriously," Ben insisted.

A little devil coiled in Jax's gut. "The way you've told Celeste how you feel?"

Ben's ears went a little red. "That's different."

"I don't see how."

"Well, Celeste hates me."

"Celeste doesn't hate anyone."

"She hates *me*. The other day at the committee meeting she actually hissed."

"You probably said something stupid."

"Hey. You're supposed to be my friend."

"Did you say something stupid?"

"Moot. Point."

Yeah, right. Jax chuckled. "Well, Nat and I have just met...again. We—"

"You don't have to defend yourself. I'm just saying, don't miss the chance to tell her how you feel. She's only here for a while."

"And she has that exciting life in LA to return to. Did you know she was nominated for an Emmy?"

"I'm a fan of the show. Of course, I knew." Ben leaned back in his chair and stared up at the sky and sighed. "But you're probably right. Why would she want to give that all up for Coho Cove?"

Chapter Six

Nat and her mother had a lovely morning together, while Celeste spent a couple hours at her favorite place, the library. They played Scrabble and chatted—about Nat's job and Amy's boys and Pepe's potty habits. What was interesting was that Momma didn't want to talk about her stroke, or any problems she was having since the stroke.

Then again, it was hardly a surprise to Natalie. Momma's modus operandi had always been to ignore any roadblocks and barrel on through. In the past, that had been annoying, but now, it gave Natalie hope that her stubbornness would prevail and help her in her recovery. She was certainly determined to walk without assistance, and to that end, had Natalie help her practice with a cane, which was less clunky that the walker, but not nearly as steady.

Celeste returned at lunchtime, carrying a pile of books, which she excitedly shared with Momma over lunch. Then the three of them went through old family albums and laughed and cried and reminisced.

To Nat's delight, Sheida stopped by in the afternoon to announce that they were going to take a walk. Momma was resting and Celeste, who had returned a few hours ago, had no objections, so Nat grabbed her sweater and slipped on. It wasn't chilly outside, but she was used to much warmer weather. "Where are we going?" she asked.

Sheida made a face. "Just come on."

Nat sighed Fine. And it was, after all, a beautiful day. It deserved some of her attention. She'd been planning to cruise around town and check out her old haunts anyway, and she couldn't think of anyone she'd rather explore with. "All right. Let's do this thang."

Sheida grinned and hooked her arm in Nat's and led the way.

There were two sides of town in Coho Cove. Everything close to the river and the marina had always been considered the touristy part of town and was mostly seasonal— the pier, with its bait shop, fish and chips place, churro stand, and the Logging Museum were open all year round, but the touristy places for bike rentals, dinner cruises and day-fishing charters were still shuttered. For Nat, that was a plus—fewer people to avoid.

But Sheida turned in the other direction. She usually did, metaphorically speaking.

The other side of town, on the inland flats, before the cliff rose to tower over them, was where most people lived and shopped. This was where Sheida headed. There was a third side to town now, the new side, out on the promontory where the old mill once stood, which was now home to the Sherrod Resort and Golf Course. And, of course, the tribal lands beyond that.

Together they headed toward the main drag, enjoying the softening sun and a kick of breeze.

"Why are we going this way?" Nat asked. It was, after all, much prettier down by the marina.

"I want to show you all the new stuff," Sheida said in a way-too-chirpy voice.

"Ah. That's new," Nat nodded at the old Five and Dime, now repurposed as Gunter's Mattress Haüs and painted a hideous shade of bubblegum pink.

Sheida growled deep in her throat. "Gunter. I was hoping you wouldn't notice that."

Nat had to laugh. The building was painted to catch attention. "I can't believe the town council isn't up in arms." The rest of the town had a cohesive vibe in architecture. And a sane color palette for a coastal town. The Mattress Haüs stuck out like a sore thumb.

"I think they are in negotiations with Gunter," Sheida said breezily. "He likes pink."

Nat nodded, and they continued on, chatting and catching up as they walked. It was amazing, the way they just picked up as though they'd never been apart. They passed the Historic Town Hall, tall and proud and made of polished marble glinting in the sunlight, and then the real town hall—a set of double-wide trailers over by the grocery store—the town square with the statue of the town founder, the bowling alley on Vine Street, the old Episcopalian Church, the library, Coho Elementary School, the trailer park. It was all so familiar, and at the same time, different. As though Natalie was looking at it all through a different lens.

She stopped short as she caught sight of a large empty lot. "Hey. The drive-in is gone."

"Yeah." Sheida shook her head. "It burned down."

"I wouldn't think a drive-in could burn down."

Sheida's grin was brilliant and oozing with irony. "Anything can burn down if an arsonist is really motivated." They turned off Main and headed down Steelhead Drive, which had been remade from an unsightly industrial complex. Brightly painted stores marched in a row on both sides of the street. "Now, this is where it gets interesting," Sheida said, by way of warning.

"Why didn't we start with the interesting part?" Nat had to ask.

"Hush, now. Pay attention. The Chamber is trying to create a shopping district. There are some cool places."

"Is this what you wanted to show me?"

Sheida didn't answer; she just tugged Nat along to a store with a sign painted in rustic, weathered pastels gently advertising that this was L'Infinity West. One whiff of sage and bergamot, one glance at the sparkling crystals in the window, made clear that this was a cool and funky new age shop, not unlike the cool and funky new age shops all over Southern California. "Oooh," Nat said, because she loved stores like this.

Sheida pulled her inside and introduced her to Gwen

Deveney, the owner and a newcomer to Coho Cove. Gwen was a truly lovely woman with a boho sense of style, long blond hair and a serene smile. They chatted for a while until Sheida decided they had to get going. She grabbed Nat's arm and said, "Come on. Much more to see," and dragged her out the door.

As Sheida towed her away, Nat waved at Gwen and called, "I'll be back!" because there were some books that had captured her attention during her scan, and she wanted to return sometime…without her bossy tour guide.

The next shop they stopped at had a shingle that proclaimed, in bright, multicolored Comic Sans, that it was Yummy.

Indeed, when they stepped inside, a mélange of scents hit Nat high in her sinuses. The store was a jumble of baskets holding soaps on one side, shelves of potions and elixirs on the back wall and, on the far side, all kinds of delicious bath accoutrements.

It took a moment for Nat to adjust to the cacophony—just so many smells—but after a breath or two, the serenity hit her. It was—

"Oh mah gawd," a chirpy voice rose from the east. "Is that Natalie Tuttle?"

The owner of the voice emerged from behind a display in distressed jeans and a Coexist T-shirt. The face was not familiar, but the hair was. It was multicolored and that, along with the *oh mah gawd*, rang Nat's memory bell. "Clara?" Good Lord. Clara Pearson. Her heart lifted a little.

Clara had been one of her few friends way back when. She hadn't thought about her for years.

She folded Nat into a hug with a low moan. "Nat, oh, Nat. I've missed your face." She went on reminiscing and chatting and bringing Nat up-to-date on everything in *her* life. Then she got serious.

"How are *you*, Nat?" she asked in a rush of curious compassion.

"Oh, I'm great," Nat said, successfully ignoring the little voice in her soul that whispered, *Liar*. She was great. She was.

"Nat's on TV," Sheida announced.

"Oooooooooh!"

Nat sighed. "I most certainly am not on TV. I work for a show. I design sets." She did a whole lot more than that, but Clara didn't need the nitty-gritty.

"She was nominated for an Emmy," Sheida said like a proud mama.

"How exciting." Clara hugged Nat again. "Of course, I don't have a television." Of course not. "But what an accomplishment."

"I didn't win." It bore mentioning. Estelle Esterhazy had won, but whatever.

"Still. It's an honor to be nominated." Clara, again, with another hug. "I am just so thrilled you are here, Nat. Oh, by the way, are you going to the reunion?" she asked.

Nat blinked. "What reunion?"

Sheida rolled her eyes. "The high school reunion. Did I not send you the email?"

"You did not."

"It's next month. Just a few weeks now!" Clara fairly quivered with excitement. "Ian McMurphy is coming back for it." Nat couldn't suppress her grin. She and Ian had worked on the school newspaper and yearbook together. They'd both been proud dorks. He'd taken her to prom because neither had a date and neither had wanted to go alone. Clara's eyes went wide. "Gosh, he's a big shot, too, now. A bestselling author. You two should compare notes!"

Nat ignored the big shot comment, because she hardly was one, and focused on Ian. Another friend she'd lost touch with when she left. She was beginning to see how she'd missed out on a lot by letting her insecurities and pain blind her to the good things in life. She had effectively clumped most of her high school friends in with Baxter and Lola and Sherill, which, upon reflection, had been dumb at worst and really inaccurate at best.

After they left Yummy, they passed by Amy's bakery, which was closed this late in the afternoon, and breezed by a few other shops. Sheida pointed one out as they passed. "This is Artsy Fartsy. Like an interactive gallery. It's a fun place. We should come here and get drunk and paint things. Angel also has a kiln, if you want to do any glass or ceramics. During the summer, it's full of rug rats, but the rest of the year, it's ours."

The store was closed, but as Nat passed, some wood carvings in the display window caught her attention and she stopped to study them. Something about them tugged at her soul. There was such beauty in their lines, and the way the artist had used the natural grain and colors of the wood to capture the sweep of an eagle's wing was stunning. She made a mental note to come back again when the shop was open and check on their prices because, while she wasn't a tchotchke fanatic, she did like incorporating fine art in her crampy little apartment.

And then, there in the mélange of her artsy appreciation, Sheida's comment hit her.

"Wait. Angel?" Her heart shuddered. "Not Angel Goulden?" Surely not. Angel Goulden had been a founding member of the Official Coho High School Cheerleader and Nerd Tormentor Squad.

Sheida nodded. "Too bad the shop is closed. I wanted you to meet her again. She mentioned she missed you at Lizzie's party." And then, "Don't make that face."

"I'm not making a face." Liar. "Why do you want me to meet her again?"

"She's pretty cool, now. You should give her a chance."

To what? Rip her heart out again? No thanks.

The next stop was the old Malt Shop which, irritatingly, was now a bar called Bootleggers. Nat had passed it on her way into town, but now, upon closer inspection, she didn't totally hate it for being, well, not the Malt Shop. It smelled of whiskey and beer and delicious food, and had a minimalist vibe with clean lines and a cave-like ambience—cool and shadowed and quiet. There were customers at tables and along the bar, and in the back the clack of pool balls served as percussion to murmured conversations, but it didn't feel crowded.

"Hey, there, Sheida," the tall, tatted biker dude at the bar said as they sidled up. "What can I get you, hon?"

"Hey, Vic. This is Nat Tuttle—"

"Nat Tuttle!" Vic thrust out a large hand. "I've heard about you."

Gosh, he had such an open, friendly vibe. She couldn't help but respond. "Not a word of it is true," she joked.

"Well, welcome. Can I get you a drink?"

"Nat's hungry. Do you have that cheese plate?" She turned to Nat. "You don't want to ruin your dinner."

"That would be lovely," Nat said. And it was, when Vic brought it by their table with two glasses of pinot gris—a full charcuterie including fresh fruit, nuts, meats and a sampler of local cheeses. It hit the spot. It hit every spot. So much for not spoiling her dinner.

"So," Sheida said as she polished off the last grape. "What do you think of the new Coho Cove?"

Nat chuckled. "Was that what the tour was about?"

"Of course. I love this town. Naturally, I want you to love it too. I'll be honest, I never really understood why you were so anxious to leave."

"It's a lovely town." Yeah. Now, as a grown up, she could appreciate the charm. "I really do like the new shops."

"Wait til summer really gets into swing. You'll see. We're becoming a destination. Some people come just for Coho Days." Coho Days was the three-day festival marking the end of the season. It had been a fun experience when Nat had been younger, but according to Celeste, the Chamber of Commerce had really upped their game. It now included other events like a full-on carnival, concerts in the park, a sandcastle sculpture contest, a kite flying festival and a beer garden.

"Sounds like fun." Nat didn't mention that she probably wouldn't be here for summer because she didn't want to ruin the mood. Instead, she said, "As to why I left, well, that's complicated. Back then I thought it was about other people—you know, the bullies, my family and whatnot—but now I think it was more about me. What I wanted, and what I couldn't have if I stayed. At the time, a small town felt, well, like a prison."

"And now?"

"It's nice." Really nice. Quiet and peaceful and, frankly, beautiful. "I do like the changes you showed me, but I have to admit, I miss the old Malt Shop." They'd hung out here as kids, after all.

"Shut up. Vic's the owner and he's cute."

Nat choked on her water. "What does Vic's cuteness have to do with anything?"

Sheida gave a heavy sigh. "All right. So, not Vic."

"What do you mean, not Vic?" Something prickled on her nape. "Sheida. Were you hoping to set me up with the bartender?"

"Not in the slightest. And he's the owner."

"Sheida…"

"We are merely exploring your options."

"My options?"

"Well, you said you're not dating."

"I explicitly said I *was* dating."

"But not seriously."

True. Carl was a coworker. They dated off and on when it was convenient to their schedules. When they didn't want to be alone. When Sheida had asked, she hadn't wanted to go into details.

She should have known better. This was Sheida. With Sheida, there were always details. "Well? Tell me about him."

Nat shrugged. "What do you want to know?"

"What does it mean to see him once in a while?"

"Wouldn't you rather know his eye color? Or his job title? Or his sun sign?"

She pretended to think about it for a minute. "No. Not really. I'm really curious to know how you see someone *once in a while*."

"Well..." Natalie sighed. "We both have busy schedules. We work in different locations sometimes—even on the same show. If we happen to end up in the same place...we keep each other company."

Sheida sniffed. "That doesn't sound like a relationship."

No. It didn't. Nat shrugged. "It works." At the very least, it kept her from feeling lonely.

"Okay." Apparently, that was all Sheida needed to know. She looked down at their empty platter. "Are you done? We're going to Smokey's next."

Nat made a face. She wasn't hungry anymore. Smokey's held absolutely no allure. "You're not taking me to Smokey's."

"I thought you were hungry?"

"Not for Baxter Vance." Besides, had they not just demolished an enormous amount of food?

Sheida sighed. "Come on. Give him a chance. He's a volunteer firefighter now." As though that simple fact erased everything.

"Nope."

"Why don't you want to be introduced to eligible men?"

Nat huffed a laugh. "Oh my God. You and your evil plans."

"Of course, I have an evil plan. Have you met me?"

"Okay. Spill it. What exactly are you trying to do?"

Sheida batted her lashes. It was irritating because she had really long, thick lashes. Nat's stubby lashes could not compete. "Well, it's pretty simple, as plans go. I figure if you meet someone and fall in love, you'll want stay in town. And then I will have you closer."

"That's not going to happ—"

"Okay. Fine. Because you need a date for the reunion, then."

Nat rolled her eyes. "Who said I'm even going to the reunion? I didn't get an invitation."

"Seriously? I emailed you the announcement months ago."

Had she? Maybe. Maybe Nat had missed it.

"Sheida, I am categorically not looking for a date—"

"A date for what?"

Nat jumped as a deep male voice surrounded her. Not because it was a male voice, though, or a deep one, but because it was Jax's.

How mortifying.

Why had he overheard that?

She took a breath, centered herself and then whirled

on him. Even though he was dressed in what were clearly work clothes, even though there was a smear of dirt on his cheek and his hair was rumpled, and he held an already-greasing to-go bag, he looked delicious. She swallowed her feelings and forced a scowl. "Your sister is torturing me."

His eyes narrowed. "Sheida. We've talked about this," he said in a tone that made even Nat burst into a laugh.

"She's trying to force me to go to prom with Baxter Vance!"

"It's the reunion, not the prom. And I am merely showing you the options."

"Baxter is *not* an option."

"You need to have a date."

"No. I do not."

For some reason, Jax snickered, and that irritated Nat and she frowned at him. He put up both hands. "Hey. I'm on your side. And here's a thought…why go at all?"

"Right?"

"Jaxon!" Sheida howled. "You're not helping."

He quirked a brow in tandem with a too sexy lip. "Helping with what?"

"She's trying to lure me into a relationship with one of these yahoos, so I'll become a pod person and never want to leave town again."

He stilled. Stared at her for a second. Said nothing.

She wished he would. She wanted to know what he was thinking just then. They were friends, but not close enough for her to ask, which, frankly, was irritating.

* * *

Something hot and cold whipped through Jax at the thought of Nat falling in love with Baxter Vance—or any of the other town yahoos. He knew damn well what that feeling was, and he struggled to push it aside. There was no place for jealousy in a friendship.

A true friend would seek only joy and fulfillment for another.

This howling beast, stuffed deep in his gut, was not that.

"Oh." Sheida said, before he could compose an appropriate response. "There's Mike Antonelli. I want to bring him over. He's a big shot at a tech company now, you'll like him. Be right back."

Once Sheida was gone, Nat turned to Jax and rolled her eyes. "Your sister."

He chuckled. He just had to. "I know."

"She's showing me like a pig at market."

"She's just missed you a lot, Nat." And, when her expression shifted into something kind of sad, he added, "She doesn't have a lot of friends." Nat glanced pointedly to the spot where Sheida stood, surrounded by friends, laughing and chatting with complete aplomb. "*Real* friends." He covered her hand with his to make the point, but then pulled back when she flinched. "There's a difference between people who *fill* your life and people who *are* your life."

She sighed. "I'm sorry. I just don't like being managed."

He had to laugh. Because Sheida was a herd dog by

nature. It was her goal in life to get everything and everyone in order and then keep them there.

Nat leaned in. "Is it so wrong that I don't want to go to the reunion?"

He shrugged. "I don't want to go." Although he would, with her. With Nat, it would be...not horrible. "We can make a pact to not go to the reunion together." He had no idea why he said that but loved her grin in response.

"Yes. Let's."

He leaned closer, too. So close he could smell the wine on her breath. See the shine in her eyes. "You can always escape, you know."

She blinked. That sweep of lashes rendered him speechless. So pretty. She was so...pretty. "Can I?" she whispered. "Can I really?"

He glanced in his sister's direction. Sheida was engaged in a conversation with Mike and a couple of other guys. At that moment they all turned. To look at *her*.

Natalie groaned. "I really should."

A little imp in his soul urged him on. "She's distracted. Now's the time. Come on. I'm heading for my studio. I'd love to give you a tour, if you want to come with."

He didn't expect her to say yes, not really. But her eyes lit up and she shifted off the high seat and collected her sweater. "You have a studio? What kind of studio?" and then, "Let's blow this pop stand before Sheida comes back."

And they did.

* * *

Fortunately, the great escape was a success. With absolutely no compunction, Nat left the bill for Sheida to pay, since she'd been kidnapped without her wallet. Then she followed Jax onto Silver Salmon Drive, which led back toward the beach through the park. It was a leafy, loamy, lovely walk.

"So, what kind of studio do you have?" she asked again as they passed the community garden, because he hadn't answered. She had no idea what Jax even did, and that realization stunned her.

He shot her a grin that nearly felled her. It glowed. It revealed him, that grin. "You know those chain saw bears my dad used to make?"

She nodded. They'd been cute.

"A little like that."

"Woodworking, then?"

He nodded. "And I have a bike I'm restoring." When she shot him a puzzled glance, he added, "It's a multipurpose space."

"A bike, huh? A Schwinn?"

He laughed. "A Harley Sportster. It's an antique, practically, but I'm determined to get her going."

"So, Jax…" She had to ask. She just had to. "What led you to woodworking?"

He retreated a little, made a face and then sighed. "Well, you know I served in the Army for four years." She nodded. She had. He'd been stationed with George before he died, Amy'd told her. "Well, it was…hard on me. I…well, I have what they call PTSD, I guess."

"You guess?"

He grimaced. "That's the diagnosis. I'm not a fan of labels. And even with labels, that's a broad diagnosis. Everyone processes trauma differently."

She nodded. "That's what my therapist says."

He glanced at her then; it was a knowing glance. In it she felt, to her soul, his appreciation of her casual acceptance of his revelation that he'd been in therapy. It kindled a tiny fire in her heart. So many people made ugly judgments about mental health—even in her circles—seeing the inability to cope with challenges as a sign of failure, rather than an opportunity to grow. It was a relief to know that he was someone with whom she could discuss, well, deeper issues.

"My therapist saved my life," he said simply. "I wouldn't be here today, if I hadn't had help."

"I'm so sorry you had to go through that."

He flushed a little, but shot her a smile. "Life is full of challenges. It's important to ask for help when you need it."

"Right? No one would resist going to a dentist if they had a toothache."

He chuckled. "Other than my father…" They both laughed because his father was notorious for just pushing through medical issues. "But you are absolutely right. And art therapy has really helped me balance things. You know?"

She smiled, because she understood. She really did. "Art releases you from all the noise," she said, off the cuff. She didn't expect him to go silent the way he did and stare at her. She wasn't sure how to respond to that, so she refocused on the path.

"It's funny," he continued after a while. "When you say PTSD, most people think of veterans. But you don't have to be in a battle or in an explosion to get PTSD. People get PTSD for all kinds of reasons. Trauma is trauma."

She nodded. "And everyone's tolerance level to trauma is different, and so are their reactions." She hated that he'd been through this and, at the same time, was so proud over how he'd handled it. "But I think the biggest problem is that people resist getting help for emotional and mental issues because there's some kind of stigma attached to it. Who we are, mentally, emotionally—that's a huge part of who we are. I'm more my sense of humor than I am my big toe. But if there was something wrong with my big toe, you'd better believe I'd be seeing a doctor. Especially if there was a risk of losing it. But losing my sense of humor? That's losing a part of *me*."

They shared a glance, one that made clear he appreciated her understanding, which was humbling.

"We're right up here," he said as they turned onto Razor Clam Way. He headed off to the left, down a rutted track until they came to a yard filled with bears and eagles, rough cut by chain saws, with a long, low building just beyond. "This is it."

She stared at the army of sculptures and laughed. "That's a lot of bears."

He nodded as he fished his keys out of his pocket. "They sell." He fell silent as he unlocked the door, pushed it open and gestured her in.

As she stepped into the dimly lit Native longhouse, the scent of earth hit her full on. Earth and sap and sanded wood. A hint of pine and lemon oil. The floor beneath her sneakers had some give. She wasn't surprised to find it covered with wood chips. It was a large space, with one side a labyrinthine jumble of raw material, from logs to slabs to fine driftwood in the rafters—and the old Harley. By the door, shelves held the smaller finished pieces—a laughing gull, a trot of sandpipers along the waves and… was that a geoduck? She barely held back her snicker. Her humor evaporated when she took note of his larger work. It stole her breath. Oh, yes, there were your typical grinning bears and an orca leaping from a wave in the wood. Very trendy. Very salable. Most would fit right in on a situation comedy set. Or maybe a Murderous Cove mystery. But it was the masterpieces behind all that pop culture kitsch that caught her unprepared.

They hit her hard. Something about them spoke to her—a familiarity, a sense of spirit, a—

She swallowed heavily as comprehension hit. Hard. "Wait. You're the artist in Angel's display window," she blurted. She knew. She just *knew*.

He chuckled. "I am the artist who *has pieces* in Angel's window." Yeah. Probably a good clarification.

"Oh my. I loved those pieces. You made them?"

He nodded.

Of course. Of course, they were his. They had resonated with her, just as each of these sculptures did. She felt his soul in them.

And then, some other, larger pieces, back in the corner, caught her eye. There were three of them. A triad. Three women emerging from the wood in exquisite splendor. The expressions on their faces were seductive,

but not in a worldly way. They whispered and wooed
their viewer to look up, to see more, to embrace life.
They were—

"Well, what do you think?" There was a catch in his
tone. As though he didn't already know the talent he silently harbored. As though he wasn't sure she wouldn't
recognize him in this, the place of his heart.

For that was what it was. *This* was the Jax she'd always seen—behind the football uniform, beyond the
smile or the lilt of his laugh or that one puerile kiss.
This was the Jax she'd always loved.

"I have coffee. But it's cold," he said into the silence,
for wont of her response.

Yeah, she was probably being rude, she should
probably be gushing. He had mad talent. All the other
women he brought here would probably be gushing.
Had gushed.

Well, crap. She didn't like the thought of other
women gushing all over him at all.

"Nat?"

She whirled toward him. "Where's number four?"
Total brain malfunction. Too much artistic beauty for
her brain to process in the moment. He should have
warned her.

"Are you crying?"

"No." She swiped at her cheeks. "Where's number
four?"

His brow rumpled. It was adorable. He was adorable.

Almost too adorable for her to remember to point
at the trio in the corner—and why the hell were they
in the corner? That was like hanging a Rembrandt in a

bathroom. Which, upon further reflection, would not be terrible. But these pieces? They deserved to be in the front of any display. They were…perfection.

But she did remember to point. At the statues. "I see Winter, Spring and Fall. Where's Summer?"

He didn't respond. He just stared at her.

She couldn't complain, because she'd just done the same thing to him, but it was concerning, especially when a suspicious dampness rose in his eyes.

"Jax?"

"You… How? How did you know?"

She made a little face, but only a little one. "How did I know there was a piece missing?"

He nodded. His Adam's apple bobbed for no reason.

"Well, I don't know how to answer that, Jax. It's pretty obvious. They are beautiful, by the way. I meant to say that right away and I didn't, but they are."

"Thank you." He shook his head and raked his stubby hair with long fingers. She suppressed a flicker of grief that he'd shed those long locks she'd lusted for, sitting behind him in Biology. "I'm just a little stunned that you got the theme of the display seeing it out of order and with one quarter of it missing."

She lifted a shoulder and smiled piquantly. "What can I say? I am an artsy-fartsy nerd. Where's Summer?"

He didn't say, but his eyes flicked to a statue covered with a tarp, so she marched over and glanced at him. "May I?" His nod was nearly imperceptible, but it was enough. She pulled off the tarp and watched as Summer emerged and— Heavens. She was, well, beyond exquisite, emerging from the wood with arms held aloft, some prayer or celebration of life. The expression on her face made clear her joy. Something about it nagged at her, some familiarity she couldn't place. It was beautiful. "Oh my." It was all she could say, all she could manage.

She'd studied art in school. She understood theme and concept and nuance, but this…

Art school had not prepared her for this.

"Oh, Jax. This is beautiful. Just…" She was tearing up. She knew it, and it irritated her, but she could not hide her response.

"Do you really like it?"

Her heart filled with ecstasy and irritation. "Do I like it?" What kind of question was that? "It's gorgeous. Just… Oh, Jax."

He came up behind her silently, but she felt his presence in a humming energy, so she turned, met his eye and shrugged. Words were stupid. Words did not and could not do this—his vision—justice.

But somehow he knew what she was feeling. And he opened his arms to her without those stupid words and she walked right in.

And oh, the hug, the enfoldment of her in him, was divine. Sacred, maybe.

She tipped her face to his and smiled and he smiled back.

"You see it, too," he said softly, and she had to nod, because she did. She saw it. She saw him, and he saw her, too.

Her heart hitched as his gaze flicked to her lips and she knew—just knew—that he was going to kiss her. And this time, it was just the two of them in his secret, sacred place. All other thoughts fell away, like sawdust in the breeze. She licked her lips. His body tightened around her. She leaned closer, welcoming the coming kiss. Welcoming the release of all her fears and wounds and barricades.

He leaned closer and she tasted the perfume of his breath, felt the warmth of his approach. Prepared for—

"Hey, Jax!" The mood exploded as the door opened, bringing in a burst of light and the breeze and, apparently, Ben Sherrod. "Oh." Ben stopped short and he stared at them as though he'd never seen two people in a—kiss-less—clinch before. "Oh, hey, Natalie."

"Ben," she said, stepping back, away from temptation, because all of a sudden, she remembered everything her overwhelming emotional response had silenced. Like the fact that Jax was her sister's man.

"Ben," Jax parroted, but in a crisper tone. "Excellent timing, as usual." He shot her a chagrined glance. Whether he was chagrined because they'd been interrupted, or because he'd been tempted to kiss his girlfriend's sister wasn't clear, but it hardly mattered.

He was Amy's. Damn it.

"Uh, sorry to, uh, drop by unannounced."

"I was just showing Nat around," Jax said.

"Ah." Ben looked from Jax to Nat and then nodded. "I see. Well, Nat. What do you think of Jax's place?"

She forced a smile, swallowed her swirling feelings and gusted cheerily, "It's amazing. He's so talented. Did you know?"

Jax grunted. "Ben's one of my best customers."

Ben grinned. "I buy the big stuff. You should come

by the resort and check it out. We have a great pool and restaurants and—"

"And why are you here again?" Jax asked pointedly.

"Oh. Right." Ben smiled somewhat apologetically. "Sorry. Danny had a cancelation tomorrow and I was wondering if you and the boys want to go out fishing with me and Quinn tomorrow."

Jax blew out a huff and crossed his arms. "You have to ask Amy."

Ben grinned. "I stopped there first. The boys are pumped."

It took a lot of effort, but Nat kept the smile on her face. The reminder of his relationship with Amy wasn't welcome but served to strengthen her resolve. "I should get going," she said, pretending to check her phone. "It'll be dinnertime soon."

"You're invited, too," Ben said cheerfully. "I'd love to have some time to catch up with you. Do you fish?"

She stared at him. "Do I fish?" *Do I look like I fish?* Dad and Nate had fished a lot and Nat had tagged along, but not because she liked worming hooks or catching slimy creatures she had no intention of eating. She'd enjoyed the quiet time with Dad—and it had been quiet because, as he kept reminding her, *you don't want to scare the fish.* And besides, she absolutely loved—

"She likes boats," Jax said. She did. She loved boats. Loved being on the water for whatever reason. How *he* knew was a mystery. He turned to her, seeping with sincerity. "You should come."

While Ben's invitation had not moved her in the slightest, Jax's did. Tremendously. That and the warmth in his eyes as he looked at her. And while she didn't care for the idea of spending a day watching Amy and Jax be a couple all over the place, the idea of a day pretending to read on a boat sounded lovely. As, of course, spending more time with the boys would be.

"Great!" Fortunately, Ben didn't seem to need a verbal response. "I'll meet you both at Amy's at five."

Wait. What? "Five? As in five a.m.?" Nearly a squawk.

Both the men laughed. "Early start," Ben crowed.

Jax caught her eye. "You'll come? I'll see you, then, okay? I'd like to…talk more. Okay?"

She nodded, then turned around and let herself out of his studio because, really, what else was there to say? And Ben, judging from the fact that he'd wandered over to the kitchenette in the corner and was rummaging through the fridge, had no intention of leaving any time soon, so clearly, any conversation with Jax would have to wait.

Chapter Seven

It wasn't until Natalie was alone and cuddled up in bed and reliving every detail of that almost kiss, that the full implication of it truly hit her. *She had almost locked lips with her baby sister's boyfriend.* Natalie flushed with chagrin. *And she'd wanted to kiss him! She still did.* Mortification swamped her.

What a horrible person she was.

She knew Amy and Jax were together. And hadn't she, just a day ago, been thankful that her sister had finally found someone? Amy had been through hell after losing George. She was raising two boys alone. She deserved to be happy. She'd seemed happy with Jax. They even finished each other's sentences, for pity's sake.

What kind of monster stepped in and ruined something like that?

No. No. She had to keep away from Jax. He was far too tempting. That *conversation* he promised could never happen.

Still, she mourned. Some small corner of her soul mourned, because just being with him lit her up, made her feel full and alive and...seen.

A good person would be able to excise thoughts of lust for her sister's boyfriend. Enjoy his company. Laugh. Smile. Not quietly plot how to get him alone for a kiss. Not lie in bed and think about him, when he'd committed to someone else—

Another wave of emotion hit her, and this one was more difficult to interpret.

Because Jax had almost kissed her, too.

She knew it had not been her imagination. He'd leaned in, dabbed his lower lip with his tongue. His body had tightened around her, the thud of his pulse had kicked up—all the signs, damn it.

That meant his relationship with Amy wasn't as solid as it could be, should be—especially with two boys looking for a father figure. That meant he hungered for her the way she hungered for him. Quietly, behind a wall.

And while that was wonderful for her tattered ego, it was not wonderful for Amy. It meant their relationship would not last. At some point there would be a breakup.

She hated that the thought lifted her heart—yes, she was a terrible person—but at the same time, she knew she could not be the *cause* of the breakup. She would not be. Her relationship with her sister was on thin ice on a good day—something like this would be irreparable. She would never be able to sleep at night if she stole her sister's boyfriend. What decent person could?

With such resolution solidified in her heart and soul, she knew the only way to proceed was to stay away from Jaxon Stringfellow altogether. Which meant canceling tomorrow. Her heart drooped at the thought because, aside from Jax's company, she'd been looking forward to spending time with her nephews and being on the water and enjoying the sunshine.

The thought of quietly packing up and leaving in the dead of night flickered through her mind—returning to LA made it easy to avoid Jax, after all—but she quickly ditched the thought.

Running away didn't solve anything. This trip had shown her that. She'd missed so much by running away, and she hadn't gained very much at all.

No. She'd stay as long as Celeste needed her. And she'd keep away from the tall, tan, lanky man whose soul called to hers. If it killed her, she would. And it probably might.

One would think making a morally right decision would set a soul at rest, allow one to fall into the sleep of the righteous. But one would be wrong. Nat tossed and turned and gritted her teeth and had conversations in her head all night, despite her best efforts to be at peace with her choice.

At four thirty she decided to get up and head over to Amy's to break the news that she would not be on the boat. Amy wouldn't care—she probably didn't even know Ben had invited her. But if she didn't let Amy know, and

Jax and Ben were expecting her, they'd probably come here to the house and wake up Momma. Besides, she needed a walk. And she'd always loved those early morning hours before the world woke up. It reminded her of the early mornings she'd spent with Dad and Nate when *they'd* all gone fishing. No one else had gone, just Nat and Nate and Dad, because Amy and Celeste hadn't liked fishing and Momma had only rolled her eyes when fishing trips were mentioned.

Indeed, it was a soothing walk to Amy's, kissed by the dampness of the marine layer, little wisps of fog, spiderwebs painted in dew. And it was quiet. Peaceful. Sacred.

Yes. She was doing the right thing.

As difficult as it was, as much as she *wanted*…she had to deny herself any exposure to her current addiction.

The light was on in Amy's kitchen, so Nat went around to the side door. She stood on the porch and sucked in a deep breath, centered herself and knocked.

Amy opened the door. She was a tousled mess in Winnie the Pooh flannel pajamas, but in the most adorable way. Her hair was askew, her face still sleep-wrinkled and her eyes were groggy. "Good morning," she said with a sniffle. "Come on in." She left the door open and padded in her bunny slippers to the coffee-pot and poured Nat a mug without asking. But then, it was almost five in the morning. No question would be necessary.

"Thanks." As Amy poured the rest of the pot into a

waiting thermos, Nat took a sip and moaned. First sip of coffee was orgasmic. "Where are the boys?"

Amy waved toward the second floor. "They're getting ready." She opened a soft-sided cooler and started loading it with sandwiches and cookies.

"You aren't dressed, yet," Nat mentioned. "Do you want me to finish that?"

Amy snorted. "I'm not going fishing. Are you nuts?"

"You're not going?" It was shameful, that flicker of excitement that arose with the knowledge that Amy would not be on the boat. Nat doused it ruthlessly. Neither would she be on that boat. Especially if Amy wasn't there.

Amy barked a laugh. "I haven't had a morning off since by last pâtissier left."

"Ah… Well, I just came by to let you know I'm not going."

Amy stared at her. "I thought you loved boat fishing."

"I, ah, don't feel well." Lame. Totally lame. But as excuses went, it was a golden oldie.

Amy propped her hands on her hips, the way she did, and tipped her head. "You walked all the way over here to tell me you don't feel well enough to go fishing?" Amy eyed her up and down. "You look fine."

"Tummy." She patted hers. Indeed, it was sloshing all over the place.

"Okay. Whatever." Amy shrugged. And then, at the top of her lungs bellowed, *"Boys! Get a move on."* A subtle thudding responded overhead. Amy sighed. "They were so wired last night, it's no wonder they're dragging butt. *Come on.*" Another bellow. *"Jax and Ben will be here any minute and they will leave without you if you're not down here!"*

Nat grinned, because that was such a *Momma* thing to say. And then… "Jax isn't here?" Amy only gaped in response, so Nat added, "I thought he lived here." Because, didn't he?

Amy snorted. "He lives in that hut down by the beach. He *stays* here, three times a week. In the spare room." She jerked a thumb toward, apparently, the guest room. "So someone can be here for the boys when I have to go in early. Didn't we talk about this? I could swear we talked about this."

Nat shook her head. They had not talked about this. "I thought you and Jax are a *thing*." Because that was definitely the vibe they gave off.

"What?" Amy stared blankly.

"A couple?" Surely they were. It had seemed that way. Hadn't it?

"A…couple?" Amy blinked. Her pupils dilated "What? Are you—? OMG. You thought…" For some reason she thew her head back and laughed. And laughed. And laughed.

Nat could only stare. There were too many swirling emotions for her to process—guilt, relief, guilt about the relief, excitement, joy, fear, hope.

"Oh, Nat." Still chuckling, Amy shook her head. "Where do you get these weird ideas? Jax is…like a brother. He loves the boys and he's good with them and since they're never going to have a—" Her voice broke a little. "Anyway, he offered to be present for them and I agreed and frankly, it's been wonderful. He's the best.

He saved my sanity, honestly, he did. After George...
well, after George."

"So, you're not... You don't..."

Amy snorted. *Oh dear.* Natalie recognized the mil-
itant look rising on Amy's expression. "You should
know. I will *never* date a military guy. Not ever again."

"But Jax isn't in the military anymore." It bore mentioning.

Amy glared at her. "You know what I mean. They
leave. They all leave. No more military men. I made a
vow." And then, after that cacophony of disjointed past
pain and emotion, she sniffed. "Besides, Jax isn't my
type. If you were ever around, you'd know that, too."

Nat's mind spun, but before she could respond, or
truly process this revelation, two things happened at
once. The boys thudded down the stairs in a riot of
chaos, and the doorbell rang. Shouts and greetings and
woo-hoos rang from the foyer and then Jax stepped into
the kitchen, haloed by the light in the hall.

God, he looked gorgeous. Jax, so tall and strong and
handsome.

And definitely not dating her sister.

Nat couldn't stop her smile.

He saw it and stilled, and stared at her for a mean-
ingful moment before he grinned right back. Her heart
fluttered. Her hope rose up. "You ready to go?" he
asked her—because everyone else in the room had
faded away.

"Absolutely, I am," she said, snagging the cooler and
the thermos of coffee.

"I thought you weren't feeling very well," Amy said.

Loyal Readers
FREE BOOKS Voucher

We're giving away **THOUSANDS** of **FREE BOOKS**

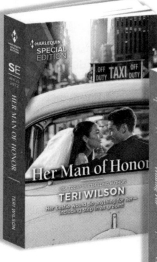

Don't Miss Out! Send for Your Free Books Today!

See Details Inside

Get up to 4
FREE FABULOUS BOOKS
You Love!

To thank you for being a loyal reader we'd like to send you up to 4 FREE BOOKS, absolutely free when you try the Harlequin Reader Service.

Just write "YES" on the Loyal Reader Voucher and we'll send you 2 free books from each series you choose and a Free Mystery Gift, altogether worth over $20.

Try **Harlequin® Special Edition** and get 2 books featuring comfort and strength in the support of loved ones and enjoying the journey no matter what life throws your way.

Try **Harlequin® Heartwarming™ Larger-Print** and get 2 books featuring uplifting stories where the bonds of friendship, family and community unite.

Or **TRY BOTH and get 2 books from each series!**

Your free books are completely free, even the shipping! If you continue with your subscription, you can look forward to curated monthly shipments of brand-new books from your selected series, always at a discount off the cover price! Plus you can cancel any time.

So don't miss out, return your Loyal Readers Voucher today to get your Free books.

Pam Powers

LOYAL READER
FREE BOOKS VOUCHER

◀ **DETACH AND MAIL CARD TODAY!** ▼

YES! I Love Reading, please send me up to 4 FREE BOOKS and a Free Mystery Gift from the series I select.

Just write in "YES" on the dotted line below then return this card today and we'll send your free books & gift asap!

➡ ------ YES ------ ⬅

Which do you prefer?

| ☐ **Harlequin®
Special Edition**
235/335 HDL GRAH | ☐ **Harlequin
Heartwarming®
Larger-Print**
161/ 361 IDL GRAH | ☐ **BOTH**
235/335 & 161/361
IDL GRA5 |

FIRST NAME	**LAST NAME**

ADDRESS

APT.#	**CITY**

STATE/PROV.	**ZIP/POSTAL CODE**

EMAIL ☐ Please check this box if you would like to receive newsletters and promotional emails from Harlequin Enterprises ULC and its affiliates. You can unsubscribe anytime.

Your Privacy – Your information is being collected by Harlequin Enterprises ULC, operating as Harlequin Reader Service. For a complete summary of the information we collect, how we use this information and to whom it is disclosed, please visit our privacy notice located at https://corporate.harlequin.com/privacy-notice. From time to time we may also exchange your personal information with reputable third parties. If you wish to opt out of this sharing of your personal information, please visit www.readerservice.com/consumerchoice or call 1-800-873-8635. **Notice to California Residents** – Under California law, you have specific rights to control and access your data. For more information on these rights and how to exercise them, visit https://corporate.harlequin.com/california-privacy.

© 2022 HARLEQUIN ENTERPRISES ULC ™ and ® are trademarks owned by Harlequin Enterprises ULC. Printed in the U.S.A.

SE/HW-622-LR_MMM22

♦ HARLEQUIN Reader Service —**Here's how it works:**

Accepting your 2 free books and free gift (gift valued at approximately $10.00 retail) places you under no obligation to buy anything. You may keep the books and gift and return the shipping statement marked "cancel." If you do not cancel, approximately one month later we'll send you more books from the series you have chosen, and bill you at our low, subscribers-only discount price. Harlequin® Special Edition books consist of 6 books per month and cost $5.49 each in the U.S or $6.24 each in Canada, a savings of at least 12% off the cover price. Harlequin® Heartwarming™ Larger-Print books consist of 4 books per month and cost just $6.24 each in the U.S. or $6.74 each in Canada, a savings of at least 19% off the cover price. It's quite a bargain! Shipping and handling is just 50¢ per book in the U.S. and $1.25 per book in Canada*. You may return any shipment at our expense and cancel at any time by contacting customer service — or you may continue to receive monthly shipments at our low, subscribers-only discount price plus shipping and handling.

▲ If offer card is missing write to: Harlequin Reader Service, P.O. Box 1341, Buffalo, NY 14240-8531 or visit www.ReaderService.com ▲

BUSINESS REPLY MAIL
FIRST-CLASS MAIL   PERMIT NO. 717   BUFFALO, NY

POSTAGE WILL BE PAID BY ADDRESSEE

HARLEQUIN READER SERVICE
PO BOX 1341
BUFFALO NY 14240-8571

NO POSTAGE
NECESSARY
IF MAILED
IN THE
UNITED STATES

"Oh," Nat gave her a smile. "I'm feeling better now." Much better. And then, to the boys, "Let's go catch some fish!"

Something had changed.

Jax wasn't sure what it was, or what had happened to loosen the mortar on Natalie's shield wall, but he sure *felt* the difference. Her smile, for one, was wide and unreserved. Her glance lingered, rather than skittering away. Her aura, well, it glowed.

This wasn't the moment to explore, but he knew he would find a chance today to ask her. A quiet moment, if such a thing were possible with George and John J in tow. And, if he were being perfectly honest, Ben as well. The three of them, together, were a circus.

It was a major military campaign getting the two boys to the car, and into the back seat with Quinn. As usual, John J sidled right up next to her booster seat and took her hand, leaving the left seat for Georgie—even though he'd called shotgun. Georgie always called shotgun, and he usually got it. But this time, there was no way Jax was letting Nat sit anywhere but right next to him. Georgie huffed and puffed just like Amy did when she didn't get her way, but Jax simply said, "Sorry, bud," and left it at that.

And then, he slid onto the bench seat of Ben's truck—right next to Nat. Hip to hip.

He tried to calm that flare of excitement at the touch, at her warmth, her presence, but he couldn't. And then he realized he didn't want to. Didn't have to. So, he leaned into it and enjoyed it. Enjoyed her.

She glanced at him then, as he pressed his thigh against hers, ever so slightly, and their gazes met. Her lips kicked up—something mischievous and playful and...was that a seductive glance? Whether it was or not, his entire body responded with a wash of heat and exhilaration.

He felt like a schoolboy sitting next to his crush. There was nothing said, nothing implied or inferred, but the mere closeness was enough to set his heart skittering with anticipation.

For what?

Well, that was half the fun, wasn't it?

"Excited?" he asked.

Her expression became even more playful. "Absolutely, I am," she said in a particular tone. And then they just grinned at each other as Ben put the truck in reverse and headed off for the marina.

"I'm excited," said John J. "Quinn is, too. We like boats."

Georgie gave a banal, stuck-in-the-back-seat-with-the-babies sigh. "Everyone likes boats," he said.

"Well," said Nat, for some reason, not breaking her gaze with Jax. "I love boats. It's been a long time since I've been boating, and I cannot wait."

Something hummed in Jax's brain. He was kind of sure she was talking about boating...but there might have been another meaning hidden there. Damn. He wished he could read her mind. Because the vibes she was giving off were...fascinating.

"You should live here," John J suggested. "We have

lots of boats here. You can go on a boat any day you want."

"I'll keep that in mind," she responded in a sedate tone, but her eyes, they danced.

"Okay, everyone," Ben chimed in. "Remember the rules of the boat?"

Georgie and John J groaned.

"That's right. Everyone wears a life jacket. The whole time."

"I'm a *dolphin* now," Georgie said in a disgusted tone, referring to his recent graduation in his swimming class.

"I know," Jax responded to him through the rearview mirror. "You're a strong swimmer, but it's important to be a good example for others, right?"

Georgie sighed, heavily.

"We're all wearing jackets," Ben said. "Danny's boat. Danny's rules. Right, Jax?" He affected a stern look that Jax knew was a sham. The life jackets were *Amy's* rule. Danny's only rule was *try not to get so drunk you fall overboard*. But life jackets were always a good idea, because not every person who went overboard was conscious, and the floaties, at least, would keep their head above water.

"I love wearing a life jacket," Nat said in a cheery voice.

"That's dumb," Georgie grumbled.

"I think it's exciting. Because it means I'm on a boat and I'm safe and I'm going to have a great day." Her smile was brilliant, so Jax responded in kind.

"Me, too," he said.

They held that look for a long while. Jax could have

held it for longer, but Ben pulled into the empty parking lot lightly spattered with moonlight, and parked next to Danny's rig. Georgie was out like a shot, but John J took a minute to release Quinn's seat belt and help her down.

Nat's hand scraped Jax's thigh as she reached for her latch as well, and he tried not to jump, but damn, it was like an electric bolt, that slight touch.

As he stepped out into the cool, quiet peace that was—as military folks called it—0-dark-thirty, he sucked in a deep breath, filling his nostrils with the scent of brine. "Nice," he said.

Nat, right there by his side, sighed. "I hate early mornings, but I do love this part."

"Me, too." Jax grabbed the cooler Amy had made up, Nat grabbed another bag that probably held a change of clothes for the boys, towels and sunscreen—knowing Amy—and they followed Ben and the kids, who were running full tilt over the tar-sealed boards onto the pier.

"She doesn't say much," Nat murmured, her gaze on Quinn and John J, who had hold of his friend's hand like he'd never let go.

"Mmm." Jax slowed his pace a little so Ben wouldn't overhear. "Quinn doesn't talk. Not since the car wreck."

Her eyes, wide and wounded, settled on him. "I heard his wife died in a crash...that one?"

He nodded. "Quinn was in the car. She was three."

"Oh, poor sweet baby. Was she badly hurt?"

"Couple bruises and a concussion. I guess her guardian angels were working overtime. If you look at pictures of the car, it's a miracle she survived."

"She's so precious. I'm sorry she had to go through that."

He nodded. "Ben's taken her to see all kinds of doctors and they can't find any physical reason for her lack of speech. So, he's hired a nanny who has a background in working with special needs kids."

"He's a good dad."

"A great dad, but don't tell Ben I said so." He raised his voice as they came up to the gangplank, because he knew Ben would hear.

"Don't tell Ben what?" Ben asked, but they both just tried to look innocent and didn't answer.

"Morning!" Danny boomed from top deck with a wide wave to the kids. Danny Proudbear was a tribe member and an old family friend who was about ten years older than Jax. He made a living chartering day-fishing trips—mostly for visitors to the Sherrod. His boat, the Jenny, named after a boat in his favorite movie, was the perfect size for day-fishing and longer trips. It had three levels, with a two-tier interior living space and nice wide decks for up to twelve fishermen. Jax lusted after it every time they went out.

"Permission to come aboard, sir?" Georgie called with a crooked salute.

"Permission granted," Danny bellowed back, as he made his down way the ladder to the main deck. He reached out a hand to each of the kids, then took their gear before welcoming the adults on board.

Jax noticed that even before everything was on board, Georgie had found the life jackets and was helping Quinn fit hers. Without being told. He clapped the boy on the shoulder. "Good man," he said.

Georgie flushed with pride and grumbled something Jax couldn't make out.

"I want one," Nat said, riffling through the pile for one her size. She found it, pulled it on and grinned at him. His heart skipped a beat because she was so damn cute. Her cheeks were pink, and the breeze teased the tendrils of her beautiful reddish hair around her face. And her lips, they were—

"Move, doofus," Ben said. And he did, because he realized he was blocking the way. But he didn't take her eyes from her. And she didn't take hers from him. Ben grunted and then muttered, sotto voce, "Get a room."

"Mmm-hmm," Jax muttered back. "Hey, isn't there a room below deck?" He was joking. Of course, he was.

But it was fun to see Ben get all huffy. "You're not leaving me alone with three kids, buddy. Don't even think about it."

Oh, he'd think about it, but Ben was right. As much as he would enjoy some alone time with Natalie in a private cabin belowdecks, this trip was really for the kids.

As Danny finished the last-minute prep, they all found seats on the bow to enjoy the feel of the sea breeze as they chugged out of the marina. Once they passed the sand bar—which could be tricky at low tide—he opened up the engine and let 'er roar.

Jax tipped his face to the wind, to the taste of salt on his lips. God, he loved this. This was heaven. He glanced at Nat and his heart warmed at her expression. Because he could tell she loved it, too. He wanted to take her hand, to touch her...but held back. Only because he didn't want the moment ruined if she yanked it back.

She probably wouldn't, but still, he resisted.

He was still kind of spinning at the realization that she's seen his work in Angel Goulden's window and loved it, without even knowing he was the artist. That she saw the value of his work in a way that had nothing to do with money. Most people, their first question was, "How much?" For Nat, it had been, "Where's the missing piece?" proving that she *got* it.

Most people didn't really understand his art. Not on a deeper level.

She did.

She was so special. It was hard for him to wrap his brain around his feelings for her, because they were all over the place, like a rubber ball—pinging from hard, hot lust to deep appreciation to irritation that she'd be leaving soon.

He decided to focus on something else entirely—just enjoying this day, this moment, with her.

It was a gorgeous day.

Nat threw back her head and just soaked it all in. By the time Danny found a good spot for fishing—based on decades of experience in these waters, and a little machine on the bridge that showed schools on radar—the sun had risen, painting the sky and the water with a wash of orange and rose.

Normally, those were two colors that didn't complement each other, but somehow, God made it work. She sighed and pulled her jacket closer, hugging herself as she braced against a swell. She loved the gentle sway of the boat, the call of the gulls as they recognized a potential meal, and the smell of the coffee Jax had brought her from the galley before joining the other men in setting up the lines.

The kids were adorable, standing in a row at the stern, in their orange life jackets waiting for a fish to bite. Nat pulled out her phone and took some pictures for Amy, and then wandered the deck, taking more shots here and there. Every shot was a keeper. It was like that on a day like today. Point and click.

She got some really good shots of John J reeling in his big catch—nearly six inches, and another of Georgie, focusing intently on baiting his hook, tongue out and all. And some of Jax, in action. Reeling in a big salmon—and then his dismay when it escaped. Then one of Ben bending down to explain something to Quinn, who stared at him with wide, adoring eyes. Another of Ben and Danny on the bridge deep in conversation.

After a while, she pulled out her book, sat in the sun on the bow and pretended to read. But really, she was just enjoying the day.

How had she forgotten how much she loved this?

"Having fun?"

She looked up as Jax plopped down beside her. It had started to warm up, so he'd stripped down to his T-shirt, revealing the forearms she'd been obsessed with as a girl. Muscled and tan and sprinkled with dark hairs. Gosh, she wanted to pet him.

Would it be rude to pet him? Probably.

"This is wonderful, Jax. I'm so glad I got invited."

He chuckled. "You can get invited any time you want to be invited."

There was something there, in his expression, that made her wonder if he wasn't just talking about fishing. But she couldn't ask, because how would she ask? What would she say?

"Hey, Nat?" The tenor of his voice shifted, just a little, and he looked around—to make sure they were alone? Her heart hitched.

She stuck her thumb in the book she wasn't reading to hold her place. "Yeah?"

"I, ah… Well, I'm not sure how to ask this…"

"Just ask." She leaned in to give him a nudge. The heat of his sun-warmed arm kissed hers. A part of her wanted to keep leaning.

"Hmm. Okay. Well, today, this morning, when I saw you at Amy's…"

"Yes?"

"Was I imagining it, or has something changed?"

"Changed?" She nearly burst out laughing. But she didn't.

"You…something about you seemed…different?"

"Ah." She glanced at him, and then away, because she couldn't seem to hold his gaze as she said her truth. "Well, this morning, I found out you're not dating Amy. Could that be it?"

He stared at her. "I… What? Why did you think I was dating Amy?"

She shrugged and said on a self-deprecating laugh,

"Because that morning you answered her door, first thing in the morning, half naked?"

"I wasn't half naked."

Uhh... "You kinda were. Any normal human woman would make the assumption that you'd slept over."

"I did sleep over."

She made a noise in the back of her throat. "Any normal human woman would make the assumption that you'd slept over...with her."

For some reason, he still looked a little stunned at her revelation. "I sleep in the guest room on the ground floor when I stay over."

"I did not know that."

"Well, why didn't you ask Amy about it, then?"

Because she hadn't wanted to hear the answer, maybe? "My family doesn't exactly excel in straight-forward communication, in case you haven't noticed."

He chuckled then, because the dysfunction in Tuttle communication was hard to miss. Then he leaned closer and sealed his arm against hers, and a shiver racked her. "Why didn't you ask *me*?" he asked in a soft voice.

She barked a laugh. "How stupid would that have looked? 'Scuse me. Are you dating this woman with whose waffle iron you are on a first-name basis?"

"That's hardly fair," he said. "That waffle iron forgets my name all the time."

She snorted a laugh, which made him laugh, too.

Then, when he sobered, he held her gaze and said, "Well, if you have anything you want to know about me, just ask." And he said it so sincerely, she had to believe he would honor that invitation.

And though the thought made her stomach churn, she sucked in a deep breath and did just that. She asked. "Would you have kissed me the other night in the studio if Ben hadn't burst in?"

He didn't answer. For a long while there was only the slap of the waves on the hull and the whip of the wind in her ear. So, she peeped at him.

His expression stole her breath. It was...*hungry*.

Without saying a thing, he cupped his hands on her cheeks and pulled her right into his face. And he kissed her. Hard.

It was a kiss that said, *You gotta ask?* But with a smile.

He pulled back to look at her, as though to assess the success of his communication. And then, he kissed her again. She loved that he moaned a little in the back of his throat as he took her mouth again. And again. As though he was starving for her. It sent a sizzle of heat up and down her spine. She couldn't help but respond and tangled her fingers in his hair to pull him closer as he deepened the kiss, only growling a little because his hair was too damn short to get a good grip.

"Hey, kids!" Ben bellowed in an overly jovial tone from just over there. "Is that a whale fluke?" And then, when the kids ran to the starboard, he clomped over in his ridiculous yellow boots and nudged Jax with a toe. "Hey," he hissed. "Kids on board." And then, to the kids, "What? Not a whale? Oh no. Maybe next time." Then he took Nat's hand and hauled her to her feet. "Come on, Nattynat. Little help with the M-O-N-S-T-E-R-S, please?"

"I can spell," Georgie warbled.

"I'll just bet you can," Ben said, rolling his eyes. Not at Georgie.

He rolled them at Jax. And Nat.

She hardly cared. Her soul was aloft, dancing with the gulls on the wind.

Because Jax had kissed her—really kissed her—leaving absolutely no doubt in her mind that as much as she ached to explore this delicious tension with him, he wanted it, too.

Chapter Eight

Even though Ben had interrupted a kiss with Natalie—again—Jax was in a great mood as the afternoon marched on. All he had to do was look at her, and he would smile. She didn't even need to look back or catch his eye. Just watching her made his soul happy.

The way the sun caught her hair, when she threw back her head and laughed with abandon at something Georgie said, the floppy hat she put on when the sun got too bright for her fair complexion—everything about her spoke to him.

He had a difficult moment after a jovial lunch of PB and Js and potato chips, when Quinn crawled up into her lap, just to be held, and Nat held her. It was a beautiful sight, the two of them, there on the bow, heads turned to the horizon, just taking in the glory of the day.

But it was difficult too, for two reasons. First of all, as an artist, he itched to sculpt this vision. And secondly, it hit him, a desire he'd never had before. A desire he'd never acknowledged or even understood. Even when he'd stepped in to provide a father figure for Georgie and John J.

Suddenly, he wanted more. He wanted a family. To be a father. And he wanted it with Natalie. This vision, of her cradling Quinn, inspired a dream in his heart that one day, she'd be cradling *his* daughter. Or his son. Or both. He didn't care. He just knew he wanted…wanted more than he'd allowed himself to want ever before.

It was a tantalizing hunger. So close, there on the bow of the boat, and, at the same time, so far away. So far away it could be a fantasy.

But it haunted him.

After lunch, Nat and the kids went below deck to rest and escape from the wind, while Jax and Ben stayed on the deck to try to catch something. So far, John J's tiny fish was their sole claim to manhood.

It didn't take long for Ben to sidle up to Jax as he stood at the stern attempting to convince a salmon to bite, and say, "Well, it looks like you and Natalie had that conversation."

Jax shot him glance. "And thanks for interrupting it." *Again.* It bore mentioning. It was, frankly, becoming a trend.

Ben slapped his palm to his chest melodramatically. "I did it for the kids."

Really? "It was just a kiss. I'm sure they've seen people kiss before—"

He grinned. It was an evil grin. "All right, I did it for fun."

Jax sighed. He'd suspected as much and while he wasn't averse to a little practical joking himself, in this instance, it had been really frustrating. All he'd wanted to do in that moment was spend more time with Natalie, exploring this...whatever this was—and Ben had dragged her away.

"It's funny, though," Ben said, leaning a hip on the transom. He didn't finish the thought. He often didn't.

Jax had to say, "What?" in a snippy tone in order to get him to continue.

"Oh, how right the two of you seem together."

"Hmm." Yeah. Jax felt that way, too. Like they fit, snapped together like magnetic pieces in a cosmic puzzle.

"I mean, get either one of you talking about art—"

Jax frowned at him. "What do you mean?" Other than *his* art, he and Nat hadn't talked art. He hadn't realized she liked talking about art—other than his art, of course.

In retrospect, he might have been a little self-absorbed in his prior conversations with her. Due to his insecurities, no doubt. He knew he'd broken a barrier, bringing her to his studio—it had been a huge step for him to share his space with someone other than Ben—but she probably didn't have a clue that no one else had ever been there. He suddenly realized that most of their chats up until now had been guided by his insecurities and protective instincts. He'd been too busy trying to assess her attraction to him than to actually explore her. Or explore *them*.

It was an important epiphany, one he tucked away for later review.

Because Ben was talking again. He did that.

"Yeah," he said, unwrapping a stick of gum and popping it into his mouth. "You're both artists and—"

Wait. *What?* "I thought she worked on a TV show."

"Duh." Ben made a wide-eyed face that was, frankly, annoying. "She's the art director for the show. She designs and builds the sets, and picks the color palettes and the furniture and the visuals. You know. All the things you *see* on a TV show."

"Okay." Okay. Yeah. He didn't know because he hadn't asked. But now that he realized, he'd rectify the issue as soon as he could.

"Anyway, I think you're a good match."

Jax huffed a laugh. "Well, thank God we have your approval."

"It's pretty clear. She likes you, dude. She likes you a lot." He turned away so Ben wouldn't notice the heat rising on his face. But the move itself gave him away. "And you like her. A lot."

"I always have liked her." What a lame word. It hardly described his *feelings*.

"Yeah, but this is different. I can tell." He smacked Jax on the back. "Don't fight it, man."

"I'm not fighting it!" He didn't intend to snap, but Ben didn't understand how far he'd moved toward Natalie, how many blockages he'd ignored or pushed out of the way—blockages that would have paralyzed him a year ago—all to get a little bit closer to her.

And Ben was his closest friend. He knew all about

the PTSD and the night terrors. If Ben wasn't aware of these monumental shifts, it stood to reason that Natalie wasn't aware, either. Which only reinforced the need to tell her. And soon. Because he had no idea how long she'd be here.

Heat walked through him as this thought trickled through his consciousness. A little horror at the real-ization that they were on the precipice of a new phase in their relationship—especially if he took her home tonight, as he fully intended to do.

And, if they did step into something inherently more intimate than sharing a kiss on a boat in front of an avid audience, she would still, at some point, leave. She'd never said otherwise. If he took this step, he took it with the understanding that this would probably be a short-lived affair—unless he moved to Los Angeles, which, given his disinclination for crowds, would be a nonstarter.

Even as his soul wailed in denial to the thought of a mere fling with Natalie Tuttle, she stepped out of the galley and into the sunshine, which caught at the gold flecks in her red hair. The vision of her in that moment etched itself on his creative mind and he knew he would be sculpting her, like this, in this moment. The rest of his mind wanted to grab hold of her and hang on.

"Hey, you," Ben called against a kick in the breeze. "Are the kids asleep?"

She wrinkled her perky nose. "Quinn threw up. She and John J are coloring now, and Georgie is napping. What are you two up to?"

Ben shrugged as nonchalantly as he could, but Jax

just came out with it. "We were talking about you," he said with a grin.

She responded with a grin that made his belly stir. "Me?"

"Yeah, Jax didn't know you were an artist."

"I did too." She'd been artsy her whole life; it wasn't like he hadn't noticed that. "Ben's just explaining what you do for work. I guess I didn't understand."

His line tugged. He ignored it. Because Natalie sauntered over and leaned against the fiberglass wall and snorted.

"Oh, it's fascinating," she said with dripping sarcasm.

"We haven't really talked about it," he reminded her, just so she would know he had realized their conversations had been a little one-sided.

"We haven't really talked about a lot of things." This, she said to him and him alone.

"Well, we should," he said, again, ignoring the tug on his line, because the gaze they were sharing was far too intriguing.

"I think you have a bite," Ben said. "Jax? Jax?"

"Absolutely, we should," she said in a playful tone. The look in her eye sent a slither of excitement through him because it made him suspect she wasn't just talking about words.

"Jax! Oh, for pity's sake." Ben took the rod from Jax and started reeling something in, but Jax wasn't, at the moment, in the least interested in a fish.

He stepped closer to Natalie, just to be closer. Just to catch a whiff of her scent, or bask in her warmth, or, maybe, to touch her. "Do you want to have dinner with me tonight?" he asked. The words barely trembled at all.

"Spend the *whole day* with you?" A light in her eyes danced. He swallowed hard at the implication that there might even be more than that.

"Mmm-hmm."

"Hey. Can someone get the net?" Ben called from the starboard, where the fish had walked him. His muscles bunched as he reeled madly.

"I suppose I could do that." God, she was adorable. Just looking at the perfect symmetry of her face—and that one little crooked tooth—made his soul happy. But it was more than her face or her body. More than her ease with verbal ping-pong or the way she made him laugh. It was something deeper and far more precious. "Where do you want to go for dinner?" she asked.

There was only one thought in his mind. "My place." Only one place that would do. It couldn't be hers, not what for what he had in mind and— And then it hit him. *Crap.* His place was a glorified man cave and she was probably thinking of something romantic with wine and flowers and metal silverware and actual napkins. "Or—"

She stopped him with a smile. "Your place sounds great. We can get takeout. I didn't notice you had much of a kitchen."

"I have a toaster oven," he muttered. "And a hot plate."

She nodded. Her grin was snarky. "So, takeout, then."

"Yeah. Takeout." Damn, but all of a sudden he wished

he'd listened to Sheida and gotten a proper house. If a man wanted to get to know a woman better—the way he wanted to get to know Nat better—the smell of wood chips motor oil might be counterproductive. And women liked nice things. Like furniture. And closets.

His refuge had been like a womb to him, a place of restoration and creative freedom, but now, all of a sudden, it was starting to feel too small, restrictive. Less a safe place and more a prison. Certainly not large enough for the life he was starting to imagine.

Abruptly, like a punch to the gut, he remembered— that wasn't what this was. That wasn't what this could become. They weren't going to set up house in his studio or anywhere. She wasn't staying.

The thought deflated him like a balloon.

Ben pouted the rest of the afternoon, because he'd lost the fish. No doubt he felt that if only Jax had brought the net, he would at least have landed something. He kept it from the kids, and Jax, but Nat could tell.

As the boat chugged back to the marina—coffers filled with John J's baby fish—Nat sat next to Ben and patted his hand. "You'll get 'em next time," she said.

He pouted a little more and then scrubbed his face with his palm. "Yeah. I know. But I was so close…"

"I know." She turned her attention to the kids, who were helping Jax gather all the equipment as Ben sulked. "This has been a wonderful day, Ben. Thanks for inviting me."

He shrugged. "I'm glad you and Jax had a chance to— Well, you know."

"Me, too."

"He's a good guy, Nat."

"He is."

Ben turned and pinned her with a steady gaze. "Don't break his heart, okay?"

She gaped at him. The blood rushed from her face. Something in her chest constricted. "I— Of course not."

"He knows you're not staying."

Again, she was gobsmacked by his comment. Had they *talked* about that? Also, in her excitement at the thought of exploring something deeper with Jax, the thought of leaving had not crossed her tiny mind. "Right."

"But he really likes you. You bring out the real Jax."

She shook her head. "I don't understand, Ben. He's always been the real Jax to me."

He huffed a laugh. "Yeah. That's the point, I think."

Even though she wasn't quite sure what he meant, she nodded. Mostly to encourage him because he seemed to want to say more. And, being Ben, he did.

"After, well everything, after he came back, Nat, he was different. Like there was a hard crust on him. He didn't laugh much, didn't interact with anyone—not even Sheida—for a long time. It's taken years for him to be like this again—"

"Like this?"

"Well, he's out in the world again. With people. Since you came back really. He went to Lizzie's party—to see you. He's talking about going to the reunion—because of you. Heck, he even took you to his studio. No one gets into his studio."

"You were there." He'd walked right in. Interrupted what might have been a fabulous kiss.

He shook his head and sighed. "Nat. It took three years to get an invitation, and even then, it was because I was bringing him some rare woods he wanted to work with. I was stunned to see you there, even though I knew that he was—" He cut off abruptly and flushed beneath his already sunburned face.

"He was what?"

Now his ears went pink. "I shouldn't say."

She gored him with a gimlet gaze. "But you will." Not a request.

"He told me he was interested in you." This he said, head down, staring at his toes like a child during a confession.

Nat's heart flipped. She caught her breath. It was confirmation beyond the hunger in that kiss, and it thrilled her. She couldn't hold back her grin. "Did he?"

"Oh, please. What man wouldn't be?"

She snorted a laugh. "You, for one."

His eyes went wide. "That's only because I'm—" He broke off again. It was getting irritating. When she glared at him, he blew out a breath and said, "I'm interested in someone else."

"Ooooh," she sang, and she nudged him with an elbow. "Does Ben have a crush on someone?" What a pity she said it out loud without checking her surroundings, because the boys heard and took up the song. Something along the lines of "Ben has a girlfriend," and "Didja kiss her yet?" Even Quinn joined into the fray, dancing and clapping in time to their chants.

Ben glared at her and then glared at Jax, who was heading their way with a glare of his own. "What are you guys talking about?" he asked brusquely.

"Nothing," Ben muttered.

"Ben has a girlfriend," Georgie announced.

Jax's eyes widened. "Who?"

"I do not have a girlfriend!" He glared at Natalie—and not in jest, she noted with surprise. "Thanks a lot."

By the time the boat docked and they had loaded all their gear into Ben's car, the sun was on its way down. It cast a soothing shadow on the marina and called in a cooling breeze. Though Jax was anxious to get Natalie alone, he took a little extra time with the boys and Quinn as they settled in the car, to get their impressions of the day.

John J was the hero, of course. Having caught the only fish.

Georgie was happy to get shotgun—as Natalie and Jax planned to walk the mile or so to his studio.

And Quinn...well, Ben's daughter was quiet, sweet and affectionate. It warmed his heart that she made it a point to hug Natalie—cling, really—before she climbed up into her car seat.

"You sure you don't want a ride?" Ben asked, but Jax could tell from his lurid expression that he knew damn well Jax wanted time alone with Natalie. And a walk would give him more time to assess her inclination to move forward.

Not that he was nervous about it. He wasn't. Not hardly at all.

"I'd prefer to walk," she said with a smile. And then, to the kids, "I need to get my land legs. I feel like I'm still moving." She wobbled side to side, and they all laughed, because they were feeling it, too; a day on the water did that to a person's equilibrium.

But this particular day had affected Jax's equilibrium in other ways, too.

They waved at Ben's truck as he pulled out of the lot and then turned to each other and locked gazes. There was a moment of awkwardness, because they both realized that they were, suddenly, finally, all alone. But she broke it with a chuckle. "Shall we?" she asked in a teasing tone.

He nodded, because words were hard to come by, and together, they turned along the sidewalk that followed the shoreline. But before he could get going, she reached down and took his hand. He stilled. Glanced at her. His heart thudded.

Her expression faltered. Her fingers loosened. "I... Ah... Do you mind?"

Did he mind? He grinned and tightened his hold, reassured and moved by the relief, the newfound playfulness that flickered over her expression. "Let's go."

So, they walked, holding hands, up Shore Drive under the leafy canopy of the maple trees marching alongside. The occasional car whizzed by, heading toward the marina, but other than that, and the call of the gulls, they were alone.

She was quiet for a time. They both were, just soaking in the day. Then she said, in an attempt at conversation that was wholly unnecessary, "This is nice."

He nodded. He'd made this hike more times than he could remember—it was a favorite path for his early morning runs. It was always nice. It was nicer with her. The warmth of her hand in his elevated everything. He instinctively stroked her with his thumb.

To his consternation, she stopped short and stared at him. She didn't say anything—while his heart pounded and he cursed himself for moving too quickly, which was ridiculous because it was only a simple touch, but he should have—

And then she smiled at him. That smile eradicated all his doubts. It was engaging and encouraging and, best of all, she then reciprocated with a slow, soft caress. Just her thumb on his hand. A simple stroke.

But there was nothing simple about it at all.

It was not a seductive caress, not in the least. But it certainly did the job, sending his blood surging in a way that made walking somewhat, ahem, uncomfortable.

"Jax," she said.

"Nat." What else was there to say? His brain was utterly empty.

Well, not empty. There were thoughts and urges and desires. Just not words.

For one thing, he wanted to pull her into his arms, here in this slice of heaven and kiss her. Kiss her again, and this time, damn it, with no damn interruptions.

She eased closer, as though she was having similar thoughts and—as simply as that—she was in his arms, her mouth on his, her body close and warm and soft. He had no idea who had kissed whom and, frankly, didn't care.

It was an easy exchange. Exploratory. Sweet. She tasted—well, she tasted of paradise. He eased back, to change his angle, to deepen the kiss, to take in her softened expression, her slightly dewy eyes. God, she was beautiful like this. Perfect like this. But before he could kiss her again, a passing car honked and the occupants whooped and bellowed at them.

And they both laughed.

It was another slightly irritating interruption in Jax's point of view, but at the same time, it reminded him of where he was and where they were going, and it reaffirmed the importance of getting her alone before even considering kissing her again.

She swept him away too easily. She made him forget so many things when he held her in his arms. Like the fact that they were smooching in a public place. He took her hand again and continued their walk with a more determined step.

It seemed she'd had a similar revelation, because she launched into a cheery monologue about how lovely this path was and her favorite beachside trails in Ventura and Santa Monica, oh, and a great place in Santa Barbara where they had an art fair along the seaward path on Sundays... And on and on.

And Jax held her hand and listened and smiled a goofy smile. Just because he couldn't stop.

Had he ever been happy like this before? Just being with someone? With Melissa, everything had been performance-based, maybe even a little transactional. What could she do for him compared with what he could do for her. They'd never just enjoyed each other for who they were. Granted, that union had been short-lived. But while their split had been mutual, he'd left feeling as though he'd failed. As though he hadn't been enough for her.

Now, years later, he realized the truth. He *hadn't* been enough for her. But that hadn't been his failing. It had been hers.

But then it was silly comparing Natalie and Melissa. Their personalities were chalk and cheese, their approaches to life so different, and their energies were vastly different, worlds apart.

"What?"

He reeled in his thoughts and focused on Nat, who was smiling at him. "Hmm?"

"You made a noise."

"A noise?"

Her grin blossomed. "A snort noise, kind of."

"Did I?"

"What were you thinking?"

He was not going to bring up his ex. Not now. So, he shrugged. "I was just thinking how much I enjoy spending time with you, Natalie."

For some reason she blinked. "Why?"

Why? Did there need to be an excuse? But if she wanted why, he'd give it to her. "Well, you're smart and funny and a great conversationalist. Not to mention, you have excellent taste in art." He waggled his eyebrows, so she knew he was referring to *his* art. "Did you enjoy fishing?"

She chuckled. "I hate fishing, but I liked being on the boat. I always like being on boats." She paused for a moment, then shot him a glance. "I enjoyed watching you with the boys very much."

He hoped she didn't catch the pinkening of his cheeks in the light of the looming sunset. "I enjoy those munchkins."

"I can tell. You're much more patient than I am." Then, "Do you think you'll ever have kids, Jax?"

His head came up so hard, he bit his tongue. He hadn't expected that veer in the conversation, so he wasn't prepared to respond, even though, earlier in the day, he'd been thinking about it. It took a minute for him to gather his words. "I... I would like to have children," he finally said. "But I don't want to be a single parent. Remember, I'm helping Amy out with the boys, but I'm not ultimately responsible for them. It's easier to be patient when you can walk away when you need to."

"Hmm." Her response was unsatisfactory. He wanted more.

"How about you?"

She threw back her head and laughed. "Oh, I'm a career gal. I always have been." And, when he glanced at her, she added, "In my line of work, you can't have responsibilities like kids. It's even difficult with Pepe. When I take a job, I know I'm all in for the duration. And it could be anywhere in the world." She shrugged, "Depending on the shoot locations. I can't even imagine having kids and doing my job."

"So, no one in your line of work has kids?"

She stopped and thought about it. The lines on her forehead wrinkled. "No. No. I suppose they do... I just don't know how they manage it, is all." She tipped up her nose then and sniffed. "What do I smell?"

He chuckled. "That's the Salmon Shack." He waved toward a bend in the road. "Around the corner."

"Oh, my goodness. I'm suddenly starving."

"We can eat there. Or get it to-go." He tried not to let his disappointment show. He was anxious to get her home, but he had to admit, he was hungry as well.

They ended up getting a table on the deck of the small restaurant with a view of the setting sun over the Pacific, and had a lovely, lingering meal of baked salmon and scallops. She had a glass of wine, and he had a beer and they talked about everything and nothing. She shared some stories about her life on a television set and he gave her an edited version of his marriage to Melissa and his time overseas. And then, because she encouraged it, he shared a bit of his journey to deal with the weight he'd brought back.

Her reaction was soothing. Understanding and sympathy and support. Nothing about how he could have been better or should have been stronger. No *why can't you just shake it off* as he'd heard so many times from so many people—including Melissa.

So, while the delay in getting her to his place was frustrating, this—were they calling it a date?—gave them both a deeper understanding of each other.

"Oh," Nat said, crumpling up her napkin and tossing it onto her plate as she finished her meal. "That was delicious."

"A good day," he responded, with a smile. Because it had been.

"Yes," she said. "A very good day."

And her smile made it clear, it wasn't over yet. Not by a long shot.

Nat's heart pattered with excitement as they came around a bend in the path and she caught sight of Jax's studio. The first time she'd been here, she'd noticed the garden of art out front, but it hadn't made much of an impression. Now she could see that there was an order to it. There were carved woodland creatures frolicking around strategically placed bushes, hand worked benches here and there, and the occasional wood sprite. And while she wanted to explore it more carefully, something else nudged at her attention. Something warm and swirling low in her gut. Heat and hunger.

And with each step closer to the door, it grew.

The day had been beautiful, dinner had been unintentionally romantic and now it was time for them to explore...this.

Oh heavens. Heat rose on her cheeks at the thought.

He paused in the act of fishing the keys from his pocket. "Are you all right?" he asked, his handsome face scored in concern.

She forced a laugh. "I'm just a little nervous."

"Ah." He jingled the keys for a minute then put them back in his pocket. "Look, we don't have to—"

"Stop right there." She firmed her resolve, and her expression. "I want this, Jax. I've wanted this for a long time. I'm just a little nervous."

He frowned. "I'm nervous, too."

For a moment, she feared he would ask her to leave,

but he didn't, so she made a little joke. "I promise to be gentle."

He didn't take it as a joke. His expression became solemn, and he looked her in the eyes and said, "I promise to be gentle, too." And then he took her hand, did that little sweep with his thumb—which she loved—and then opened the door.

"Well, all right, then," she said, putting on a brave face and marching inside.

The scent of wood and varnish greeted her, along with the dryads she'd noticed last time, although they all stood—together—by the door. "You finished!" she said. She hadn't meant to start talking about his work— she'd meant to get him on the couch over there and start the yummy kissing again—but her delight in seeing the set as a whole overcame her.

He tossed his keys in a bowl by the door and grinned. "Do you like them?"

"I love them." She drew her hand down the Summer statue in sheer appreciation of the way a man could recreate such a perfect human form. His skill was astounding. She glanced up at the dryad's face and her heart stalled.

It was like looking in a mirror. Down to the dimples on her cheeks as she smiled.

She glanced at him. "She looks like me."

He was quiet for a second then said, in a deep voice, "Everything looks like you to me now."

And, oh. His words, his expression, everything about him made her want to be close. Closer.

She was in his arms before she even realized she'd moved.

The kiss was hard and whole, each of them giving, yet taking with a ravenous hunger. It made her mind spin, made her heart thud, made her body melt. His hands roved—tentatively at first as he explored her curves— and then, more deliberately. Consumed with emotion, she explored him as well. His hard, well-formed pecs, his firm chest, his nape—incongruously soft, like velvet. She shifted her position so she could break the kiss and taste him there, on his neck, where he smelled like earth and musk.

He groaned and pulled her back, closer, against him. He was hard. Hard all over, but in one place in particular. And her body reacted with a gush of pleasure. His mouth found and settled on that little spot beneath her ear, the one that made her head spin, and he suckled her gently. Her knees locked.

She tried to lead him then, to the sofa over there, because standing was annoying, but he countered with pressure in another direction as they feasted on each other. It took her a moment to realize he was leading her to a door she'd not noticed before. "What?" she snapped. She didn't mean to snap, but he understood.

"Bedroom." A growl, guttural and commanding.

But she required no commands. Once she understood his direction, she was all in.

He opened the door with force; it bounced back against the wall, but they both ignored it. She had only a second to take in his most private of havens before he lifted her bodily and carried her to the bed.

It was a shadowed bower, dominated by a large bed with a chunky headboard and matching footboard carved from natural wood. The floor was wood as well, ancient planks that had been expertly refinished. The walls were a dark sage. She recognized, in that flash of a second, the desire to recreate the feel of nature in his retreat.

Gently, he laid her on the bed, and she took a moment to appreciate the soft, fuzzy and welcoming bedspread—it might have been fleece, hard to tell because seconds later he was there beside her and all other thoughts fled.

"Natalie," he said before she silenced him. Before she took him by the ears—because his hair was too damn short—and pulled him to her. After that he said very little, other than to moan or groan and mutter her name as she methodically removed his clothing and explored his body.

And what a body.

He'd been hot in high school, lanky and lean, but now he'd added layers of muscle that fascinated her. There, on his belly, she found some scars and she traced them gently. She didn't ask where he'd gotten them, because she knew. Somehow, she knew.

He'd spoken at dinner of a stint in the hospital after an explosion, and these scars were jagged and coarse. The violence in them was implicit and heartbreaking and, before she could stop herself, she kissed them.

He stilled. His breath stalled in his lungs, and she felt his intensity rise.

She glanced up at him, just to check in, and his expression burned her from the inside out.

"Natalie." His voice broke on her name.

She returned her attention to the scars and stroked them, as though she could make them disappear—and it was at that moment that she realized, well, just how close her mouth was to another part of him. With a spurt of humor, she realized his reaction had nothing to do with her discovering his wounds at all. Her concern morphed into playful glee, and she shifted downward, settling her fingers on the snaps of his jeans. But she paused, and flicked a look at him.

"May I?" she asked in a prim voice.

He stared at her, veins bulging, eyes wide, and croaked, "What?"

"May I?" she repeated. Then she batted her lashes at him. "I mean, I wouldn't want to take advantage of you, and I did promise to be gentle—" She allowed her fingers to drift, ever so gently over the bulge before her. Just that simple touch, through denim, even, made her blood simmer. She wanted, more than anything in this moment, to *taste* him.

He shuddered, which she took as assent, and she went to work releasing his thickness from its prison and—

She caught her breath as he was revealed to her in all his perfection. Heavy and hard and ready. When she wrapped her hand around him and tested his weight, his resolve, he groaned. "Nat—" A warning, perhaps? Or a plea?

She didn't wait to find out. She took him into her mouth and tasted him.

She did so gently, but he sucked in a breath and fisted his fingers in the covers and arched into her. "Ah."

Oh, yes.

She loved this. She loved the way he tasted, the way he smelled and the way he felt in her mouth. The way he begged.

She was not ready to release him when he pulled away. So, she frowned at him.

"Too soon," was all he grumbled as he rolled her over onto her back. She allowed it, because he insisted and, after all, she wanted what he had to give as well.

Still, it took an effort to lie still as he undressed her, explored her, inch by inch with his lips and his fingers and his tongue. By the time he got her bra off, her nipples were hard and tender. He encased one in his hot mouth and gave it a suckle and she nearly came out of her skin.

There was no more lying still after that. She came at him like a wild creature, and he responded in kind. After that, nothing was particularly gentle—and neither cared.

It was a hard, hot joining that left them both breathless and sheened with sweat.

And he was fabulous. As though he read her, knew her. His thrusts seemed to hit home with delicious precision as he moved over her and in her, staring down at her with an expression she could not decipher, though she did not need to try. His body spoke for him.

As hers spoke to him. Urging him on, to move faster and harder. To bring her to heaven with him.

And there, in that moment, when she spiraled into bliss, and he released everything to her, their gazes locked. Held. In that moment she saw it, she caught a glimpse of all of him in a way she had never imagined.

In that moment, they were one.

In glory, in delirium, in total unreserved acceptance.

And it was like nothing she'd ever known before.

In fact, it was beyond anything she'd ever imagined could be hers.

Chapter Nine

It took a while for Jax to recover from the bliss. His body, of course—his thumping pulse, his breathless-ness, that welling joy—but it took a bit for his mind to return as well. And when it did, he cuddled closer to Natalie, limp and lambent beside him. He stroked her shoulder, her hip. Reveled in her warmth.

"Mmm." Her response was nearly a groan. Hard to hear, because she'd turned her head away. Something in him needed to see her, so he eased her hair from her face and curled it around her ear. His heart clenched when he spotted tears on her cheeks.

Tears.

Something cold clutched at his chest. God. Had he hurt her? "Are…you okay?" he asked. He had to, though he dreaded the answer. He'd kept himself on leash so long, he'd hate it if, the first time he'd released complete control with her, he'd ruined everything.

She huffed a breath and murmured, "Am I okay?"

With a gentle thumb, he swiped at the moisture. "Are you crying?"

She rolled over to face him, to draw her finger down his face as well, to caress him with what felt like reverence. "Are you?"

He frowned. "I don't cry."

"Then you're leaking." Her smile was playful, and her mood was light and the knot in his stomach melted away.

"You're leaking more," he said. And then, because it needed to be asked, "I wasn't too rough?"

Her response was a laugh. He took that as a no and relaxed a little more. Thank God. Because, and he burned to say it, "That was amazing."

"So amazing." She cupped his cheek in her palm and then drew him closer. Kissed him. It was a long, lingering kiss, one of reflection and tender exploration. He wanted it to go on forever.

Sadly, nothing lasts forever, so when she drew back, he allowed it. But he didn't want to.

Did she know? Did she really understand what this had meant to him? Probably not. He hadn't told her that he hadn't been with a woman, like this, for years. He hadn't been able to open his heart, or he hadn't had the inclination. Or the courage.

And now that he had, there was no going back.

She'd opened a need in him.

Filled a hole—one he hadn't really understood until now.

She stretched and struck a pose; her skin was an alabaster counterpoint to his black sheets. His artist's eye took her in, memorized her. Studied each ripple in her areola, the lift of her breast, the dip from her ribs to her belly, the perfection of her hip, her leg, her perfect toes… He would sculpt her, just like this…

Color filled her cheeks beneath his scrutiny. "Why are you looking at me like that?"

He forced a laugh. To lighten the mood. To distract himself from ruining this by being needy. Even though he felt needy. "Like what?"

She shrugged. "Intently?"

How did he answer that? With a responding shrug apparently. "Don't all men stare at you intently after making love?"

Her laugh was a surprise. "Most men fall asleep."

"I'm not tired." He wasn't. And even if he was tired, he couldn't fall to sleep with her here. Couldn't expose her to the violence of his dreams. Besides, he was awake. Wide-awake.

In fact… He glanced pointedly at his, well, rising interest.

Her eyes widened. She chuckled. "Oh my. You are wide-awake, aren't you?"

He hadn't intended to push for another go. She probably hadn't intended it, either, but they came together in concert for a kiss, one tangled in a laugh, but it grew into something more.

And as much as he had loved the wild ride the first

time, this, the slower exploration, gentle teasing and rise to passion… This, the taking time with her and she with him, filled his soul in a way he had never expected, sated him in a way he had never been sated.

This time, afterward, she did fall asleep.

And he held her. And reveled in the fact he no longer felt so alone, simply because she was here.

When Natalie woke up, it took a minute to realize where she was and what had happened and…that Jax was gone.

His enormous bed with the fuzzy bedcover was empty.

She found her clothes strewn here and there, and dressed. When she came out into the studio, she didn't see him immediately. And then she located him in the corner of the room, hunched over a worktable and utterly absorbed in a task.

"Hey," she said, and even though she said it softly, he jumped. Whirled around.

"Hey. You're awake." And then, "You're dressed." There might have been regret in his tone. He rearranged the papers he'd been working on and slipped them into a folder, then came to her and wrapped his arms around her. She cuddled in, reveling in his scent, his warmth.

After a while, she sighed. "I should go," she said.

Oh, there was definitely regret in his expression. "So soon? Can't you stay a while longer?"

"It's late. Celeste will be wondering where I am." She fished around for her phone and then groaned. Indeed, there were a number of missed calls and texts. Most from Celeste, but a couple from Amy as well.

He sighed. "I'm sorry. I should have woken you. I... ah...was hoping we could have a talk before you left."

"A talk?" Her heart thudded. His expression was harsh. Had he decided he'd had enough of her? Had he not loved every second of their tryst? Trysts?

He pulled her closer and kissed her in a way that washed all those doubts away. "About this. About us."

Her heart warmed. "There's a lot to talk about." She loved that his eyes shone at her little joke. But it wasn't a joke, really. Was it?

He scrubbed his face with his palm. "Aw, crap. I'm not good at this, Nat. I just want to say, well, how much I enjoyed today. Everything."

"I enjoyed it, too." She had. Tremendously.

"And I know you're only here for a while..." Well, why did he have to go and bring that up? And why did the reminder irritate her? "But, well, I'd really like to..."

She squeezed his hand when he trailed off. "Explore this?"

"Yes." Relief washed his face. "Could we?"

"Yes, Jax," she said. "I'd really like that, too."

"Good." He kissed her gently.

"But..." she had to ask. "What do you think about, well, keeping it to ourselves?" Was that selfish? Maybe it was. She glanced at him and winced at the flash of pain in his expression. "Is that okay? I mean, your sister, my sisters... I don't want to get their hopes up." The prospect of talking about all this to them, just to turn around in a week or two and explain why she was leaving, was exhausting to think about.

"They have hopes? About us?" His smile was a wraith on his face.

She huffed a breath. "They would. If they knew. Your sister, especially. I mean, she was pretty clear about it with all that matchmaking. I would hate for her to start thinking that I'm going to change my mind and stay."

He swallowed hard. Looked away. "No. Of course not. I understand."

"So, you don't mind? If we keep this to ourselves?"

It took him a minute to look at her, but his eyes were sincere. "I'm not going to lie, I'm not a fan of secrets."

"It's not a secret, it's...well..." She sighed. "They just make everything more complicated. And I want to enjoy myself while I'm here. Can we just avoid the drama and enjoy our time together?"

He nodded then, and she breathed a sigh of relief. Thank God he understood.

Keeping this between them would make everything so much easier in the end. Especially when she had to say goodbye.

The thought made her chest hurt, but she pushed the pain away.

Because this would be best in the long run.

For both of them.

He blew out a breath and retreated a little. His demeanor sobered. "So, if we are going to explore this. Well, there...are some things you should know about me."

She nodded. She was pretty sure she knew what was

on his mind, but wanted to give him the space to tell her in his own words, so she took his hand and led him to the sofa, and they sat side by side. She was prepared, ready, to hear whatever he had to say.

"I really enjoy spending time with you, Nat, but it may not be a good idea for you to sleep over."

Not what she expected. Her chest constricted. "Um, okay."

He winced. "That was too straightforward, wasn't it? It's not how I meant to say it."

"It's okay. Take your time."

He did. He stood and started to pace, like a cornered animal. She hated that he might feel that way—with her.

"Jax." She waited until he stopped. Until he met her eye. "You can say it. You can say anything. We can deal with it."

He blew out a breath. She hoped it was a relieved breath, but it didn't matter if it was or not, because this was his story. She was determined to hear him.

"Okay." He sat down again, but didn't touch her. Didn't look at her. He stared down at his hands, his tangled fingers. "First of all, let me clarify. I would love for you to sleep over. It's just not a good idea. I don't sleep well. And sometimes... Sometimes..."

She didn't respond—trying to give him space and all—but he glanced up at her as though he'd been expecting...something, so she said, "Go on. I'm listening." She'd never been a good listener, but she knew, if she valued him—and she did—she had to try to understand what he was going through. More than that, she wanted to. Needed to.

One of the hardest parts of listening was waiting, and Jax tested her here, as he searched for words. Finally, he blurted, "I have dreams." His expression darkened. "Bad dreams."

"I see." She knew she didn't, not really, but he seemed to relax a little with her acknowledgement.

"My therapist calls them night terrors. I'm in battle. Or hell. Or whatever—I'm under attack, backed into a corner, helpless…and when I wake up, well, sometimes it takes a while for me to realize it's not real. I… Sometimes… Well, I just don't want to hurt you."

She took his hand, because he was hurting himself, twisting his fingers into knots. It took him a moment to stop. "It's okay, I don't need to sleep over if it makes you uncomfortable."

He snorted a denial. "Oh, it's not that. I would love to fall asleep with you in my arms. And I would love to wake up with you there as well. But you need to know that something like that could happen. You need to be prepared. It's…not pleasant. I'm not myself."

"Does it happen often?"

His eyes were haunted. "Sometimes I don't even know something happened, until I wake up in the morning and something's broken… But as far as I can tell, it hasn't happened for some time. But that's not really the issue. I don't always know *why* it happens, what triggers it, so I don't feel…"

"Safe?"

"Yes." He stared at her, his eyes wide, sincere and impossibly beautiful. "I would never forgive myself if I hurt you. Could you… Are you…?" He gusted a sigh and wiped his face with his palm. "If this is too much for you, I understand. Really, I do—"

She had to shut him up, because his words were too painful. And the quickest way to do that was simply to kiss him, so she did. When he finally relaxed into it, when the thudding in his pulse had silenced, she whispered to him, "We can work through it, Jax."

"Can we?"

"Of course, we can. Together, we can. And Jax?"

"Hmm?"

"Thank you for telling me."

Jax stared at Natalie in awe. Her understanding, her support, her willingness to step up and face his challenges with him was more than he could ever have expected.

She'd taken his greatest fear—that she might reject him because of the trauma that still haunted him—and had turned it on its end. *Of course, we can. Together, we can.* The most beautiful words he'd ever heard.

While a part of him really didn't like the idea of keeping their relationship a secret, he knew it was probably a good idea. This was so new and raw for him—for both of them. They both needed time alone together without outside interference to figure out what this was and where it might lead. And as much as he loved his sister, and hers, if either of them had an inkling that some kind of romance was brewing between Jax and Natalie, there would be pressure. There would be expectations. So, yeah, she was right on that note.

Aside from that, as much as he didn't want to focus on Nat's impending departure while they were together...

she *was* going to leave. No secrets there. No pretending. When it was time for her to go back to California, she'd be gone.

She said she wanted to explore this attraction, but that was what people said when they weren't sure if this was something they wanted.

While he appreciated the knowledge and the understanding that this relationship probably wouldn't end in a happy ever after, it didn't keep him from wanting more. At the very least, being open to it if it did happen.

But if she decided she didn't want that, what could a guy do, but let her go? What could a guy do, but be who he was, and hope he could be enough?

Better to focus on the fact that she was interested in him and she *did* want to explore whatever this was. So he set his concerns aside and relaxed and smiled at her, and she smiled back. "Good talk," he said.

"Great talk." She slid into his arms, and he cradled her, held her. He would have continued doing so, had her phone not pinged just then. She pulled it out and made a face. "Celeste. Again. I should probably go."

Probably. Still, "I don't want you to."

She nibbled on his earlobe. "I don't want to go, but I'd better, before Celeste sends out a search party."

Yeah. She probably would. "Go ahead and text her you're on your way home while I get my shoes. I'll give you a ride."

"That would be nice." She tapped away as he found his slip-ons.

And then, once they were in his SUV, he said, "When can I see you again? How about tomorrow?"

She shook her head. "Celeste has to work, so I have Momma all day."

"Dinner, then?"

She made a face. "Your sister is taking me to dinner."

"Cancel it."

"I promised, Jax. I keep my promises."

"Okay." He had to respect that. But still, he muttered, "Sheida's a pain."

"She's such a nudge." They both laughed. "She's taking me back to Bootleggers. She's adamant. I told her it's a bar, not a restaurant, and she went into some paroxysm over baked Brie *en croute*."

He chuckled. "They do have great baked Brie."

"Well, she's adamant, and you know your sister when she gets that way."

He rolled his eyes and grinned at her. "Tell me again why we have families?"

It was silly for Natalie to be disappointed that Jax didn't walk her to the door and kiss her good-night, because this was what she'd asked for. If he'd walked her to the door and pulled her into his arms, someone might have seen, and that would have complicated everything.

And someone *would* have seen. Because when Natalie walked through the front door, Celeste was waiting in the foyer, arms akimbo. She'd probably been peeking through the curtains. "Where have you been?" she said in an unusually snippy tone. Celeste rarely snipped.

"I'm sorry, Celeste. I lost all track of time." Natalie brushed past her and into the living room, then stopped short. Because Amy was there as well, cross-legged in

Dad's easy chair, nursing a cup of tea. There was no sign of Momma, but it was kind of late. She was probably in bed.

"Look who finally decided to show up. Gosh," Amy gushed. "The boys got home from fishing hours ago."

"And where are the boys?" It was a lame attempt to divert attention, and Amy knew it. Her expression made that clear.

"They're sleeping over at Dylan's," she said, and then, without so much as a breath, she added, "How's Jax?"

Celeste frowned at her. Then frowned at Natalie. "Wait. You were with Jax all this time?" And then, "I called and called. Why didn't you answer?"

Natalie sighed. She could hardly say she'd fallen asleep in Jax's bed after a wild, amazing bout of sex, at least not without starting yet another conversation in which she didn't want to engage.

Amy answered for her. "I told you. She was with *Jax*." She said it as though it were an accusation.

Celeste's brow wrinkled. "You spent the whole day with Jax on the boat. Why didn't you come straight home?" Damn, she was like a mother hen.

"Can't you figure it out?" Amy muttered. "She was *with* Jax," she repeated. With precise enunciation.

Celeste frowned. "That doesn't explain why she missed my calls." And then, to Natalie, "Why do you have a phone when you don't check your messages?"

"I'm sorry. I didn't check my phone. We were... busy."

"Busy." Amy snorted. "Georgie said you were kissing on the boat."

It took everything in her not to groan. Of course, the boys had talked about that. They were boys. "It was nothing." A complete lie, but a necessary one.

Celeste stilled. She looked from Natalie to Amy and back again. "You kissed Jax?" A little more than just kissing, but her sisters had no need for details. "Why were you kissing Jax on the boat?"

"Oh, for pity's sake, Celeste." Amy blew out a breath. "Isn't it clear? Nat has the hots for Jax. And, I'm assuming, based on the reports from the boys, Jax feels the same."

"It was just a kiss." A desperate wail. Nat could feel control of the situation, and their secret, slipping away.

Celeste just gaped. "Jax?" she said on a breath. "And Nat? When did *this* happen?"

Amy snorted. Again. "Tonight, I think."

"We had dinner," Natalie repeated. "I lost track of time. I didn't check my phone. I'm sorry."

"Oh, don't worry about that. I'm glad that you and Jax are reconnecting." Celeste made no attempt to hide the delight in her eyes. "I know you had a crush on him in high school, but I didn't realize you were still interested in him. Why didn't you say something? I could have set you up together."

"Apparently," Amy said in a grandiose tone, "she doesn't need help with that."

Well, damn. "Look. We're friends. We had dinner…"

"I lost track of time," Amy finished for her. And then, for some reason Amy glared at her. It seemed as though she were...jealous. But this morning she'd been clear. More than clear, that she had no interest in Jax—

Honestly. Her family was impossible. This was exactly why she hadn't wanted to tell anyone. People had a tendency to make more of a simple thing than it was. Yes. She and Jax had had a wonderful evening and yes, she fully intended to do it again. But she didn't want to get anyone's hopes up and, judging from the expectation in Celeste's eyes, her hopes—for whatever—were way up.

"Look, we went to dinner at the Salmon Shack, then went back to his studio to talk—"

Another snort from Amy.

Nat frowned at her.

"He took you to his studio?" Celeste shook her head. "No one gets to see his studio."

Amy frowned. "Nat does."

Celeste's jaw dropped. She stared. "Oh my."

"It's no big thing. Really." She looked from one to the other. Neither seemed convinced. "We had dinner. We caught up." Good glory. "Can we talk about something else?"

Oh, please, A change of topic.

"Okay," Amy chirped. She turned to Celeste. "Did you know Nat thought Jax and I were dating?"

It took some effort, but Nat didn't groan.

"Really? You? And Jax?" Celeste gaped, and then snorted a laugh.

The tiny hairs on Nat's nape prickled. "Why are you laughing? I showed up at her house and he answered the door half naked." Toweling his hair. Looking yummy. Half. Naked.

"Okay." Celeste nodded solemnly, but Nat could tell she still wanted to laugh. "I can see how that could have been misleading."

"They finish each other's sentences, for pity's sake—"

For some reason, this seemed to irritate Amy. "Well, what would you know? You're never here." Nat reeled at the gut punch—even though it was true—but Amy didn't give her time to process. She just barreled on, as she did when she was really mad. "You can't just cut us out of your life and then get annoyed that you don't know what's happening in our—"

"I hardly cut you out—"

"Jax and I have developed a system that works—for all of us. He saved my sanity, and he's wonderful with the boys."

"The boys do love him," Celeste added.

"And he deserves better than to be your vacation *fling.*"

Ah. The source of her annoyance revealed. This was why she'd come over tonight and lain in wait.

"He's not my vacation fling—"

"Some kind of *boy toy* that you use and then toss to the side when you're done with him."

Oh, that hurt. That was not her intention. It was not. "Oh, for pity's sake—" Nat muttered. It was like this, an emotional tumult sometimes, with everyone coming at her from every which way. *This* was why she didn't want to share with them the intimate details of her relationship with Jax. Her family would never understand or approve. Even though Amy didn't want Jax—not like that, anyway—she acted as though he was hers.

"Or worse," Amy continued, with something akin to a sob. "Taking him with you when you leave! The boys would be devastated. He's the only father figure they have."

"Taking him with me? I never said I'm taking him with me!"

"Amy, Jax isn't leaving this town," Celeste said soothingly. "And it's not fair to put all that weight on *him*. If you want a father figure for the boys you should start dating again."

Amy made a face. "In this town? Hah. Who? Baxter Vance?"

"Luke Larsen is nice."

"Oh, please." Amy rolled her eyes. "You're just saying that because you want your best friend Lynne to be your sister-in-law. Why don't you push Luke at Natalie?"

"She picked Jax."

"I didn't *pick* him—" He wasn't an ice cream flavor.

But, as usual, Amy wasn't part of the conversation. She was directing it. "I'm fine without a man. We are fine." Meaning herself and the boys of course, not the family at large. "I'm happy, damn it." And this last bit, she snarled, which kind of undercut her point.

"I know you're fine. You're doing a great job, Amy-Mamie." Celeste was so good. So good at soothing ruffled feathers. Then again, she'd had a lot of practice. "I'd just like to see you, well, not so alone."

Amy straightened her spine and huffed a breath. "I'm perfectly fine. Why are you trying to fix me, Celeste?" She pointed at Nat. "*She's* the one who needs to get her life together."

"Me?" Nat gaped at her. "My life is just fine." It was. It was perfect. Wasn't it? She huffed a breath and turned to Celeste, determined to end this conversation here and now. "Do you still need me to take Momma in for her therapy tomorrow?"

"Yes, please." Celeste's calm smile was a balm. How was it that one sister was a soft breeze, and the other a tornado? And what did that make Nat? Stuck there in the middle?

"Great. Then I'm going to bed. Night, Amy," she said breezily as she headed for the stairs.

But once she got into bed, she didn't sleep. Altercations like that always got her riled up. That, and the milling thoughts in her head about her day with Jax—and the way it ended. Why did she feel guilty? Why did she wonder if it had been a mistake to ask him to keep their relationship—such as it was—on the down-low?

Why couldn't things just be easy?

And what a pity none of those questions had any answers.

Jax didn't sleep well at all that night. For one thing, Natalie's scent lingered on the sheets, which only reminded him of how amazing making love with her had been, how well they'd fit, how joining with her had solidified his nebulous feelings into something that went way beyond sexual attraction.

Being with her, like that, had shifted something in his soul.

He'd caught a glimpse of the kind of life he could have, if he allowed the changes they required. They were scary changes—stepping-blindly-out-of-the-nest kind of changes. Which was terrifying.

But birds would never learn to fly if they never stepped out of the nest.

For Jax, those changes, and the fears around them, had deep roots entangled in a heightened sense of self-preservation and the revelation of just how brutal and careless other people could be—some so, with great glee and intention. That realization had shattered his life-long belief that people were basically good. He'd come out of that nightmare raw, ragged and bereft of faith in humanity.

And, while change was hard, even destructive, when the roots ran deep, he could see how the work he'd done in the past several years—through talking therapy, art therapy, and reaching out to help the boys—had helped him get to this place. A place where he was able to consider possible changes. Where he was willing to make them.

So, finding Nat again, reconnecting, deepening their relationship, had been transformative. All of a sudden, he was thinking in a larger scope than his tiny—safe—studio. He was thinking picket fences. Wondering if Natalie liked dogs. Imagining what a life with her could be like…together.

A part of him, that fearful part, had trouble seeing how such a relationship could work, with her so attached to her work, and so resistant to moving to Coho Cove. Natalie was definitely drawn to him on a spiritual level, just as he was drawn to her. There was no doubt she was eager to explore this connection they shared. That, in itself, at least as far as he was concerned, made it worth taking the chance.

And as far as her desire to keep this fledgling fling to themselves, she was right on point. Both their families required expectation management. He understood that. He got that. He just wished there was another way to manage expectations.

So, yeah, he didn't sleep well, and he tossed and turned and ended up working on a project into the wee hours—which was a mistake because he wasn't in a good place for his muse to visit. In the end, he went outside, started a fire in his firepit and sat in meditation watching the flames and listening to the crash of waves on the beach until the sun arose.

It didn't solve any of his problems, but it brought him closer to peace in his contemplation of his feelings for Natalie, and her desire to remain emotionally unencumbered to preserve the life she'd created.

How could he really complain, when he'd done, essentially, the same on his journey?

But he didn't have to like it.

When his phone pinged over breakfast, announcing a text message, his heart skipped with excitement.

But the message wasn't from Natalie. It was from Pops.

The roil of disappointment irritated him, because he'd been waiting to hear from his father for weeks.

But he was able to brush that aside. Because Pops was home now, and, frankly, Jax could really use a chat.

He hopped in his SUV, stopped by Amy's bakery to grab Pops's favorite bear claws, the ones with almond filling, and headed out to his place.

Pops had always lived on the tribal lands—even when he'd been married to Mom, who hadn't wanted to live so far out of town. They'd simply had two residences and, while it had been a little confusing for Jax and Sheida, identity-wise, it had somehow worked. Pops's home was very modest, and now, after decades of pleasing only himself, was less a residence and more a storage facility for his rocks. One room was filled with raw materials, and another with completed pieces. The living room was always scattered with projects-in-process as well as the tools of the trade, including an industrial tumbler, bales of jewelry-grade copper wire and several soldering irons. Somewhere in there was a fridge and a hot plate.

Sheida often squawked that he needed a proper home, with furniture and stuff, but Jax could relate. He felt the same about his wood.

He knocked before he opened the door—he always did because he knew how jarring interruptions could be to a man deep in his work—but he didn't wait for an invitation to come in. "Hey, Pops," he called as he stepped into the living room. It was more cluttered than usual because, apparently, Pops had unloaded bins of rocks from his truck right into the foyer when he'd arrived home.

Pops was sitting at the old dining room table, the

one from Jax's childhood, bent over his project with an etching tool. When he heard Jax's voice he set the tool in a holder and came straight over to give his son a hug.

Though he was in his late fifties, Pops was still a strong and vital man. His shoulders were broad, his back straight, and the long ponytail hanging in a braid down his back was only lightly dusted with gray. His hug was powerful enough to realign a couple vertebrae. Jax chuckled at the snaps and cracks that resulted.

"My son." Pops stood back to give him the once-over. Then, after a moment, he nodded. "Looking good," he said with a quiet smile. And then, "What has changed?"

Jax stared at him. How like Pops to just cut through all the niceties straight to the bone. And while he wanted to talk to his dad about recent developments—in addition to being a mentor, he was an excellent counselor—he didn't want to start like that. So, he deflected. "How was Arizona?"

Pops chuckled and waved at the stacks of bins by the door. "Abundant." His grin was broad. Pops was a seeker of abundance. And he always found it. "Come. Let me make you a coffee."

He'd already had a coffee, or two, but he didn't demur, because what Pops really meant was, *let's have a talk*. "I brought bear claws," Jax said, holding up the box.

"From Amy's." Pops's eyes lit up. "Excellent."

"Is there any other place?"

"Nope." His father chuckled as he poured dark brew into two fat mugs. He handed Jax his mug in exchange for the box of carbs, and then led the way to the back porch of his house, which faced the shore and always boasted a sea-kissed breeze. They sat in the rocking chairs Pops had made, years ago when he'd been into woodworking, and Jax sipped as Pops tore into a pastry. "Man, I have missed these."

"Don't they have bear claws in Arizona?"

"Not like this." Pops grinned, utterly oblivious to the crumbs clinging to his tightly trimmed beard. Or maybe not oblivious. Maybe he didn't care.

They talked a little bit about his trip to the south, the old friends he'd connected with and the people he'd met down there, but Jax was aware that Pops was just letting him ease into his own issues. He loved his dad, for so many reasons, but most especially because he was so good at reading people and knowing when someone needed a little time to get to a point.

"So," Pops said, after he'd answered all of Jax's questions about his spirit quest. "What's been happening here?"

Jax lifted a shoulder. "Not a lot. Natalie Tuttle's back in town. For a while."

"Mmm." Pops nodded. "Sheida told me." And at Jax's surprise, "She called after she got my text."

Well, yes, that sounded like Sheida. "She's happy that Nat's back. But it's only for a visit. Pearl had a stroke, so she's helping Celeste and Amy with everything."

"Mmm." Pops did that a lot. Just a simple *mmm*. "And how about you?"

"Me?" He wasn't sure where this sudden reluctance to discuss his feelings about her came from. That was a big part of why he'd come today, after all. To get his father's take on things. But it was impossible to buffalo Alexander Stringfellow. Pops just knew things sometimes.

He nodded. "How do you feel about seeing her again?"

Jax sucked in a breath and tried to organize his thoughts. He knew whatever he told Pops would stay between them, and he knew there would be no judgment, so he had no worries about telling him the truth. "I... I really like her, Pops. We've become close."

"Not terrible." As usual, his responses were clear and concise.

"*Really* close." He winced a little, because he worried that he felt more deeply for her than she did in return. "It's...challenging."

Pops nodded. "Because she's only here for a short while."

"Yes. And..." Damn, it was hard to say. "She wants to keep our...relationship a—" that word stuck in his throat "—secret."

"Mmm." Another sip. Another bite from his bear claw. "Why do you think that is?"

"She told me. She doesn't want her family—and Sheida—to know. Doesn't want to get their expectations up."

"Because she's not staying."

"Right."

"And you're not happy about it—this denial of what you have."

Yep. Trust Pop to zero right in. "I hate it. But I don't want to push. It's still early."

"Early." Not a question. Just an observation. Just him saying, *Look at this word you used.*

"We've had one real date, Pops."

His father threw back his head and laughed. "Feelings don't understand time, though, do they?"

"No." No, they didn't.

"I fell in love with your mother the moment I saw her. I still remember her, the way she looked that day on the beach all barefoot, with her hair loose and her smiling eyes. That was immediate. It's all the rest of the nonsense that kept us apart for so long. Now, as an old man..." He smiled because he considered that a joke. "I wish I had done things differently. The things that kept us apart, the things we thought made us incompatible, despite our attraction, were like waves in the wind. We should have laughed them off and simply enjoyed our time together, however long we might be allowed." His expression softened as he thought of Mom and the love they'd shared—despite all of their challenges. "Life is too short to miss those opportunities to love and be loved."

Jax swallowed heavily. *Love.* That was a scary word, at least in his vernacular.

But love itself wasn't scary. It was a beautiful gift when given freely.

The trouble started when a man wanted something back.

And the fact was, the only reason he wasn't using the word *love* to describe how he felt about Natalie was because he wasn't sure she would or could love him back.

"So, what would you do? If you thought you might,

I dunno, love a woman, and she might not love you in the same way?"

Pops finished his bear claw and riffled around in the box for a second. "First of all, it's foolish to try to rank love. Or to expect someone else to feel the way you do. That's not the point of love. It's not even stephen. It never is. Second of all, if you see the magic in her, and you're drawn to explore it, you take the risk. Knowing that it may only be for a short while because, son, it is always, only for a little while. You take the risk, knowing that your feelings might not even out on some cosmic scale, because love is always its own reward."

"So, lean into it?"

"Life is about experiences. So, go experience it."

"And when she leaves?"

Pops narrowed his eyes. He was probably thinking about Mom. "Then you have great memories of a great love to carry with you."

"And what if I want more?" More than memories? The stupid picket fence? Kids? Maybe a dog?

"Well…" Pops leaned back in his chair and rocked a little. "You have a choice. You can accept that she's just not the one—by her choice—and find a woman who fits your lifestyle, or you can dig in and fight for what you want. And by fight, I mean sacrifice. Make those hard decisions to be there for her, with her, no matter what."

Jax leaned back and stared out at the sea—it wasn't as calming as it usually was, but that was probably a reflection of the churning in his soul. Pops was right. The choices were simple. And excruciatingly difficult at the same time. He didn't know if he could be happy, or healthy, in a bustling city filled with unfamiliar noises, unwelcome intrusions and, well, people. But he also knew that he wouldn't be happy without Natalie in his life, in some way.

But he could be open to exploring the possibilities. Couldn't he?

"At the very least, son, you have clarity. If you know what you want, and you search for it with an open heart, you will find it. If it's not this woman, it will be another woman."

Jax's gut tightened at that. A visceral rejection of the thought that he'd be happy with just anyone. Not now. Not after Natalie. He'd known many women, but none of them made him feel *seen*, not the way she did. She was the one he wanted all this with.

Only Natalie.

No one else.

So, yeah. That was his answer.

He'd have to fight. Change. Evolve.

While the decision gave him a measure of peace, and a whiff of excitement for the future, he was, at the same time, terrified.

Chapter Ten

Natalie spent the next day with Momma, because Celeste had to work. In the morning, they putzed around the house, having breakfast, watching Momma's shows together and playing with Pepe. She even sat for a portrait that Nat painted of her. When Momma napped, she went online and started researching PTSD, which led her to an article on night terrors. One website in particular, nami.org—the National Alliance for Mental Illness—had a lot of information not only on how to deal with night terrors, but also how to prevent and manage them.

Throughout the morning, Natalie found her mind wandering to Jax, again and again. Reliving last night, certainly—and the deep feeling of rightness being with Jax engendered—but also contemplating the future.

Could she blithely go back to her life the way it had been—living alone with occasional bursts of unsatisfying and temporary lovers—now that she knew something else was possible? Now that she knew she *could* have the kind of relationship she'd always craved in a partner?

How hard would it be to walk away from Jax? Now? Could she?

Well, of course she could. She'd spent her life walking away—from places, from identities she'd created, from friendships. You just cut emotional ties, boxed up those feelings, put them in storage and moved on.

But the costs were high. She was beginning to realize just how high a price she'd paid when she'd left Coho Cove. And now that she'd allowed Jax into her heart—and she most certainly had—the stakes were even higher.

Fortunately, it wasn't a decision she had to deal with right now.

Right now, she could relax and enjoy his presence.

What a shame that her whole day was booked out—taking care of Momma, and then dinner with Sheida—because all she really wanted to do was be with him. But this was what being a grown-up was, wasn't it?

In the afternoon, Momma had a physical therapy session at the Elder House. The plan was for Natalie to take Momma in, then hang out until the end of Celeste's shift. Then Celeste would take her home, while Natalie and Sheida went out for dinner at Bootleggers.

Natalie was struck by the childlike joy on her mother's face when she announced it was time to go. It felt, in a strange way, that roles had been reversed and, all of a sudden, she was the parent taking her child to a play date.

Once they walked into the bright and breezy Elder House, there was even a spring in Momma's step as she—and her walker—blazed a path to the rehab center.

Not surprisingly, Sheida was there to meet them. "Hey, you," she said, giving Nat a hug. "And how are you today, Pearl?"

Momma frowned and looked around. "Where's Rico?"

Sheida laughed. "Don't worry, Pearl. I'm not taking over for Rico. I promise. And look. Here he comes now." She sketched a wave at the long, lanky athletic type loping toward them. "Natalie, this is Rico. Rico, this is Pearl's daughter, Nat."

His handshake was strong, and he met her eyes and smiled, and she liked him immediately. "Come along, Pearl," he said as she gazed up at him adoringly. "Today we're going to practice stairs!"

"We'll be in the community room," Sheida said as Rico led Momma through the mock kitchen to a set of stairs in the corner. And then, to Natalie, "You do want coffee? Don't you?"

"Always." But wait… "*Real* coffee."

"Oh." Sheida put out a lip, but there was a teasing glint in her eye. "You didn't like the mushroom coffee?"

"Real. Coffee."

To which she laughed. But she did order, specifically, *real coffee* for Natalie, along with a croissant—because they were just baked and there was nothing more wonderful than a just-baked croissant. Sheida ordered a lemon bar for herself—she'd always had a penchant for anything lemony.

An art class was starting up as they headed for a table by the window and, as there were empty easels, the instructor waved them over and they headed that way instead.

"Gosh, I haven't painted in years," Sheida said as she stared at the watercolors and paintbrushes scattered on the table.

"Me, either. I miss it," Nat said. And oh, it felt good to have a brush in her hand for no other reason than pleasure. Since she'd made art her living as well as her life, the joy had been elusive. But today, as pure fun, it swept her away.

They chatted a little as they painted. Specifically, Sheida asked about Carl, and Nat had to tell her that no, he hadn't called. In fact, she'd called him a couple times and gotten voice mail and he hadn't yet called her back.

What she didn't mention was that she'd been calling Carl to let him know she'd met someone, and that she'd been relieved that he hadn't picked up. He often went off the grid when they were on hiatus—and she didn't particularly care that he hadn't called back, because she'd been busy with another man. That would have required telling Sheida the identity of said man and that would have become messy.

It made her feel a little uneasy, not mentioning that she and Jax were exploring things, because Sheida was her friend and Jax was Sheida's brother, and she would definitely want to know something like that. But she didn't veer from her decision to keep it private. It was too new, too fragile and definitely too triggering. For everyone.

Look at how Amy had reacted—just because they'd shared a kiss on the boat.

No. This was a short visit and Natalie did not want to spend it defending her choices—which would certainly be the case. If things between her and Jax worked out, there would be plenty of time to tell Sheida.

So, she shut her piehole and painted. And it was lovely.

After a bit Sheida leaned over to look at her canvas. "Oh, Nat! That's pretty."

Nat smiled. "I'm an artist. It better be. That's how I pay the rent."

"I thought you built sets," she said.

Nat chuckled. "Well, I'm the art director. I design the sets, manage the construction team—who then build the sets. My team and I create the mood for the feel of the whole show. Every lamp, every painting… I designed or selected that on purpose for a reason."

"Hmm. Sounds very focused and deliberate."

"It is."

Sheida was silent for a moment, which gave Nat a little warning. With Sheida, silence was usually followed by something pithy. Or at least attempts at pith. "Wouldn't it be nice if you could apply all that focus and deliberation to your *real* life?" she said in an aside that made no pretense at subtlety.

"I'm sure I don't know what you mean." Nat took a swipe at an evergreen tree on the cliff she was painting.

"Yes, you do. Your work, it's all on purpose, but your emotional life, hon, it's a mess."

"Is it?"

"Yeah. Take this Curt guy."

"Carl."

"What kind of man never calls?" She waited for an answer, but not long. "A man who knows you're not committed to each other. I guarantee you, he's seeing someone else."

Nat nodded noncommittally. She was pretty sure that was the case as well. They'd never agreed to be exclusive. And frankly, she didn't care. "Can we talk about something else?" she asked. "You're harshing my art buzz."

Sheida huffed a sigh. She jabbed her brush at the canvas. "All I'm saying is, you should be as honest and deliberate about what you want for your life as you are about what you want for your career. You are kicking ass in your career. In your love life, though… Is this guy what you really want? A part-time lover?"

Nat wished Sheida would stop talking about Carl. She hadn't even really thought about him since…well, since Jax had kissed her. "Please do *not* quote song lyrics at me."

Sheida lifted one shoulder to show the full depth of her apathy at the accusation. "If the shoe fits…" She painted a little more, then said, "Tell me honestly. Are lukewarm dates really the emotional life you want?"

Simple question. Nat shrugged. "It works for now."

Sheida snorted. "Good for now has a tendency of becoming adequate forever."

Natalie stilled. An adequate forever? That didn't sound appealing. Not really. Not after the flash of fabulous last night had been. And Carl forever? No. He wasn't even a reasonable facsimile of Jax. Not a shadow of Jax. After the depth of her experience with Jax last night, it was clear that she and Carl were just placeholders for each other. Nothing more.

Which begged another question—what was this thing with Jax? What *could* it be?

It could be a fling. Easily.

But Jax wasn't Carl. Jax wasn't a man she could stop thinking about just because he wasn't there. And Jax was not the kind of man she could share.

So, if a fling, or part-time lover wasn't enough for her, what were the options?

She shivered at the thought that descended from some higher place in her being.

It could be something *real*.

Something…permanent.

Another shiver wracked her, because in her life, nothing had ever been permanent. She didn't trust it as a concept, and she didn't know if she ever could.

The only element of her life that hadn't changed over the years as they moved from base to base had been her family. They'd been always there, always available.

And now even that was an illusion. Dad had died. Then Nate. And now Momma was getting older. One day Momma would be gone as well.

So, what was permanence anyway?

And what was the benefit of trying to keep things the same?

And—more to the point—what was the cost of *staying* the same? Of never stretching. Never risking?

Could she be happy with a life with Carl? Or a string of Carls wandering in and out of her life? A string of adequate, totally acceptable men? Probably. Many people settled for adequate. Before last night, she would have. She had.

But now…things had shifted. Now she knew that there was a difference between being happy and being completely and totally fulfilled.

She knew she could have that fulfilment with Jax. She knew that if she chose to, she could have it forever.

But the cost was high. For one of them, at least. One of them would have to make a life-altering change.

And after everything he'd been through, fighting for his hard-won peace, it seemed unfair and unrealistic to expect *him* to be the one to compromise.

But could she? Could she walk away from her life? Her career?

Her job had become her identity in so many ways. Everything flowed from it. Her joy, her satisfaction, her money…

What would she do without it? Who would she be?

She sat back and stared at her painting, her mind reeling and oddly detached as she realized she'd painted the town, Coho Cove, from the sea to the cliffs. She hadn't intended to. She hadn't intended to make it look like such a lovely place, either, but she had.

And she wasn't sure how to feel about that at all.

* * *

After his visit with Pops, Jax sequestered himself in his studio and caught up on work. Not the creative side—his mind was too distracted for him to submerge in creation—but the business end, the stuff he hated, yet had to do. It wasn't good for much, but it definitely distracted his overactive brain.

Funny, it was almost a relief to calculate quarterly taxes and update his inventory. Summer was coming and, other than the fancy-schmancy customers Ben brought him, tourists were his bread and butter. Though it had started as art therapy, it was damned satisfying to see his work turn a profit.

The main trouble he had all afternoon—all day, really—was that the only thing he wanted was to be with Natalie. Everything else felt like, well, filler.

So, when his alarm went off at six, he decided to clean up and head for the place he knew she'd be, having supper with his sister.

A man had to eat, right? And if he could convince her to come home with him after dinner, so much the better.

When he pushed through the door of Bootleggers, he saw her right away. His gaze tracked to her like a magnet—and his heart lifted. Just seeing her made his day better. They were still in the bar, nursing wine and chatting, so he joined them at their table.

"Good evening," he said to Nat, as he took the empty chair at her side.

"Jax!" Her delight, her smile, thrilled him to the core.

Sheida, on the other hand, glared at him. "What are you doing here?" she said.

"A man's gotta eat."

The frown darkened. "You hate eating out."

He shrugged. "I'm hungry." He glanced back at Vic, who paused by the table, and ordered a beer.

Sheida's eyes went wide. "You're not staying!?"

Jax glanced at her. "I thought I would. Surely you don't mind?"

"I don't mind," Nat said.

He nearly jumped out of his skin when her knee brushed his. Then pressed against him. His pulse shot into gear and he grinned at her.

"Well, you can't stay," Sheida muttered, then she glanced around the bar and checked her watch.

And all of a sudden it hit him. He realized that this wasn't some simple dinner. His sister was up to something. Again. "Um," he cleared his throat. "Are you expecting someone else?" He asked Nat—who shook her head—but Sheida responded.

"Luke Larsen is meeting us. You're in his seat."

Natalie choked on her drink. "Luke's joining us?"

Jax liked that she'd been unaware, but it was clear to him what was going on. Sheida was still trying to matchmake. It was a damn good thing he'd decided to show up. It was a damn good thing he'd taken a minute to clean up. He leaned back in his seat—*his* seat—and gave his sister a long, slow smile. "We'll pull over another chair."

"We can do that," Nat said. She even stood, went to an empty table and dragged over a fourth chair. He didn't miss the fact that she set it between himself and his sister. And when she settled back in her seat, she scooched hers ever so much closer to him, then rested her thigh against his. They exchanged a smile then, one he wanted to sink into. And he would have, had Sheida not been there.

"Jax," his sister said in something of a hiss. "You're ruining everything."

He batted his lashes at her, because he knew what he was ruining, and he was fully complicit. He didn't mind keeping his new relationship with Natalie from Sheida—in fact there were definite benefits. But he wasn't going to step to the side and let another man try to woo his woman.

"It's okay, Sheida," Nat said.

"No. It's not. Luke will be here any minute. He's expecting to have dinner with you."

Yep. Just as Jax expected. This was a stealth fix-up.

Natalie leaned in so she could whisper, "Sheida, I told you, I'm not interested in Luke. Not like that."

"But he's so perfect for you." Something in Jax's gut grumbled. It might have been hunger, but it probably wasn't.

Natalie laughed. "He's a nice man. He's probably a great catch, but Sheida, he's not perfect for me. He's not even close."

"Okay. Fine. But give him a chance. Let him take you to the reunion."

Natalie sighed heavily. "Why are you trying so hard to fix me up with Luke?"

"Would it be so terrible if you fell in love with him and stayed here? I miss your face. I want my friend back."

"Oh, Sheida." Nat took her hand across the table. "I will always be your friend."

"I just want you to stay. Is that so terrible?"

"Hon," Natalie said in a gentle tone. "I'm not going to stay. Not for Luke, at any rate."

Silence crackled, and while Jax felt uncomfortable, he was more than happy to sit here by Nat's side in silent support. She glanced at him, and he read the frustration in her expression—because Sheida wasn't listening. She rarely did, especially when she wanted something.

In the end, Sheida gave in, because it was clear Nat would not. "Well," she huffed. "You can't blame me for trying."

Natalie physically relaxed. "Thank you, Sheida."

"What about as a date for the reunion? Surely that's not too much to ask? You are planning to go?"

Nat shrugged. "Sure. If I'm still here." She shot a look at Jax, a question really, which he interpreted immediately and gave her a small nod. "But I was planning to go with Jax."

Sheida stilled and stared at her. Then stared at him. "What?"

"Yeah," he said, straightening in his chair. "We thought it would be fun."

"But Jax, if she's hanging out with you, how can she find the love of her life?"

Natalie laughed. "At the Coho High Reunion? Really? Look, Sheida, I'm not planning to find the love of my life. I just want to relax and enjoy my time off."

"With *Jax*?"

The little hairs on his nape prickled. *Why was that so outrageous?*

"Yes." She set her hand on his. "With Jax. So, please. Just let it go, will you?"

"All right," Sheida said after a long minute. Then a small smile curled on her face as she realized Nat's hand was still on Jax's, because she hadn't moved. And neither had he.

Dinner with Luke and Sheida had been fun, once everyone understood it wasn't a date of any kind. At least, not a date between anyone but Nat and Jax. *He* was certainly counting it as a date. Luke talked a lot about real estate, which Jax found interesting, as well as the plans for Coho Days and some other projects the town council was working on. Natalie told some funny stories from work and there was, in general, a lot of laughter and lively conversation. It was a nice evening.

But all Jax could think about was getting her alone.

When they left the restaurant, they walked away together to his SUV, without any explanation or discussion; they both knew they were heading back to Jax's place.

He loved that Nat took his hand after they got out of the car, as they walked along the shadowed path toward the studio. Loved that they didn't need to chat incessantly to communicate.

When they reached his place, they made love—more than once—then curled up together in the covers.

"I think Sheida suspects," he murmured into her hair as he drew ellipses on her so-soft skin.

Natalie sighed. "You're right. I think Amy suspects, too."

He chuckled. "Already?"

"I think she smelled it on me when I got home last night."

"Amy was there?"

"Waiting." She glanced at him. "The boys told her about the kiss on the boat."

He rolled his eyes. "Of course, they did."

"I think she's afraid I'm going to steal you away from her, or ruin the relationship you have, or something."

"Never happen."

"Of course not. I wouldn't want it to. I think it's a wonderful arrangement for Amy and the boys, but also for you."

"So do I."

She was silent for a little bit, and then she huffed a sigh. "I can't believe Sheida tried to set me up on a blind date."

Couldn't she? He could. "She didn't know we were seeing each other." If she had, this nonsense would never have happened.

"That's not an excuse for an ambush."

"She just misses you. She always has," he said.

He didn't expect such a simple and obvious observation to hit Nat so hard, but her eyes widened and filled with misty tears. "I've missed her, too. I didn't realize how much until I came back. It's horrible the way we forget how much we love our friends when we're apart."

"You were making your life. It's what people do."

"I could have done a lot of things differently. I don't know why I didn't."

"You were a kid. You were in a hurry to start your life. I remember that."

"I wanted to escape." She sighed and the scent of her breath teased his nostrils. He loved having her this close. Just the two of them. Alone. Together. He felt... like himself. Without even trying.

"Escape what?" he asked, a whisper. He wished he hadn't when she sat up, pulled back her hair and then pulled away.

"That's the really stupid part, Jax. You'd think after a lifetime constantly on the move, I would have known that you can never escape the things about yourself you don't like by packing a bag. You have to deal with those things and fix or change them or simply accept them."

He sat up, too, so he could see her eye to eye. Because this was an important conversation and he wanted her to know he saw that. "Where are you now? In that journey?"

She smiled. She glowed. "I like myself now." Her smile faltered. "At least I did until I came back here—" She cut herself off. "No, that's not it. I do like myself. Love myself, really. But coming back here made me face a lot of things I've been avoiding." She made a face. "And then, on top of all that, coming back, and realizing that I missed so much time with everyone. The boys aren't babies any more, and my mom... The stroke. The physical changes. The way she struggles with words sometimes. Even calling us the wrong names..."

He gave her a hug. "That's got to be difficult."

"Oh, Jax." He hated seeing that telltale tear in her eye. Hated that he couldn't make it all better for her. But he knew, from experience, simply having someone to listen could help, so he did. "It's made me realize that she's not going to live forever." She let go a not-so-amused, wet laugh. "You'd think that after losing Dad and Nate I would get it. But I didn't. Some part of my brain just assumed she'd always be there. Or just did not want to process the fact that she could...die."

"I know." He pulled her closer. "When my mom passed, none of us expected it. It's a shock. And your mom's stroke was a reminder that she's mortal. That shakes you."

"It bothers me that I lost hold of that truth."

"You have hold of it now," he said. "And it's not too late. She's still here. You still have time with her."

"Yeah." She snuggled in and he held her and stroked her for a while in silence. Then she blew out a sigh. "Ugh. It's not a lot of fun, all this self-introspection. I never bothered with it in LA. Too busy. Probably on purpose?"

He chuckled. "Well, that's the thing about family. They will make you challenge yourself and your assumptions about life and what really matters. I guess the real question you have to answer is, what really matters to you? What do you *really* want?"

She huffed a sigh. "Is it silly that I'm not sure? At my age?"

"I hope not, because we're the same age and I'm not always sure what I want." A partial lie. He knew what he wanted now. He just hadn't realized it before.

She threw back her head and laughed. Something musical and stirring. He wanted to cover her mouth with his again and consume that laugh. And more. He wanted so much more.

She shifted over to face him, her cheek on her hand, which was resting on his pillow, and she smiled at him. Just smiled. It was a sight he wanted to memorize. A feeling he wanted forever.

Natalie didn't mean to fall asleep at Jax's that night. And he probably didn't mean to let her. But after a long day, a couple drinks and the mind-blowing sex that followed...it just happened.

She was roused from her sleep by a cry. It was followed shortly thereafter by thrashing on the bed beside her. She knew at once this was no normal dream. Though Jax was sitting straight up, and his eyes were open, she could tell he wasn't present. His gaze was trained on something that wasn't there, his pupils dilated, his skin flushed and sweaty and his expression a mask of panic.

Panic flashed through her as well, because she knew this was the event he'd warned her about. Her first instinct was to try to soothe Jax or wake him up, but she remembered her research and just sat close by—and out of reach of his flailing limbs—speaking softly to him. She remembered reading that people with night terrors were unlikely to wake up—because they were in a deeper sleep state than when dreaming. And trying to wake them up could trigger a defensive reaction which, in the instance of a night terror, could lead to unintentional lashing out.

No doubt, that was his greatest fear—that he might hurt her.

"It's okay, Jax," she said, over and over. "You're not alone. I'm here." And, as frightening as this was for her, she could only imagine how scary it must be for him, in that state, wherever he was. But her tone seemed to reach him, somewhere in that mélange of terror. And slowly, he quieted and calmed. And then, after a long, long while, he exhaled a deep breath and lay back down.

She waited a while, calming herself as best she could, and then slowly eased in next to him and stroked him and murmured sweet nothings. She didn't go back to sleep—she was far too alert now. Instead, she lay there and thought about everything she'd read, and tried to develop a plan for next time.

When he awoke, just before the dawn, she was still there, holding him.

He turned in to her and caught her gaze and offered a sleepy smile.

"Good morning, you," she said. "How are you feeling?"

He yawned. "Still tired."

She nodded. "You know, you had a bad dream last night." She wished she didn't have to bring it up, because it would shatter the peace of the morning, but they had to talk about it. He needed to know she was all in on supporting him—no matter what.

He stilled. His eyes went wide. That panic flared in

his expression again and he looked away. Swallowed heavily. "I did?" A croak. "Did I…"

She stroked him gently. "No. You didn't hurt me, Jax. And because we'd discussed it, and I'd done some reading about it, I understood what was happening. So, I want to thank you for that."

He met her gaze then. Stared at her. "You're thanking me?"

"Yes." She took his hand. "Things aren't so scary when you understand what's happening. And I know it was hard for you to share. But it really helped me cope—just knowing what was happening and what to do." Also, what not to do.

"How, uh, bad was it?"

She shot him a grin. "I don't know. It was my first. But after a while, you calmed down and went right back to sleep, if that helps."

He sat up and turned away from her—which was crushing—but then, he said, in nearly a whisper, "I don't deserve you."

She turned his chin, making him look at her, and she looked deeply into his eyes and quipped, "Probably not, but you're stuck with me." It was a joke and, as intended, it cracked the rigid mood and he chuckled. And, though it was a joke, it really was true. He was. Stuck with her. Because, somewhere in the darkness of that night, she'd decided that they would make this work. They could.

She didn't know how yet, but she was certain that she would give this relationship every chance for success. It was too…important to her.

"You know, Nat," he said into the silence. The slight tremor in his voice caught her attention. "We really do have something special."

She chuckled. "I was just thinking that, too."

"I love spending time with you. Talking with you. Sharing my life with you." He stroked her hand with his thumb, the way he did, the way she loved. Then he drew his warm palm down her bare flank, sending shivers through her. "And this."

She couldn't hold back her smile. "I'm enjoying this, too." Yes, she certainly had not expected this when she arrived. Would never have dreamed she could wander into a romantic relationship with him.

All right. She might have *dreamed* about it, but she'd never expected it to actually happen. And now that it had—well, she was torn. Now, when she thought about going back to LA, there was no excitement. In fact, there was even a little dread.

As though he read her mind, or her mood, her energy, her something, his smile faded. "You'll be leaving soon."

The catch in his voice hit her harder than she expected. "Yeah. I'll get the call." She thought about it now, every morning when she woke up. Would today be the day?

"I..." He paused, collected his thoughts, then met her gaze. "I just want you to know that when you leave, I'm going to miss you. A lot."

"You can always come to LA for a visit," she said because she'd been thinking about it.

He huffed a laugh. "I'm not much of a big-city guy."

"But a visit?"

He winced, but said, "I can manage a visit. I think I owe it to us to try, at least."

"I don't want you to feel pressured, though."

He blew out a breath. "Avoidance was my favorite strategy for a long time. It's not a healthy strategy in the long run. Not if you want to have a full life. My therapist taught me about a window of tolerance—the space where you are comfortable interacting with the world. It's a small window at first, but then, hopefully, you develop strategies that allow more and more exposure. If we can move slowly, strategically, I think changes like that could be doable—" He broke off on a laugh.

"What is it?" she asked. Nothing he'd said had seemed funny to her. In fact, she'd been in awe of his courage. His willingness to open himself up to things that were, on some level, terrifying to him.

He turned to her, his face alight. "I can't believe I just said those words. I've been struggling with this for years—and my therapist told me a day would come when I would be ready to open up to new experiences and, well, I didn't believe it."

"So, this is a good step?"

In response, her kissed her.

And then, he kissed her again.

And then the kisses became something more—a glorious and intimate celebration of small steps, trust and communion that left them both breathless and sweaty.

He took a shower while she made them both breakfast, and over the meal they talked more about the strategies he'd learned, and others she'd found online.

He'd already incorporated many of those tactics in his lifestyle, including minimizing drugs and alcohol, healthy eating, meditation, daily exercise, creating a safe sleep environment—which explained why his bedroom was so spartan. But he was still enthusiastic to her suggestions as well.

Simple things like playing classical music at night, deep breathing, focusing on random sights or smells for calming—for rooting in reality, and intentionally holding good thoughts. They talked about how laughter and singing rewired the brain neurologically and healed the vagus nerve, about aroma therapy, weighted blankets and more.

Together, the drew up a plan to try to incorporate as many of these strategies into their days as they could. It wasn't a magic wand. It wouldn't fix many of the problems they had moving forward, but it was a productive and hopeful exercise. And finally, for once, Natalie could see the possibility of a future for them. And so, she could tell, could he.

In the next couple weeks, things got even easier. Balancing time between Momma and Jax wasn't difficult, especially once they stopped caring if family knew about their blossoming relationship. In fact, Amy's nagging actually decreased and Sheida's matchmaking efforts ceased entirely. When he wasn't working, Jax came over to spend time during the day, playing cards with Momma, doing silly arts and crafts projects and making lunch for the three of them.

Once school got out, they included the boys in their

activities as well—which Natalie enjoyed tremendously. And so did Momma. It was particularly fun when they did day trips out of town. Nothing strenuous, so Momma could keep up—but the times when they needed to, they brought her wheelchair, and Jax charmed her into letting him push her around. Momma allowed herself to be ferried—by Jax. No one else got to push her. It was simply accepted as law.

They made a visit to Northwest Trek, a wildlife refuge in Western Washington, and spent a day at Mount St. Helen's to explore the museum on an active volcano—which kept the boys intrigued. And while Pike Place Market was crowded and bustling—and a challenge with a wheelchair—with Jax there managing their path with the clarity of a military campaign, it was easy and delightful.

Everything seemed so much easier with him around. He had a natural charm that had Momma fluttering her lashes and going along with ideas she might have rejected from any other person. Amy loved and trusted him, and Celeste thought he walked on water. In short, he was a great fit with her family.

More than once, when he walked out of a room, Momma leaned over and said to Natalie, "I like that boy." Which was high praise indeed.

Beyond that, Natalie simply enjoyed his company. Whether it was just the two of them, wrapped in each other in an intimate embrace, or they were with other people—including her family—it was simply free and easy spending time with him.

As time passed, their conversations delved deeper

as well. She learned more about his marriage, and she told him about her past relationships—including Carl. He shared more about his journey through trauma and the strategies he used to balance his emotional, physical and psychological needs. She loved that their conversations could veer wildly from deep philosophical ruminations to fart jokes.

On the day before the Coho High Reunion, Jax planned a trip with the boys to Point Defiance in Tacoma, which boasted a zoo and an aquarium. When they pulled up to Amy's house to pick the boys up, Jax stayed in the car with Momma while Nat went in to pick up the boys because getting in and out of Jax's large truck was a challenge for her.

Amy met Nat at the door. The two of them hadn't been alone since the spat they'd had that night after the fishing trip, so Natalie was a little leery. Though they'd been together, it had always been in a group setting, or with the family. That fight had been the last time they'd had a real conversation, and Amy had been very upset about Nat's relationship with Jax.

She forced a cheery smile, hoping to keep things light. "Good morning," she chirped.

"Morning." Amy ushered her in. "The boys are running a little late. Sorry. They just finished breakfast and are getting ready."

"No worries. We're not in a rush."

Amy nodded. And then they stood there, looking at each other awkwardly for far too long.

"I—"

"Hey—"

They both winced when they spoke at the same time. "Sorry," Nat said.

"No. I'm sorry." Amy locked her fingers together and sighed. "I, ah, really appreciate you and Jax taking the boys. I've been meaning to say so, but—"

"But there hasn't been a chance. I know. We've all been busy."

"Right." Amy shifted her feet. "Look, Nat, there's something I want to say. I…" She trailed off and Natalie tried not to wince, because she wasn't sure which way this would go. Amy continued in a rush. "Look, I'm sorry I was such a big baby about you and Jax. No. No," she said when Nat opened her mouth to reply. "Please. Let me get it out."

"Okay." It was only right. Nat had it coming. Amy had every right to complain. She had kind of stolen Jax away. He certainly hadn't been sleeping at Amy's house much in the past two weeks. So she steeled her spine for the onslaught.

Amy sucked in a deep breath. "I just want to say I'm sorry for the things I said about you and Jax. I have to admit, he is so much happier with you in his life. He smiles now. He laughs. And I realize I was just being selfish—"

Nat's heart thudded. Not what she'd expected. She swallowed heavily as tears pricked at her lids. "Oh, Amy—"

Again, Amy cut her off. "Celeste was right. It's wrong of me to put all the weight of being a father figure for the boys on him. I thought I needed him, but now I realize that I just liked having a partner. I wasn't fair to him and I wasn't fair to you, and I'm sorry for being a brat."

"You're not a brat."

She snorted, because there had been many times, when they were kids, that they'd called each other brats. And some of those times, they'd been right. "I just want you to know that I'm happy you and Jax are together."

"Thank you." Natalie pulled her into a hug, one she didn't want to end. "I'm sorry I wasn't here for you when George died. I should have been. I should have... Well, I should have...so many things. I'm going to be a better sister, I promise."

"Me too."

It was still awkward, looking at each other with suspicious dampness in their eyes, but they both bore it with grace.

When the boys thudded down the stairs with their backpacks in tow, Amy hugged and kissed them both and told them in no uncertain terms to behave. And then she hugged Nat again with a warmth and sincerity that filled her heart.

Oh, it wasn't a perfect relationship, there would always probably be bumps and bruises here and there, but she loved Amy and it gladdened her heart that they weren't at odds. At least for the moment.

The boys barreled to the driveway and piled into the back seat of Jax's SUV with Nat—Momma was in the front seat for comfort—and they were off. Nat waved to Amy on the porch until Jax turned the corner and she disappeared from view.

It was a beautiful day, with blue skies and big fluffy

clouds, and Natalie, with an especially light heart, appreciated strolling from enclosure to enclosure, experiencing the animals from her nephews' point of view. When Momma got warm, they stopped for shaved ice or popped into an air-conditioned exhibit.

"You are so great with the boys," Jax said to her as they ran over to a face painter.

She leaned against him. "You are."

"They're great kids."

They were. Oh, John J was still prone to temper tantrums and Georgie was as stubborn as...well, as Amy. But she couldn't imagine her family without the boys. They brought such joy and depth to life.

She directed her attention to John J, who was wriggling excitedly in his seat while the artist attempted to draw tiger stripes on his adorable face. It was so much fun, just watching the boys explore the world. Life felt... fuller with them in it. Life had, well, context.

She stilled as something moved inside her, a desire she'd never really felt before. Granted, she'd wiped the prospect of children from her heart and mind a long time ago, because she'd had other things to do—finish art school, get the job, keep the job, learn more, get the promotion and on and on and on. And even though she'd always had very clear goals for her career, there had never been a through line. Not really.

There'd been lots of who, what, when, where and how, but she'd been missing the most important element. The *why*.

It hit her suddenly and it hit her hard. What was the

point of accomplishing all these things if there was no one to share it with?

She'd been feeling that her life was missing something, but she'd been hiding from that truth. Now it was blindingly clear. She couldn't hide from it anymore.

This break from her *normal* life had been causing her to challenge *all* the elements of her life. To ask what she *really* wanted in a broader scheme of things. And almost every one of those answers conflicted with the life she'd built.

Her reverie was shattered when John J leaped at her with a roar. "Look at me. I'm a tiger!" he cried.

She stared at him, unable to respond, her heart filled with love and regret and questions…and, poor thing, his excited expression melted into concern. His lip trembled. "Did I scare you?" He took her hand. "Don't worry Aunt Nat. I'm not really a tiger. I'm just pretending."

She went down on her knees to hug him, this fierce, adorable tiger cub. Because she could relate. She'd been pretending to be a tiger most of her life.

Chapter Eleven

The next night, when Jax arrived at Natalie's door to pick her up for the reunion, she almost didn't recognize him. They'd both agreed to dress up, but she was not prepared for the sight of Jax in a sharply tailored suit. The black fabric against his tanned skin and a snowy white shirt was stunning, and the lines of the coat accentuated his wide shoulders and slim hips.

He was, in a word, *hot.*

The bouquet of flowers he proffered, with a little flourish, didn't hurt.

"Wow," he said as he took in her sparkly dress—the only dressy dress she'd brought. "You look fantastic."

She grinned. "You clean up pretty well yourself."

Celeste, being Celeste, insisted they pose for pictures by the mantel—as Momma looked on murmuring, with each new pose, "Hubba, hubba." As a result, it took them longer to get out of the house than they intended.

"Nervous?" Jax asked as she settled into the passenger seat of his SUV.

She laughed a nervous laugh. "Why do you ask?"

"Hey." He leaned over and kissed her. "Relax. It'll be fun."

"Will it?" she muttered, but at the same time, she appreciated his tone, his words and his intent. What a man, to focus on her, even though he must be crawling out of his skin at the prospect of a party of this magnitude. On that thought, she stopped him before he started the car, turned his face to hers and kissed him, too.

He grinned. "What was that for?"

"A thank-you."

"For what?"

She tried not to let her lip wobble as she responded. "For being you. For making this easy for me. You know."

He held her gaze and then he nodded. Because yeah. He did. He knew.

And that was one of the things that was so great about him.

But only one of them.

It was a little surreal, stepping into the Coho Cove High School gymnasium after all these years. Funny how it still smelled the same—of rubber and sweat— even though it was decorated with all the folderol of a prom. *Their* prom, to be precise. The theme had been

Seaside Paradise back then, but had felt more like Enchantment Under the Sea. It still did.

Apparently, the decorations committee hadn't changed—and they were really missing their high school glory days—because it looked exactly the same, down to the cheesy sailfish nailed to the wall and the bejeweled jellyfish hanging down from all the overhead lights.

Nat glanced at Jax and they both grinned. "Some things never change, I guess" she murmured, and he chuckled.

At the entranceway they stopped at a long table covered with name tags and guarded by Sherill Scanlon, the terror of Coho High. From head cheerleader to prom queen to the arbiter of all that was cool and all that was dross, she'd ruled with a ruthless cruelty toward anyone whom she deemed a lesser soul.

Still, somehow, Natalie forced a smile. "Hi, Sherill." The cheery tone nearly gagged her.

Sherill smiled at her—a smile Natalie had never experienced before. She wasn't sure how she felt about the fact that Sherill bounced out of her seat, came around the table and hugged her.

What she was certain of was the fact that she didn't care for Sherill's perfume, or the fact that it clung to her long after she'd been released from the embrace.

"Wow, Natalie. You look great. And hey, Jax. You look nice, too." He looked better than nice. He was scorching hot. So hot, Nat had been tempted to blow off this party and get him alone somewhere on a bed with a fuzzy comforter. Still, Natalie bit her tongue, because she'd made a vow not to let anything trigger her—or him—tonight. "Look. Here you are, right next to each other."

It took a moment for Natalie to realize she was talking about their name tags. Jax was an *S* and she was a *T.* "There we are," she said to him. "At the end of the alphabet."

He grinned. "Just like old times."

"Well," Sherill gushed. "That's the fun of reunions, isn't it?" Her expression shifted from friendly concierge to curious housewife. "So, Natalie, I'd love to hear about your life. What's it like working with all those movie stars? Have you ever met Jason Statham?"

Nat blinked. Really? She worked television shows, not feature films. But then, civilians, as she called them, rarely made that distinction. And while the very last thing she wanted, when she could be slow-dancing in Jax's arms, was to have a conversation with the Gorgon of Coho High about *work*, she smiled and shook her head. "No."

"Oh." Her still-beautiful face drooped into disappointment. "Who *do* you know?"

Without intending to, Nat shot Jax a glance, which he correctly interpreted—bless him—and he said, "Oh, Ben's waving us over. Come on, Nat. Thanks, Sherill." And he took her arm and literally dragged her away from the heinous welcome table into the gym. Of course, it wasn't much of a drag, because Natalie was more than willing to abet his efforts.

"Where's Ben?" She scanned the milling crowd, though it wasn't much of a crowd yet.

Jax shot her a grin. "I have no idea. I just figured you didn't want to get sucked into Sherill's gravitational pull for long."

Oh, good glory, was he right. "Thank you," she murmured.

He chuckled. "I was expecting something like that. We should have decided on a safe word."

She stopped short and gaped at him. "What?" she blurted.

He waggled his brows. "Surely you know all about safe words. You live in LA."

"Of course, I know what they are." She had to laugh. He was just so adorable, talking about safe words in the high school gym decorated a little like Davy Jones's locker.

"Okay. So, pick one."

"What?"

He paused at the bar, ordered a white wine for her and a beer for himself, and then fixed her with a steady gaze. "Pick one. That way I'll know when you need rescuing tonight." *When*, not *if*. Gosh. He did know her, didn't he?

"You're serious." His expression made clear he was. While she was amused, she was touched at the same time. She'd never had a rescuer before. Granted, she hadn't needed one, because generally she rescued herself when such a thing was necessary. But it was a very nice thought. Having a partner. Someone to watch her back. Someone to look out for her. And how much did she love the fact that he was worried about protecting her? When he was just as terrified. "That's sweet, Jax."

He shrugged. His ears went a little pink. "I just want you to have a good time."

"We could have had a good time at your place." It bore mentioning. Maybe not in quite that lurid tone, but whatever. His ears went all the way pink, and she gave a laugh. She loved that he was all man, and still humble enough to be self-conscious when she complimented his prowess. She wanted to kiss him, but because she suspected it might embarrass him further, especially in public, she didn't. Instead, she sucked in a deep breath and said, "All right. Safe words. Do you have any suggestions?"

His expression was priceless. "I don't know. What kind of words do people usually use?"

"I'm sure I don't know," she said. "It should be a word you don't usually use in normal conversations, I guess."

He thought about it for a moment, then said, "How about strawberry cheesecake?"

"Hmm. I might use that in a normal conversation." At any moment. "How about broccoli?" That would probably never come up.

He wrinkled his nose. "That's not very exotic."

"Does it need to be exotic?" Her smile was easy, because as silly as this conversation was, she loved it. "How about magma?"

"Can you work magma into a casual conversation?"

"Oh, new rules now?"

It was adorable, the way he rolled his eyes "All right. Fine. Broccoli it is."

"What's broccoli?" They both swung around at Sheida's voice.

"Sheida!" Nat wrapped her into a hug. "I wasn't sure you'd make it."

She made a face. "And miss the event of the year?" Sarcasm dripped from her tone. "Nice to see you out of the cave, Jax." She adjusted his collar, though it required no adjustment. "You look nice."

He shrugged. "It's just clothes."

"Well, good job anyway. So…" Sheida's gaze was laser-sharp. "Why are you talking about broccoli?" This she said in a tone that made clear she saw no reason for anyone to discuss broccoli, like ever.

"It's our safe word," Natalie said, if only to see Sheida flush. And she did.

Nat and Jax exchanged an evil grin, then Jax explained, "In case she needs saving tonight."

"Ah." Sheida took a sip of her drink and scanned the assemblage. "Well, that's not a bad idea." She winced when she saw Sherill Scanlon and Lola Cheswick heading their way. She made a face. "And on that note, I better skedaddle. And oh, look. There's Angel. I need to talk to her about…something."

"Coward," Jax whispered as she whisked herself away. "She's such a coward."

"Is she, though?" Nat had to ask. If she could have whisked herself away, she would have. "Don't leave me," she murmured as Sherill and Lola descended.

And he didn't.

The conversation with Sherill and Lola was pretty much what Natalie expected. Lots of questions about

Hollywood icons she'd never met—and a couple she had—as well as a preponderance of information about their current lives that made clear they were both unhappily married, unhappily mothers and unhappily unfulfilled.

It was obvious to Natalie that the husbands and the children and the lack of meaning were not the core problems with their lives. Rather the fact that neither had grown nor changed in all these years, and had no inclination to try.

In short, it was a banal conversation that would have sent Natalie running back to LA if she hadn't had Jax at her side muttering about broccoli. Every time he whispered that word, she had to fight back the urge to laugh. As miserable as this little reunion could have been, he made it fun.

But then, something really amazing happened.

Nat had been scanning the gym during Lola's monologue about her recent cruise to the Med with her extraordinarily wealthy husband...who drove a *Tesla*, so she'd seen a particular knot across the room and, with lust in her heart, had wished she was over there. It included Sheida and Angel, of course, as well as Clara Pearson, her sister Celeste's best friend Lynn, with whom she'd yet to catch up, and Ian McMurphy, the dear friend who'd taken her to prom. Well, technically, they'd taken each other. Gosh, they looked like a fun group. They were laughing and joking and smiling—

But Sherill and Lola were really good at holding civil people prisoner, and every time she tried to disengage, one of them would launch into another long rambling hostage conversation. Short of walking away or invoking the vegetable that shall not be named, she was stuck.

Except she wasn't. Because here they came, her buddies, in a pack, enveloping her person, surrounding her, hugging her and, in general, cutting Lola off mid-brag.

No one was rude. Not really. But when the conversation shifted from being all about them, the two remoras lost interest and wandered away.

And then, oh, and then, things got fun.

They found an empty table and sat and chatted and ate canapés and laughed…a lot. Clara had brought her yearbook and pulled it out so they could all laugh at the things they'd written to her, and really laugh at how goofy they'd all looked on Senior Picture Day. Then they all reminisced about their favorite teachers—Mr. Walden, with his deep, booming voice who'd taught history, Mr. Booker the tall, skinny science teacher Nat and Sheida had called an armpit with teeth—on account of his overbite and unfortunate facial hair—Mrs. T, the librarian, and Coach Granger, who'd run the gym like a military general.

And even though Angel hadn't been one of the nerds in high school, she seemed to fit right in. Even Jax relaxed in her presence, which said a lot. He was laughing and chatting along with everyone, which Nat hadn't really seen him do up until now.

She didn't realize what a change this was until Sheida leaned over, squeezed her hand and whispered, "You're so good for him."

The comment warmed her, and she glanced in his direction, catching him in the middle of a laugh. His smile was wide, his eyes crinkling with delight, his entire aura alight.

She was good for him?

Hell, he was good for her.

Their gazes tangled and he sobered. He leaned closer and took her hand under the table. "Are you okay? Do you want some broccoli?"

It wasn't something others were meant to hear, but they did.

"Oh, they have some broccoli over on the snack table," Clara said cheerfully. "I can go get you some."

"No," Sheida said with a glare, leaving no room for discussion. "No broccoli. We're having fun."

Nat had to laugh, because no one really understood the reference—other than herself, Jax and Sheida—and the confused expressions around the table were hilarious. Especially Clara's. She was, apparently, a fan of broccoli.

"No. Thanks," she said. "I'm fine." And she was. Heck, she was better than fine. "I don't think I've had this much fun for…well, I can't remember."

Funny. But it was true.

Despite everything, Jax had a blast at the Coho High School Reunion.

The thought was mind-boggling. But then—so much of the last month had been. From the moment he'd seen Natalie fall down the stairs at Smokey's, to laughing with her tonight, surrounded by all their friends. The way his feelings had shifted, the way his chains had loosened and fallen away. The way he was thinking, considering, planning changes. Huge changes.

It felt like a miracle, and it probably was one. And it had all happened because of Natalie.

In the past, that alone would have triggered him into panic mode. Depending on one element of your life to hold everything together was not sustainable. Counting on Natalie to keep him afloat was also not sustainable.

But it wasn't like that. Not really. She certainly had been the agent of many of his changes, his evolutions, but they weren't dependent on her. He knew she was leaving. If this was all about her presence in his life, he would have been a mess, thinking about her leaving, and that wasn't the case.

Oh, he didn't like the thought. And he really didn't like the knowledge that he was going to have to deal with it, when it happened.

But it didn't send him to a dark place. It didn't trigger panic.

It made him even more determined than ever to be a whole man, a healed man—for her.

She'd worked so hard to create her career, and she was very good at what she did—even Ben raved about the sets on her show. Jax knew he would never ask her to give it all up.

He was just thankful that he was in a place where he could stand up and support her when the time came for her to leave. They both valued what they had together, and they'd both decided to make it work…some way.

And as long as two people shared that common dream and were willing to fight for it, to adjust and to explore possibilities—they could work it out. He knew it to the depth of his soul.

Natalie was flying high on a cloud of renewed friendships and wine spritzers as Jax drove them back to his studio. Her eyes sparkled as she related, or recalled, one conversation after another. Her enthusiasm was contagious. They both were reduced to laughter more than once.

"Oh," she sighed after a long moment of contemplative silence. "I had so much fun tonight."

"Me, too."

And then, she added on a little laugh, "I never would have imagined such a thing."

"It was great."

"*They* are great." She shook her head. "Great people." Her phone pinged just then as though one of those great people had been reading her mind.

Indeed, she laughed. "It's from Angel. It just says, *broccoli.*"

He chuckled, too. "We're going to have a hard time living that one down."

"Right?" She scrolled further. "Oh, here's one from Ian McMurphy. Do you want to meet him for lunch tomorrow?"

"Sure." It had been great reconnecting with Ian. Contrary to expectations, he hadn't become some snooty celebrity, even though he had five books on the New York Times Bestseller list. He turned out to be a really decent guy. Once he understood that Natalie wasn't up for grabs, that is.

Jax glanced at her, because she'd been quiet for a bit,

scrolling through her phone. Her face was in profile as she stared at it, and illuminated only by its glow, but he knew immediately that she'd scrolled down her list of messages and seen something bad. Something horrible. Maybe something they'd both been dreading.

His heart clenched and his lungs locked, but he kept driving—thank God he knew the route by heart. And he didn't say anything, even though his silence didn't change a thing. It certainly didn't stop a ticking clock. Once he'd parked, though, he turned to her, in the shadows of the cab, and she turned to him.

"I have to go back." Her eyes shone, but not from happiness, and her lips curved, but not with joy. As beautiful as she was, he would never want to sculpt her like this. It would break his heart to do so.

"How soon?" he attempted to say, though it came out all rusty.

She sniffed. A long tear tracked a path down her cheek. "Soon. Tomorrow, if I can get a flight. There was a fire on the set and they're calling my team back in to fix everything before taping starts up again. It sounds pretty significant."

He drew in a deep breath. *All right.* "Let's go inside," he said. Because, honestly, what else was there to say?

Natalie was devastated, gutted, at the message from one of the producers asking her to return immediately. It surprised her, how much.

She wasn't ready to leave. Not now. Not so soon. She hadn't expected to find a connection like this— certainly not with Jax, certainly not in Coho Cove—

but now that she had, she wanted to keep it. Somehow. Things were complicated, yes—but when had they ever been uncomplicated?

It was one thing to make a vow to explore and enjoy their time together, and another entirely to seriously contemplate what the future might look like—especially since their lives were so vastly different. Her life was all hustle-bustle, production schedules and far-flung locations. His was more centered, stable, built around a core of maintaining a calm environment. There had to be something in between, some place they could meet, but as much as she wracked her brain, the solution continued to elude her.

And now her time had run out.

When Jax made love to her that night, it was unlike any other time. Unlike any other man. But they were both emotionally wrought, sensing the looming separation like the cloak of winter, and they could not get enough of each other. It wasn't until the next morning before Natalie realized she hadn't shared the news that she'd been called back to work with anyone else yet.

It did not go over well. Not with her family, or her friends, or her heart.

"But you just got here," Amy blurted, when she broke the news to everyone who had gathered over brunch at her request the next day.

Natalie was gutted to see tears glimmering in her younger sister's eyes. In fact, it hit her hard. So hard she went over and gave Amy a hug. Neither of them were casual huggers, but they both clung. "I'm coming back as soon as I can," she said.

John J put out a lip. "Do you promise?"

She knelt down to meet his gaze. "I promise."

"And can we go fishing again when you do?" Georgie asked. He didn't understand why all the adults laughed; this was clearly a very important point.

"I would love that."

Georgie threw himself into her arms then, with an enthusiasm that made Nat choke up a little. She'd become so good at compartmentalizing and focusing on what needed to be handled in her life, she'd somehow forgotten to appreciate the people who truly brought her joy, simply by being.

This trip had helped her remember.

And now she had to leave.

Saying goodbye to Celeste was rough too, because Natalie could see how hard she was trying to be cheerful. She could also see the pain behind her smile.

"Thank you for coming," she said. "You've been such a great help."

"Will you be okay when I leave?" Nat had to ask, because nothing had really changed in Momma's condition, or the demands on Celeste's time.

"Of course. We'll figure it out. I'm just glad you had time with Momma. It was good for both of you." It had been.

Nat glanced over at her mother, who was sitting at the table and watching everyone's reaction to Nat's news with a dour expression. Yikes. Saying goodbye to her would be the worst.

Momma had always been a constant in Natalie's life, indestructible, but this experience had brought home the truth. That change is inevitable, and no one is in-destructible. That every interaction with a friend or a loved one is precious and fleeting. That choices have consequences.

"Hey, Momma," she said, sitting next to her and tak-ing her hand. "I'm sorry I have to leave so soon."

Momma sniffed. "Well, you have things to do, I sup-pose."

"I'll be back soon. I promise." And heavens, she meant it. Felt it to her core.

Damn, but it *hurt* to leave.

After she'd packed, Jax took her around to let Ben and Sheida know she was heading out, and that wasn't any easier.

"Stay in touch," Sheida admonished her, through a brutal hug.

"Of course. I will. I promise."

Because Momma and Pepe had bonded, it only seemed right to leave him here. If nothing else, it gave her a reason to come back— She nearly laughed at the thought, because she didn't need an incentive to come back.

There were many.

But the biggest reason was Jax—this relationship, this experiment. She wasn't ready for it to be over, and neither was he.

It irritated her how quickly those last hours with Jax and her family flew by. Before she knew it, she was on the road, on the way home, and leaving them all be-hind. It was harder than she could ever have imagined.

Natalie's apartment was cold when she opened the

door. And musty. It usually was, when she returned from a long absence, but somehow, this time, it seemed even more soulless. Granted, her furnishings were spartan, chosen for utility rather than style, so that didn't help much. It hadn't bothered her before, living in a glorified hotel room, but now, she had a sudden urge to add something... A nice warm wooden sculpture leaped to mind.

But her home wasn't the only thing that appeared lifeless, she noticed. As she arrived at the studio the next day, there was none of that tickle of anticipation that she usually felt. The movement around her in the warehouse seemed mechanical and two-dimensional. Even catching up with her crew—usually a raucous exchange in which she reveled—lacked depth.

She knew why, of course. *He* was superimposed onto every thought in her head.

She missed *him*.

More than she ever thought possible.

It was so hard for Jax, watching Natalie go. Hard standing there, waving with a fake smile on his lips and a tinny taste in his mouth as he watched drive away.

It didn't get any easier after she was gone. Even when they texted. Even when they talked on the phone. It was nice to know she was safe. It was nice to hear her voice. But it wasn't the same as having her here, in his arms, in his bed.

He refused to let it consume him. He had to look forward. He had to use this discomfort to make progress on the life, the haven he could offer her when she returned. Because he knew she would. He knew she would return to him.

Jax began on a new project the day Natalie left and he worked on it every day after that. He got the usual complaints from Ben and Sheida and Amy that he was hiding again, but he wasn't. This was different. This passion had purpose. This sculpture was for her. For Natalie.

He met with Luke Larsen, too—to start checking out *real* houses, as Sheida called them. Houses with real kitchens and real living rooms and bedrooms that weren't refurbished storage rooms. To his surprise and delight, the old Windwalker Cottage, up on the bluff, the one he'd always admired as a boy, had just gone on the market and Jax snapped it up. It was a three-bedroom and two-bath house with a loft overlooking the sea, and a nice-sized shop nearby. It needed some work, but as Pops always said, no one was allergic to work.

So, while he missed Natalie terribly, he put all of his love for her and all of his hopes for the future into fixing up this little house, so they'd have a real place to stay when she came. He ripped out the old countertops and remade them with planed oak, then varnished the heck out of them. He enjoyed that so much, he designed and carved matching lintels. Then, of course, the color of the walls wasn't quite right, so he had to change that...and so on.

But it filled his soul in her absence, and it grounded him in his determination to make things better. And making things better, well, made them better.

* * *

Natalie struggled over the next few weeks. Leaving Jax had been the hardest thing she'd ever done.

She missed his scent, and his laugh. The feel of his palm on her breast, his mouth hot on her nape. His presence.

And, well, hell, she loved him.

It wasn't a high school crush or admiration because he was so amazing and strong. It wasn't an appreciation for his intellect and empathy, or the fact that he always managed to say just the right thing. It wasn't hot, hungry lust that wanted to scatter the buttons of his shirt across the floor.

It was something even more. Something greater. Higher.

Along with it came a mortifying realization and a humbling feeling. She'd never truly *given herself* to someone before—she could see that now. And she could even see the why of it.

She'd never truly given herself to anyone before because she hadn't felt safe.

Jax made her safe.

Jax was her heart home.

And damn, if that wasn't love, whatever could it be?

To her annoyance and despite her emotional distance, Natalie got sucked right back into the mayhem at work. Things got so chaotic that first week—trying to get everything done before the hard deadline hit—that she barely had time to think about Jax and how much she missed him. She called him when she could, but during work there were interruptions, and after work she was exhausted.

How had she ever sustained this lifestyle? How could she continue?

As much as she loved connecting with him over the phone, it just wasn't the same as being with him. And she felt the same when she talked to her sisters, the boys, Momma and Sheida... Just not satisfying at all. As though she craved the physical. She'd gotten so good at phoning it in over the past seven years, she realized. So good at pushing away the desire for deeper relationships. So good at skating on the edges.

But now...now she wanted more. Craved it.

Now she felt...alone.

She'd never felt alone before. Not like this.

Even when Sheida called to tell her that Angel wanted to display the watercolor she'd painted at the Elder House in her gallery—which was a wonderful validation—it only made Natalie feel lonely and sad. One bright and chirpy conversation with the boys left her in tears because she missed them so much.

But she sucked it up, and even threw herself more deeply into work—as though she could make time pass more quickly if she just didn't think about it.

It didn't work.

The only thing that had felt good was when she and Carl sat down for coffee, right after she arrived, and she told him she'd met someone, and yes, it was serious. Contrary to her expectations, he was happy for her—which was a relief. She'd been worried how he might react—even though they hadn't spoken for weeks. Aside from that, his reaction only served to underscore the fact that they'd just been keeping each other company. They chatted a while longer, just catching up, as old friends did, and then she went her way and he went his. It was a lovely farewell, filled with good wishes and affection and appreciation for the times they'd shared. But now it was time to move on.

The only real respite she knew was when she was talking to Jax. It wasn't the same as chatting while he curled around her in bed, or sharing wisecracks across the table or holding hands and walking on the beach. But it was better than the whistling wasteland her existence felt like without him.

She tried not to talk about the minutiae of work with him on the phone, but since her life consisted only of work now, she found herself struggling to come up with other topics. Jax was always full of stories—updates on Ben and Quinn, a quip about Amy or the boys, hot gossip about someone in town that made her laugh, but after he hung up, she was right back to being sad. And while she tried not to constantly talk about how unhappy she was, she couldn't keep that a secret from him.

"If you're not enjoying it, you can always come home," he said on one late-night call.

She sighed because she'd had similar thoughts—all of which she'd shot down. "I need this job."

He was silent for a minute. "You don't need *that* job. I mean, if it's not fulfilling anymore. There are other options." Then he laughed. "But I'm biased. I don't want to push you into making a decision you'll regret, Natalie. If you want work, you should work. I'll be here for you when you come home. But if this is about money, we can figure something else out. I just want you to be happy."

"Even if that means we're not together?"

There was a crackling silence on the line for a long while. "Yeah." A sigh. "Honestly, if you were with me and not happy, I can't see how I could be happy, either." He went on to add, "Just know, you have a home with me, no matter what."

Home.

Her heart thudded.

Funny thing, she didn't reject that thought any more, that Coho Cove could be home. Simply because he was there.

Jax paused in his delimbing of a large log, turned his face up to the sun and mopped up the sweat on his brow. He loved physical labor these days, hard work that required effort and concentration. Work that kept his mind busy. Otherwise, his loneliness would swamp him.

He tried to stay cheerful and uplifting when he talked to Natalie, because he could tell she needed it, but to be honest, the world was kind of a desert without her. Nights were long and cold—even though it was summer—because his bed felt empty. Every interaction he had with other people reminded him how much he wanted her here.

Still, he had to stand firm on his decision to let Natalie go. And, more to the point, to support her decision to do so. He suspected he could probably convince her to leave her job and move in with him, in the cottage on the cliff he'd been renovating. But he also knew it would be wrong to pressure her. Melissa had pressured him to fit into her world and he'd hated it. He could hardly do the same simply because he wanted Natalie here.

Thank God they lived in an age where they could FaceTime. Even though—even seeing her face—it wasn't the same as having her close. It couldn't be.

She'd been particularly sad last night. She hadn't been able to hide it. But other than sending her flowers—which she said was a waste of money because she was always at the set—the only other option was hopping on a plane and flying to Los Angeles. While he shuddered at the thought, he knew that was the only way he could see her, hold her, if only for a while.

He heaved a heavy sigh and reached for his water bottle—it was important to hydrate when he was working in the sun—when something, a mirage, maybe, caught his eye.

He stilled and stared at the figure moving toward him through the garden.

Yep. He needed to hydrate all right. He was hallucinating.

Surely it wasn't Natalie?

Ah, but it was.

His heart leaped. His soul soared. He secured his saw, dropped his water bottle and headed toward her in a rush.

"Nat?" he croaked. She opened her arms to him and the met in a hard, harsh hug. God, it felt good to hold her. "Is it really you?"

Her grin was brilliant. "You don't mind the surprise?"

Don't mind? He shook his head. "I'm over the moon. How are you here? When did you get in? What's happening?" So many questions.

She made a face. "Well, after we pulled double shifts to get the set back in place, the actors went on strike and production is on hold while the producers try to work everything out. Since there was nothing to do in the downtime—and I missed you so much—I decided to fly up until it's resolved."

"God, I've missed you." It was all he could say. All he could think.

"I've missed you, too."

"You don't know how long you're here?"

She shook her head. Her smile curled mischievously. A glint shone in her eye. "We have no time to waste..."

He knew immediately what she had in mind, and he threw back his head and laughed, from pure joy. And then, "I'm all sweaty." He'd been working for several hours; his T-shirt was drenched.

"Stop trying to seduce me," she said wryly, and then they both laughed. Then she took his arm and led him to the studio.

They showered together, and made love twice—with a quick snack in between—and then curled up together on his bed and cuddled.

"Hmm," she grunted after a while.

He levered up on an elbow to look at her. "What?"

"Did you change bedspreads?" A frown. "I really liked the other one."

"Did you?" He couldn't help smiling. Because he still had that bedspread—it was his favorite—but he'd moved it. And though he knew he should probably share her with her family, at least a little, while she was here, he wasn't ready yet.

He hopped out of bed and pulled on a clean pair of jeans and T-shirt. "Come on. Get dressed," he said when she squawked. "I have something I want to show you."

"Where are we going?" she asked as he bundled her into his SUV.

He shot her a grin. "It's a surprise."

"Ugh," she said on a heavy sigh, with a hint of a smile. "I hate surprises."

"Really?" He shot her a sardonic look. "I'm a fan of surprises right now. Like a really big fan."

And of course, she had to laugh.

Oh, it was so wonderful being with Jax again! Something about *him* just filled her up. His smile, his laugh, his energy, his scent. Or all of that. Natalie wasn't sure exactly what it was about him that made her feel the way she did, but it didn't matter.

It was pure joy.

She didn't know where he was taking her, especially when he turned off onto a westward road she wasn't familiar with, but she didn't ask. She just sat there next to him, with her hand on his thigh and enjoyed being with him.

He turned from the road and followed a track up the hill, then pulled in beside an adorable cottage overlooking the sea. It had a turret. *A turret.* She grinned at him. "I love turrets."

He grinned back.

As she got out of the car, she got a glimpse of the view, which was—stunning. From this vantage point, she could see the town in the distance as well as a great swath of sea and sky. "This is so pretty," she said as she got out of the car.

He nodded as he came to her and took her hand. "One of my favorite places."

"Is this what you wanted to show me? This view?" It was breathtaking.

"No. Here." He led her around to the seaward side of the place and Nat saw it immediately. A gorgeous sculpture in the yard, an exquisite mermaid yearning for the sea.

"Oh, Jax. Is this new?" She didn't have to ask if it was his work, because his soul was in every line. "I love her."

"Do you?"

"Of course." It was a shame someone who lived so far out had bought it, because she deserved to be seen.

"Do you want to go inside the house?"

She turned to him. Quirked a brow. "Can we?"

He grinned. "Yeah." He opened the door and ushered her inside and she caught her breath.

It was beautiful, an eclectic mix of comfortable furniture and fat, carved wood accents. The colors were the palette of a shadowed forest, mosses, dark browns and mustard golds, all elevated by the shafts of sun warming the room. The windows, which were broad and wide and open, showcased the great expanse of the sea fading into mist at the horizon. "Oh, it's magnificent," Nat gasped as she stared out at this panoply.

"Come see the kitchen."

She made a face and laughed. Who wanted to see the kitchen when there was a view like that? But the kitchen was amazing, with the most beautiful countertops she'd ever seen, set off by brushed stainless steel appliances that looked as though they'd just been installed. There was a circular nook off to the side—the base of the turret she'd noticed on the east side. "Oh, this is cute," she said, running a hand over the slender carved columns that framed the open doorway.

"It gets the sunrise," he said.

Something in his tone made her still. She glanced at the column, stroked it more carefully. And then she narrowed her eyes on him. "Did you do this?"

He grinned like a little boy. "You noticed."

Oh, heavens. Had she noticed. He was all over this place and, "I love it. I absolutely love it. Jax, you should do this for a living."

He ignored the excellent suggestion—he really could make a living at this—and took her hand and tugged her to the staircase. "Come see the loft."

She followed. Of course, she did. She loved this side of him. He was giddy and excited and irresistible.

The staircase was narrow and curved a little, and opened to a large bedroom. Although, to call it a bedroom was understating it. The bed was the center point of the room, certainly, but the space was large enough for a sitting area on one side by the hearth and a desk on the other. There was a glorious bath en suite—with a claw-foot tub—and a large rain shower.

But it wasn't just the fabulous accommodations or the decor that caught her eye. Not here in the bedroom.

Because there, on the bed, was his fuzzy bedspread. The one she loved so much.

She jerked her gaze from the blanket to him in a quizzical glance. "Jax, why is your bedspread on the bed?"

He shrugged. "Well, it's my house."

Her heart thudded. She gaped at him. "What?"

"I bought it."

"You bought a house?"

"Yeah. I thought we could stay here when you're visiting. I, uh, fixed it up."

He certainly had. Her pulse pounded. Hard. He'd bought a house so she would have a place when she came home. For her. He'd fixed it up. For her. The thought nearly brought tears to her eyes.

He jammed his toe into the carpet. "Well, what do you think?"

She was so choked up she could barely speak, but she finally managed, "Oh, Jax. It's absolutely perfect. I love it." She threw herself onto the bed—loved the bounce.

Loved the fact he joined her there.

Loved even more the passion that followed.

How could she have walked away from this? From him?

She'd been asking herself that same question since she went back to work—maybe even before then. But now the stark differences between her two lives was undeniable. She'd always loved her job—and the sheer energy of it. But something in her had changed. She didn't want that life anymore.

She wanted this.

She wanted him.

And honestly, even if he did move to Los Angeles, her job, as exciting as it was, didn't make her happy anymore. She wanted to create art and beauty—like Jax did—to feed her soul. And all the busyness of the life she'd made only served to do just that. Keep her busy. Like her relationship with Carl, it was filling, but not fulfilling.

She wanted more.

She deserved more.

And she knew that she was the one who had to make the changes—the difficult changes in many ways—to build a life that fed her soul.

"What is it?" Jax murmured.

"Hmm?"

He traced a finger along her cheek. "Your expression is fierce."

"Is it?"

"Tell me."

Yeah. It was time to say the words. It was time to tell him. She was ready.

She sucked up a deep breath and said the words that had been haunting her for weeks. "I've decided to… quit my job."

Jax stared for a second, gaped, really. "Are you sure?"

"I… Yes—" But before she could elaborate on all the whys and wherefores, he leaped from the bed and pulled her into his arms and twirled her around, whooping with joy. And she laughed all the while.

He set her down, breathless and dizzy. "Are you sure? I mean, Are you sure?"

"Oh yes, I'm sure. I'll finish the season, of course, and give them time to replace me, but… I just don't want to be without you anymore, Jax."

"I don't want to be without you, either."

"It's not a commitment," she said, just to clarify. "I'm not asking for a commitment from you."

His Adam's apple bobbed. "Are you saying you're not interested in a commitment?"

She kissed his frown away. "No, Jax. I'm not saying that. I just don't want to pressure you… I mean we haven't really talked about the future or what that might look like. And I—"

"Natalie." He cut her off with a glower. "I am so in love with you sometimes I can't see straight. All I want is to be with you, in whatever form that takes."

Her heart soared. *He loved her.* They were simple words, but they changed everything. They always did. But— "You're in love with me? Are you sure? It's only been a couple months…"

His smile was serene. He cupped her cheeks in his palms. "A couple months? Natalie, it's been years. And even if it had been minutes, it makes no difference. I want you in my life, somehow, no matter what. Forever."

She pulled him into her arms. "I want the same, Jax. I do. All I really want is to be here, with you." She sucked in a breath. "I love you too, Jaxson Stringfellow. I never expected it. But it happened. You are the most important thing in my life. You are what I want. And whatever happens, whatever we have to face, we'll do it. Together."

He kissed her then, and kissed her hard. But then, just when things were getting interesting, he pulled away. She would have complained, but before she could, he fished in his pocket and pulled out—her heart skipped a beat—a *ring*.

It was unlike any ring she'd ever seen—a gorgeous, intricately etched ring made of jade.

"It's not a commitment," he said, parroting her ridiculous words. "Not unless you want it to be."

There was nothing she wanted more. "Oh, Jax."

"May I?" he asked, and when she nodded, he slipped it on her finger.

She stared at his ring on her finger. "Oh, Jax. I love it."

His grin was brilliant. "Pops made it."

"He made it?"

He lifted a shoulder. "He likes to make things, too."

"It's so beautiful." It was. And it was exactly the kind of ring she liked—earthy and natural and one of a kind.

His grin was broad as he pulled her into his arms and kissed her. "I'm glad you like it."

"I love it. And the house. It's perfect. You're perfect. Everything is perfect."

"We'll still have challenges," he reminded her.

"Of course." She needed to find a job, here in this small town, but there were so many options. The difference was, now she was open to seeing those possibilities, and all the possibilities that they could create, as a team.

"Whatever comes, we'll figure it out...together." He smiled, that little crooked quirk that always warmed her heart.

"Together," she repeated on a whisper.

That sounded pretty perfect indeed.

* * * * *

Look for Amy's story,
the next installment in
New York Times *bestselling author Sabrina York's*
new miniseries for Harlequin Special Edition,
The Tuttle Sisters of Coho Cove.
On sale January 2024, wherever Harlequin books
and ebooks are sold.

COMING NEXT MONTH FROM

ℍ HARLEQUIN®
SPECIAL EDITION

#2989 THE MAVERICK'S SURPRISE SON
Montana Mavericks: Lassoing Love • by Christine Rimmer

Volunteer firefighter Jace Abernathy vows to adopt the newborn he saved from a fire. Nurse Tamara Hanson doubts he's up to the task. She'll help the determined rancher prepare for his social service screening. But in the process, will these hometown heroes find love and family with each other?

#2990 SEVEN BIRTHDAY WISHES
Dawson Family Ranch • by Melissa Senate

Seven-year-old Cody Dawson dreams of meeting champion bull rider Logan Winston. Logan doesn't know his biggest fan is also his son. He'll fulfill seven of Cody's wishes—one for each birthday he missed. But falling in love again with Cody's mom, Annabel, may be his son's biggest wish yet!

#2991 HER NOT-SO-LITTLE SECRET
Match Made in Haven • by Brenda Harlen

Sierra Hart knows a bad boy when she sees one. And smooth-talking Deacon Parrish is a rogue of the first order! Their courtroom competition pales to their bedroom chemistry. But will these dueling attorneys trust each other enough to go from "I object" to "I do"?

#2992 HEIR IN A YEAR
by Elizabeth Bevarly

Bennett Hadden just inherited the Gilded Age mansion Summerlight. So did Haven Moreau—assuming the two archenemies can live there together for one year. Haven plans to restore the home *and* her broken relationship with Bennett. And she'll use every tool at her disposal to return both to their former glories!

#2993 THEIR SECRET TWINS
Shelter Valley Stories • by Tara Taylor Quinn

Jordon Lawrence and ex Mia Jones just got the embryo shock of their lives. Their efforts to help a childless couple years ago resulted in twin daughters they never knew existed. Now the orphaned girls need their biological parents, and Jordon and Mia will work double time to create the family their children deserve!

#2994 THE BUSINESS BETWEEN THEM
Once Upon a Wedding • by Mona Shroff

Businessman Akash Gupta just bought Reena Pandya's family hotel, ruining her plan to take it over. Now the determined workaholic will do anything to reclaim her birthright—even get closer to her sexy ex. But Akash has a plan, too—teaching one very headstrong woman to balance duty, family *and* love.

YOU CAN FIND MORE INFORMATION ON UPCOMING HARLEQUIN TITLES, FREE EXCERPTS AND MORE AT HARLEQUIN.COM.

HSECNM0523

Get 4 FREE REWARDS!

We'll send you 2 FREE Books plus 2 FREE Mystery Gifts.

FREE Value Over **$20**

Both the **Harlequin® Special Edition** and **Harlequin® Heartwarming™** series feature compelling novels filled with stories of love and strength where the bonds of friendship, family and community unite.

YES! Please send me 2 FREE novels from the Harlequin Special Edition or Harlequin Heartwarming series and my 2 FREE gifts (gifts are worth about $10 retail). After receiving them, if I don't wish to receive any more books, I can return the shipping statement marked "cancel." If I don't cancel, I will receive 6 brand-new Harlequin Special Edition books every month and be billed just $5.49 each in the U.S. or $6.24 each in Canada, a savings of at least 12% off the cover price, or 4 brand-new Harlequin Heartwarming Larger-Print books every month and be billed just $6.24 each in the U.S. or $6.74 each in Canada, a savings of at least 19% off the cover price. It's quite a bargain! Shipping and handling is just 50¢ per book in the U.S. and $1.25 per book in Canada.* I understand that accepting the 2 free books and gifts places me under no obligation to buy anything. I can always return a shipment and cancel at any time by calling the number below. The free books and gifts are mine to keep no matter what I decide.

Choose one: ☐ **Harlequin Special Edition** ☐ **Harlequin Heartwarming**
(235/335 HDN GRJV) **Larger-Print**
(161/361 HDN GRJV)

Name (please print)

Address _____ Apt. #

City _____ State/Province _____ Zip/Postal Code

Email: Please check this box ☐ if you would like to receive newsletters and promotional emails from Harlequin Enterprises ULC and its affiliates. You can unsubscribe anytime.

Mail to the **Harlequin Reader Service:**
IN U.S.A.: P.O. Box 1341, Buffalo, NY 14240-8531
IN CANADA: P.O. Box 603, Fort Erie, Ontario L2A 5X3

Want to try 2 free books from another series! Call 1-800-873-8635 or visit www.ReaderService.com.

*Terms and prices subject to change without notice. Prices do not include sales taxes, which will be charged (if applicable) based on your state or country of residence. Canadian residents will be charged applicable taxes. Offer not valid in Quebec. This offer is limited to one order per household. Books received may not be as shown. Not valid for current subscribers to the Harlequin Special Edition or Harlequin Heartwarming series. All orders subject to approval. Credit or debit balances in a customer's account(s) may be offset by any other outstanding balance owed by or to the customer. Please allow 4 to 6 weeks for delivery. Offer available while quantities last.

Your Privacy—Your information is being collected by Harlequin Enterprises ULC, operating as Harlequin Reader Service. For a complete summary of the information we collect, how we use this information and to whom it is disclosed, please visit our privacy notice located at corporate.harlequin.com/privacy-notice. From time to time we may also exchange your personal information with reputable third parties. If you wish to opt out of this sharing of your personal information, please visit readerservice.com/consumerschoice or call 1-800-873-8635. **Notice to California Residents**—Under California law, you have specific rights to control and access your data. For more information on these rights and how to exercise them, visit corporate.harlequin.com/california-privacy.

HSEHW22R3

HARLEQUIN
PLUS

Try the best multimedia
subscription service for romance
readers like you!

Read, Watch and Play.

Experience the easiest way to get
the romance content you crave.

Start your **FREE TRIAL** at
www.harlequinplus.com/freetrial.

HARPLUS0123